Savaged Dreams

SAVAGED ILLUSIONS TRILOGY · BOOK ONE

JENNIFER LYON

Savaged Dreams
Copyright © 2017 Jennifer Apodaca
All rights reserved.

Cover and Savaged Illusions Logo Designs:
Jaycee DeLorenzo of Sweet 'N Spicy Designs
Editor: Sashaknighteditor.com
Copy Editor: www.kimberlycannoneditor.com/
Formatted by: Author E.M.S.

Published by JenniferLyonBooks
www.jenniferlyonbooks.com

ISBN: 978-0-9984595-1-6

*For all those who ever dreamed
of becoming a rock star.*

Or falling in love with one.

This story is for you.

Chapter 1

JUSTICE CADE SQUINTED IN THE vicious sunlight of San Diego, California, as he parked his car. He'd had hangovers that hurt less than the sleep-deprived headache pounding in his skull.

Your own fault, dumbass.

Yet the pain, frustration and fatigue didn't do a thing to diminish a streak of triumph when he spotted the marquee blazing over the front of the auditorium.

COMING SOON: *COURT OF ROCK*
FEATURING THE BANDS:
FURY RUN, JAGGED SIN & SAVAGED ILLUSIONS

Savaged Illusions. His band. His dream. The one single thing in life he didn't fail at—music. He and his band had made it this far in the eliminations. Two more shows and they could win, capturing the one-year contract with a top record label.

Winning was everything. The only thing. Justice had nothing else but his band and music. He wouldn't let anything stop them now. Which meant it was time to quit admiring the sign and get his ass into practice.

After getting out of the car, he grabbed his guitar case from the backseat and juggled to carry two coffees across the parking lot. At the steel door of the theater, he handed one of the drinks to Colin, the security guard for the *Court of Rock* reality TV show.

"Thanks, man."

"No prob." He winced at the rough sound of his voice. His singing was going to be shit today. He really should have gotten some sleep. Nothing he could do now but power through. Once inside, he got halfway across the lower level of backstage when he heard the shouting.

"You son of a bitch!"

What the fuck? That was Simon's voice. The lead guitarist of their band rarely lost his temper. Justice ditched his guitar case, set his coffee on a table and launched into a run. Hanging a hard right into the greenroom, he skidded to a halt and took in the scene. Two camera guys were filming as the Savaged Illusions drummer and bassist held Simon back, the man's face a murderous shade of red.

Ace, the obvious troublemaker from their rival band, Jagged Sin, bellowed back, "You either replace my guitar, or I'll tell the whole world you're such an asshole, your own wife killed herself to get away from you." He glanced at the cameras then back to Simon and smirked. "Oh wait, I just did."

Simon roared, breaking loose from the two men holding him, and lunged.

Holy shit. If Simon hit the other man—on camera—they'd be fucked. Thrown off the *Court of Rock*. With zero choice, Justice dove, getting his arms around Simon, spun and slammed him down to the couch.

Caught by surprise, Simon sat dazed for a second.

Taking advantage of his shock, Justice slapped one

hand on the sofa arm, the other on the back, using his body to block the cameras and trap Simon at the same time. He had to talk his lead guitarist down. "Cameras are rolling, dude. Get your shit together."

The other man's eyes scorched with fury. "I'll kill him."

It was all Justice could do to keep from killing that weasel Ace himself. But first he had to keep Simon out of jail. What the hell had he walked into? The feud between Simon and Ace was mounting every damned day, making this competition a powder keg.

"Listen up, man. It's a setup. We're being played. Why else would there be cameras here?" There were no shoots scheduled for today. The bands had a day or two to practice without being recorded. Another question occurred to him. "How did Ace know about Julie?" Very few people knew about Simon's deceased wife.

Simon stiffened, his entire body vibrating. "I never told him."

"Shit. This is bad." He glanced over his shoulder. Their three other band members, River, Gray and Lynx, had spread out, forming a wall to block the cameras.

Returning his attention to Simon, he said, "Someone did." Hot anger jacked his pulse and made his muscles twitch to kick some ass. "The ratings whores strike again."

Simon's eyes narrowed. "Bastards."

The show execs were always looking for ways to create more tension between the bands. Especially now that the show was heading into the final two episodes. They'd done extensive backgrounds on all the band members, so they'd know about Simon's wife. It'd been a few years since Julie died, but for Simon it was an open wound. "You need to hold it together. Or leave. Let me handle this."

He took a deep breath. "I'm staying."

Yeah, he figured. Simon didn't talk about Julie much, but he was fiercely protective of her memory. "You hit Ace and we'll be tossed off the show. They'll have you dragged out of here in handcuffs and put it on the air. You hear what I'm saying?" The show played hardball. The group had known it going in, but the payoff if they won was worth it—a contract with the record label, Tangent.

Their ticket to the big time.

"Got it," Simon said, back in control.

After pushing off the couch, Justice crossed the room to the show's producer, Frank. "What's going on? It's our practice time. Ace isn't supposed to be here." His band practiced after Savaged Illusions was finished. All this was usually tightly scheduled.

"He trashed my guitar." Ace's thin face contorted as he waved around the two pieces of his Gibson Les Paul Standard electric guitar.

"Didn't ask you." Justice's hands twitched with the need to punch the lies out of Ace's mouth. Fucktard. He'd disliked the guy before, but now after baiting Simon with his wife's death? What kind of scumbag did that? Hatred brewed in his belly.

"Give it a rest, Ace, you made your point," Frank said, resignation riding every word. The last eleven weeks of traveling around the country, dealing with rock bands and drama, had left the man looking like a candidate for a massive heart attack. He faced Justice. "Ace's story is that he'd put his guitar in his car yesterday, and he found it broken in the greenroom this morning. He's sure that since he and Simon were at the same club last night, Simon stole it out of his

4

car and trashed it, then left it for him to find today."

Justice rolled his eyes. "Bullshit." One look at the instrument's broken neck told him exactly what happened. He glared at Ace. "You got drunk or stoned and did it yourself. Showing off for some chick, or were you raging? Woke up this morning and realized you're out almost a thousand bucks."

Ace's cheeks mottled. "You savages are going down." He stormed out, dragging his busted guitar with him.

Jesus. One problem down, but they had more to deal with. Spinning to the producer, he snarled, "Don't use that footage."

"Not your call."

His head pounded. Violence gripped his muscles. They were fucked. They'd signed the contract, giving *Court of Rock* the rights to all their footage, including editing it. They wanted to make Jagged Sin the underdogs to manufacture a fiercer competition. He glanced over at Simon, who was flanked by their other bandmates.

That was the one thing all five of them could count on—they had one another's backs. Always.

But there was a publicity shitstorm brewing. Justice could accuse the show of telling Ace about Simon's wife's suicide, but they'd edit it out. Frustration added to his fury. "Let's go practice. No cameras." Not that he could enforce it, but—

"One more thing," Frank said.

"What now?"

"Your publicist will be here to meet you during practice."

If ever they could use a publicist, it was now. Ace's accusation that Simon's wife had killed herself to escape Simon was a time bomb that could explode in their faces. Women were a huge chunk of their fan base, and that lie could easily turn them against Simon, and by extension, the band. They needed every single fan vote to win *Court of Rock*. So yeah, a publicist was a godsend. "Who is it?"

"Liza. She's a student at UC San Diego."

"What?" He barely held on to the last brittle strand of his temper. "A college student? Our contract says if we made it to week eleven, we'd get a publicist, not a college kid." The show and the record label were jacking them around mercilessly.

"This is what Tangent Records wants, and they're the sponsor. They ran some contest. Our biggest demographic is college-aged—"

"Screw the bullshit. It was in our contract."

"You don't have a choice, Cade. You were promised a publicist, and they consider her qualified enough." The producer scowled. "Either suck it up or quit the show."

Remember the cameras. But damn, he'd spent his whole fucking life without choices and sucking it up. No way was he quitting the show. They'd eat shit until they won and got that one-year contract with Tangent Records—their ticket to real fame.

Then no one would fuck with them.

"We don't quit. Not now or ever." He stormed out. Once in the hall, he slapped his hand against the wall. *Calm the hell down.* He was too fried, the pressure riding him relentlessly. All of them were showing the cracks.

"You gonna puke or something?" Lynx, their drummer and his longtime friend, leaned next to him, eyebrows raised.

"Something. Not hungover, just strung tight." So damned tired and angry. They had too much on the line in the next couple weeks. He pivoted in time to see River and Gray flanking Simon as they walked to the stairs leading up to the stage. Suspicion took shape. "The suits engineered this. They've been sitting on the knowledge that Simon was married and his wife..."

"Creepers."

He nodded. "Yeah, but they sprang it now, then tell us we get a kid as our publicist. My guess is they're creating fires for the publicist in some other game we don't have the rules to."

"For ratings," Lynx snapped. "But Ace, he's smacked. Guy's so messed up he doesn't know reality."

More than likely. "Coke?"

"Or meth. Don't know, don't care. What he did to Simon today, man, that's twisted."

"Yeah." Justice glanced around the lower floor of the huge auditorium close to the University of California's campus. It had all the equipment the show required, but at this point in the season, after traveling to so many locations near colleges—*their demographic*—it all looked the same to him. He closed his eyes, needing a minute to get his head to stop with the drilling.

"No sleep?"

He pulled in a breath. Lynx saw too damned much. "Back off."

"You went looking for him, didn't you?"

"Get off my ass. Had business to take care of." He opened his eyes and shoved off the wall. "Where's my coffee?" After storming to the table, he snatched it up and drank the lukewarm brew.

"Your voice is shit today. You didn't sleep, and you're cranky as a crack baby. You spent the night out on a futile search instead of getting the shut-eye you need."

His gut burned. They'd just gotten into town last

night after weeks of traveling and performing, fighting not to get eliminated every show. He'd barely put his stuff down in his house before he'd been out the door, only returning home in time to grab a shower before heading to practice. And now Lynx was dogging him. "You're two seconds from my foot up your ass."

"Try it."

The silky invitation tempted him, but he was too damned tired. Lifting his gaze, he admitted, "Couldn't find him. He might be dead for all I know." And Justice would have failed. Again. He'd sworn to his grandmother before she died that he'd take care of his father.

So far he hadn't lived up to his deathbed promise.

The old anger stewed in the mix of everything else. He just needed this day to be over. Done.

"Your dad doesn't want to be found, J. That's reality, and you need to deal. We didn't get the full house in our family hand, we got the jokers."

Justice eyed the drummer, catching the strain around his eyes. They'd both grown up in San Diego, but at least Justice'd had his grandmother until she passed away last year. Lynx had definitely gotten the worse deal. "You have a key to my house, crash there. Take a break from the sterile hotels for a while." They might not be blood, but Lynx was a brother to him. And they both had the band, their only real family.

"Nah. I can't bring chicks to your grandma's house."

Nostalgia swept over Justice. "Still afraid of her, huh? You think her ghost is going to smack you upside the head?" Not that his grandmother had ever smacked Lynx, but the image amused him.

"Respect, asshole. Not fear." He tapped on the table in time to some beat playing in his head. "She let me live there when I got sprung from juvie."

Being back in their hometown made them both edgy, a reminder that they'd been judged and labeled losers. Justice hadn't even lasted a day before he'd been out on the streets, scraping his childhood wounds open to expose the festering sore. "We're going to show them when we win *Court of Rock*."

Lynx nodded. "Damn right. I'm going up." He tilted his head to the stairs leading to the stage.

"I'll be there in a sec." Just one more minute to get this headache under control and get his shit together. He finished off his coffee, tossed the cup, grabbed his guitar and headed up the stairs to the big stage facing the five-hundred-seat auditorium. Gray sat at the piano, while Lynx took a seat at the drum kit. They were both at the back of the stage. Justice took center, with Simon on his right. River, the bassist, fell in behind them. After all the weeks of performing in various locations all over the country, it was a familiar routine. They automatically adjusted positions to make sure the two in the back weren't blocked during a show.

After freeing his guitar from its case, he strummed it, the sound helping soothe his head and focus him on what really mattered—their music.

Simon tuned a few strings on his BilT Revelator guitar. "I'd have killed him if you hadn't walked in."

"Any other time I'd have grabbed some popcorn and pulled up a chair." Happily. He shot Simon a hard look. "They're going to use the footage. We can't stop it."

"I know."

The quiet acceptance ripped a hole in Justice's chest. Simon had watched all their backs time and again, loaning Justice the money to cover his grandmother's funeral before he got the estate settled.

God knows what he'd done for the others, and none of them could stop the pain train coming for him. Whatever had happened, Simon had loved his wife. "Look, maybe we can hire a real publicist."

"Can't. In the contract, remember? No unfair advantages."

Damn it. "We're up shit creek. Not only aren't we getting a real publicist, but we have to babysit some sorority girl whose only experience at promotion is taking selfies."

"Or a groupie," River added. "More interested in snagging a rock star than doing the job."

Justice fought a groan. He loved groupies, they needed them. But right now they needed an experienced publicist more.

"Actually..." A voice came from the wings at the top of the stairs. "I'm not in a sorority, I'm a bit old for a babysitter, and I don't even like rock stars."

Justice spun around to see a woman who was barely five and a half feet tall, wrapped up in jeans and a blue T-shirt with a long, dark open-front sweater over it. Her reddish-brown hair was scraped back into a low ponytail, and nerd glasses finished the look. She wore credentials around her neck, which explained how she'd gotten past the show's security. There was only one person she could be.

Their new publicist.

Liza tried not to laugh. Justice Cade pulled up short, his blue eyes going wide as he took her in.

Surprise.

Not a sorority girl or groupie. Nope, Liza rocked average so hard, people forgot her before she left a room. Exactly as she wanted it—for now anyway. The other band members were spread out on the stage with their instruments, or she guessed it was them. Liza was sure she'd recognize them from the hours she'd watched the show and videos—except she couldn't drag her gaze away from Justice long enough to really look.

The lead singer and front man for Savaged Illusions packed a lot of talent in his six-foot-plus frame. Sex-messy hair with surfer-blond streaks that stood out against darker strands. Black T-shirt and jeans molded to lean muscle.

No wonder girls lost their minds for Justice Cade.

Not her, she reminded herself harshly, and shifted her scrutiny away from him. She was immune to rockers and musicians in general. She'd learned that brutal lesson, and she wasn't likely to forget. Ever.

"You must be Liza."

The sound of his voice yanked her attention back to him. Smooth and rich with a hint of the deep resonance he sang with when he really opened up his vocals.

"Yep, I'm Liza Glasner. I'll be Savaged Illusions publicist for as long as you remain on the show." She took in the grim mood. What was going on here? She'd figure it out, but right now, she had to establish her place. "Whether you want me or not."

She needed this gig. First, if her band won, she'd get the paid summer internship with Tangent, which she required for enough credits to graduate after the fall quarter. Second, her roommate was moving in with her boyfriend, and Liza had to be out of her apartment in three weeks. If she didn't get the internship that came with the studio apartment, she'd be forced to go home for the summer. The thought of going back to her aunt and uncle's house in Santa Barbara made her chest tighten. But the band didn't need to know how desperate she was.

Or who she was. For the three years she'd been in college, she'd been just Liza—an average college girl.

Justice twisted his full lips. "Yeah, sorry. It's not personal, Liza."

"I'm not taking it personally." Nope, this wasn't her first experience with rock-star arrogance. Of course they thought they deserved better than a student. "But here's the deal. I met Karl and Nikki, the publicists who got the other two bands. Both are college students and go-getters. They're each going to work hard to help their band win. But I'm going to make sure Savaged Illusions wins, so get used to the idea."

He raised his eyebrows. "How?"

His doubt grated on her nerves, but she tried for a conciliatory tone. "I realize you don't know me, but—"

"You don't know us either."

Fine, he wanted to challenge her? "Wrong. I did my research, Justice Noah Cade." She took one step closer, keeping an arm's length between them. "You're the lead singer and front man of the band. You also write songs, have a juvie record, are quick-tempered, impulsive, stubborn and insanely talented. And you obviously like to prejudge people before meeting them."

He opened his mouth, but Liza turned away before she got sucked into those penetrating blue eyes. Something about his gaze unnerved her. She focused on the tall man holding the gorgeous guitar. "Simon Bender with the lion eyes. Although they look more brown than gold to me, at least in this lighting. You're the lead guitarist, backing vocals, with enough talent to head up a song if you chose."

Simon held out his hand. "Liza. Nice to meet you."

After shaking his hand, she covered a few steps to the man with long dark hair leaning on the bass guitar. She could feel Justice's stare on her, almost a weight on her skin. Which was ridiculous since she had on a shirt and cardigan covering it. She'd needed the extra layer of protection, even with the weather in the seventies. *Focus.* "River Donovan, the playboy charmer. You're the bassist and can play anything with strings. And backing vocals too. You add a dark throb to the band's savage sound. Think you can focus on winning for the next few weeks and not college girls?"

"I can multitask. Don't wanna disappoint the pretty chicks."

Time to shut this down with some bluntness. "The last thing I want to do is clean up one of your sexcapades gone bad. That stuff catches fire on social media." She knew all too well how easy it was to twist facts. It was one of the reasons she'd been drawn to communications and publicity—learning to control the story.

River laughed, regaining her attention. "I'll try to be a good boy."

She stopped next at the keyboard rig. "Grayson Price, nice to meet you. You're the newest member of the band, can play piano or any keyboard and some guitar. Went to Juilliard, impressive." Curiosity propelled her to add, "You were a classical music prodigy. Interesting that you ended up in a rock band."

Gray stared back with zero expression in his piercing blue eyes. "Is it?"

Right, he didn't want to talk about it. She was the last person who would poke at old wounds. "I can barely eke out 'Chopsticks,' so yeah, talent and commitment like that are fascinating." As she turned away, she noted that he could use some coaching in coming across as more accessible in interviews. He seemed to have an automatic shutdown that made him distant.

"Liza?" Gray called out.

Liza returned her attention to the pianist. "Yes?"

"Most people call me Gray."

Awesome; she'd cracked the ice with him. She smiled. "Gray, then." She headed to the drum kit. The percussionist watched her with the amused expression of a cat toying with a mouse.

"Lynx Steele. I'm curious, where'd you come up with Lynx?" His real name was Aiden, which didn't fit the hard-angled man.

"Street name."

"Oh. Tough guy, huh?" Rather cliché for a drummer.

"Like, a literal street name I saw once and thought was cool."

Liza blinked, then laughed. "Okay, that's awesome. We're so using that. But the name fits you." The man definitely had an untamed edge to him. "So you and Justice started this band together. You're not only the drummer, but under all those tats, leather and party attitude, you're also a writer and composer. You're driven in everything you do, including drinking." Liza glanced at his water bottle.

Lynx scooped it up and held it out. "Wanna check?"

A chill rippled down her spine, chasing out her earlier amusement. It wasn't the drummer, but the sight of his hand holding out the drink. *Stop. Don't think about it.* "Pass." She had to swallow the sudden wave of nausea.

That hadn't happened in a while. Stress maybe? Didn't matter, she had a job to do and ignored the queasy reaction.

"Done showing off?" Justice said. "We're burning practice time here."

Spinning to face him, she sensed confusing undercurrents, like she'd walked into the middle of something, but she had no idea what. Right now she needed to work on gaining their trust and cooperation. "I was making a point. I've prepared for this job, and you need to check your ego so we can work together. I want the same thing you do—to win."

"Ease up, Justice," Simon cut in. "She's all we have."

Dropping his crossed arms, Justice sighed. "Okay, I get it. What do you need, Liza? We really are short on time. Our practices are tightly scheduled."

Well that was marginally better. "I'm going to be with you guys for the next couple weeks. Pretty much everywhere you go, I'll be tagging along."

"With all of us?" he asked.

The suspicious note in his voice made her uneasy. What was he looking for? Attention all on him? Or was it something else—maybe the underlying tension she'd picked up on? It was unnerving the way all five band members seemed to be silently communicating with one another. "Specifically with you. Tangent wants me to focus on the front man. Both your professional and personal life."

"Oh hell no." His shoulders swelled beneath his T-shirt, and his eyes narrowed. "That's where I draw the line. Savaged Illusions is the five of us, not just me."

"They're pulling more bullshit," River snarled.

"Fucking typical," Lynx added. "We're getting cut out."

Whoa. Justice was pissed, whereas she'd half-expected he'd just assume it was his due. But no, he was insisting that all the members of the band mattered. Gazing around, she noted that no one was surprised by his reaction. Huh.

"Okay, hang on," Simon said. "If we win, the deal is that Tangent has to sign the band, all five of us. There are no exceptions, no substitutions. We had the contract checked for exactly that."

Justice nodded. "With you so far."

"If that means you're featured in our media campaign, big deal. As long as we win, we get the contract."

"I still don't like it." Justice compressed his mouth, his full lips whitening.

"Look, man, it's shitty, yeah." Lynx snatched up his water bottle and strode over. "But what can we do? We gotta play the game."

These guys really had her interest now. It was the whole loyalty thing. The way they watched out for each other intrigued the hell out of her. That kind of allegiance had been scarce in her life. What was it like to trust like that?

But she wasn't there to answer a question about trust, she was there to do her job. Didn't mean she couldn't be creative about it though. Ideas began buzzing and taking shape. "I don't have a lot of choice, but I can find a way to do both. Keep Justice front and center, while working in things that show the five of you together are the heart of the Savaged Illusions band." The challenge of that fascinated her. She loved creating and controlling the story. "I'll start with you, Justice, so I'm going to need an interview and see a bit of your daily life with the band and away from them to satisfy Tangent." She swept her gaze over them. "Then I'll figure out ways to do features on all of you that appear organic."

Justice turned the full force of his attention on her. "You'd do that?"

"Well yeah. Look, I get that you don't like me, or you're pissed that I'm not a real publicist. But I'm here. Let me do my job, okay?" She hated having to beg. That old fear that if she said or did the wrong thing she'd be sent away crept up. But these guys were a job, not a life partner. "It's two and a half weeks and you'll never see me again."

Justice took a deep breath and closed his eyes, then opened them. "I'm sorry about being an ass to you. It was totally uncalled for."

The apology caught her off guard. "Uh, thanks."

He nodded. "We have a party tonight at Screech's Nightclub. I assume you'll want to go?"

Tonight? Damn, that was jumping right into the fire. Nerves jangled her stomach, but she had to do it. "Just long enough to get some pictures. If you give me the address and time, I'll stay an hour or so." She'd be in the background, so no one would notice her.

"Won't work. Screech closed the club to the public. It's invitation only. Meet me at my house, and I'll get you in."

His house? "I'd rather meet you at the club." She was stubborn on that point. Always.

His gaze stayed level. "Do you want an interview? We could get started on that at my house before we leave."

"Why not now?"

"Practice. We only get four-hour slots and then have to be out. Things like interviews have to be outside of practice time."

They were serious about their music. She was supposed to follow Justice, and getting a few pictures of him at home would be good. She could do this. "Okay."

Taking out her camera to grab some shots as they began warming up and playing, Liza told herself over and over that she could handle it.

The last time she went to the house of a rock star had ended with her in the hospital, her dad dead and her mom under arrest.

But she knew better now. She'd never again trust the wrong person like she had that horrible night.

Chapter 2

LIZA FOUND THE ADDRESS EASY enough. Streetlights illuminated an older house set on a large piece of property. Someone had mowed the weeds in the front. Had it been grass once? A couple rosebushes beneath a window were overgrown and sad.

As she walked to the door, a band formed around her chest, and her pulse pounded. *Don't back down now. Do it. Knock on the door. And look confident, you're not a scared teenager.* Before she could lose her courage, she rang the bell.

One minute passed. Then two. Liza peered around. Did she have the right—?

The door opened.

She started to speak and froze. Despite a screen door between them, she had a clear view of Justice wearing nothing but a pair of dark jeans riding low on his hipbones, several tats and a few drops of water sliding over his collarbone from wet hair. Her gaze snagged on the ink of a blue jay with wings spread over his heart. The image had a tenderness to it that didn't seem to match the rest of Justice.

"Hey, you caught me just out of the shower.

Come in." He pushed open the screen and stepped back.

She hesitated, thrown by his half-dressed appearance. "You said eight o'clock, right?"

"Yeah, sorry. I crashed for a couple hours and woke late." He studied her while holding the door wide open. "I'll grab a shirt. Wait here or come in, whatever you like." Pivoting, he strode away.

Spread over his back was a lion wearing a ferocious expression, one paw raised as if he were stalking prey. Then Justice vanished from view.

Well crap. What should she do? Curiosity tugged her into a living room with a chocolate-brown couch and love seat on the right. Ahead of her was a dining room with a dark oval table and a matching hutch filled with flowered dishes. "What guy has flowered dishes?"

"They came with the house." Justice leaned one shoulder against the wall of what looked like a hallway. He'd pulled on a shirt, and his hair was drying in casual, sexy waves.

"You rent it?" she asked.

"Nope. It's mine."

He owned a house? "Uh, are the other guys staying here with you?" This Justice seemed very different from the man she'd met earlier today. That guy had been angry and sharp-edged. This man was easier going, softening her unease.

"Simon has a house. The other guys can crash here if they want, but after weeks on the road, we all like our own space for at least a few days. Everyone needs to decompress." He headed toward her and stopped before getting into her personal space. "I'm starved, how about you? Want a sandwich?"

"Uh, don't we need to do the interview and...?" She

glanced at the opened door. Since she'd only closed the screen when she came in, she didn't feel trapped. Justice wasn't scaring her, but she wasn't entirely comfortable either.

"Liza."

His voice compelled her to look at him. Three feet separated them, which was wide enough to make her feel safe, but close enough to get the full impact of Justice. His hair begged for a woman's fingers, and those eyes, blue with gray flecks, were captivating. A flutter touched her stomach. Not attraction, he wasn't her type. Maybe appreciation?

"We don't need to be at the club until around ten. I have some things I really want to talk to you about. But we can go out to a restaurant if you'll be more relaxed in public." He sighed, his mouth tightening. "This morning was a total clusterfuck, and you walked into the aftermath. I wasn't thinking, or I wouldn't have insisted you come to my house if you're uncomfortable."

There was a ring of truth to that, especially since she'd sensed a lot of tense undercurrents with the whole band. "You wanted to talk in private?"

"I did, yeah. Restaurants can be tricky if people happen to watch the show."

His frankness tugged out her bravery. She had to get used to him if she was going to be working with him for a few weeks. "Here's fine. Want me to shut the door?"

"Leave it if you want. Kitchen's this way." He headed through the doorway.

Open worked for her. She set her camera bag on the big dining table. Gathering her courage, she followed him into a square kitchen and stopped in surprise. Linoleum floors, old antique green cabinets, cracked tile countertop and chickens? Copper and ceramic-shaped chickens hung on the walls and lounged by the sink and stove. "You must like chickens."

"Not me, my grandmother." He stuck his head in the fridge and came out with a bunch of deli-wrapped meats and some plastic containers. After shutting the fridge, he dumped everything on the counter and looked around. "Told her I'd buy her a brand-new, fully updated house one day. She didn't want that."

"No?" Why was he so different now than he'd been at practice? Fascinated, she rested against the sink. Oddly enough, the well-loved kitchen made her feel safe. She hadn't really felt safe...ever. And she'd never lived in a house like this. It reminded her of an old TV sitcom where the worst thing that happened was a burned dinner and a bad grade in school.

"She was a tough woman with a soft center. This was her home, where she raised her sons, and then me." His gaze slid back to hers.

Love for his grandmother blazed in his stare. Raw, unfiltered and so real, it made her ache for him. "I read in your bio that your grandmother passed a year ago."

"Yeah. Bad case of pneumonia got her. I've been traveling since then. Let the house get ahead of me. She'd be furious about her yard. She loved her flowers, especially in the backyard. Now it's a mess. I cut the front and back grass, but I don't know shit about flowers or how to get it all in shape again."

On firmer ground, she said, "You cut weeds that choked out the grass. It needs to be dug out and replaced with either seed, sod or drought-resistant landscaping. And the rosebushes need to be pruned back and fed."

"You know about gardening?"

"A little." While Justice pulled more things out of

the fridge, she walked to the back door and looked out the window. Yep, dead yard surrounded by overgrown shrubs and plant corpses that might have once been flowers. "I worked at a nursery and took care of the yard at my aunt's house." One day, she'd have her own home. A real one like this. But that took money, so graduating and getting a good job were first on her agenda.

"Turkey or ham?"

Crossing to him, she eyed the bread on the plates. "How about I make mine?"

"Perfect."

They worked together for a few minutes, making sandwiches and scooping out deli salads. While he made a second sandwich, she examined the inked skull and clock wrapped in a rose vine that covered his entire upper arm. That tat was very different from the blue jay on his chest. That one had been poignant and soft somehow. And her thoughts were wandering off topic. "So, you wanted to talk to me?"

He glanced over. "About a couple things, actually. I meant what I said at practice today. I don't want the other guys cut out of the publicity you do." Seriousness hardened his features. "This band, it's the five of us. I don't mind being the front—hell, I love it. But the band is all of us, and I want to make sure that comes across. Don't cut them out, Liza."

Damn. She liked that fierce loyalty in him. It tugged at the raw, empty place in her. "I'm not going to. But as Simon pointed out, Tangent has to take you as a band if you win."

"Yeah, but it doesn't mean they won't try something underhanded. I want us to go in strong as a clearly defined group. We need you to help us with that so we have some leverage, or Tangent could keep us languishing for a year by having us open for weak acts on their way out and delay getting an album recorded. Then when the year is up, they may decide they'll only re-sign me as a solo artist. Or maybe cut me and choose another."

He'd thought this through, and it made sense. "After looking at your schedule, I have a few ideas on how I can work in some individual features on the other guys. I'll show you once I grab my phone." She'd left it tucked in her camera bag. "What's the second thing?"

"Working up to it."

For the first time, she caught a flash of uncertainty in him. "Don't trust me, huh?" Was it a personal issue for him? Or something potentially explosive?

"No more than you trusted me when I opened the door."

"Touché. What are you worried about?"

"Loyalty. *Court of Rock* and Tangent are playing games to increase ratings."

"And Tangent's more or less my employer." Even if she wasn't getting paid at the moment, she did answer to them. She got the conflict, but she needed the band's trust to do her job right. Leaning a hip against the counter, she pushed up the sleeves of her cardigan she'd pulled on over her green tank top. "We need to find a way to work together. I'm not reporting every conversation to Tangent. They picked me based on my proposal. Basically I'm a finalist in a contest, and there are now three of us competing to win a summer internship with them. My win is tied to yours. So why would I give them information that they could ultimately use against me to manipulate behind the scenes?"

He studied her. "Good point."

"But you're still not sure."

"I don't know how you can help. I mean, you don't have any real experience." He ran a hand through his hair.

She had up-close-and-personal experience with bad publicity, but that wasn't the kind of experience he was referring to. "You're really worried." Without thinking, she touched his forearm. "Is it about you?"

He shook his head. "No, it's Simon. He was blindsided this morning. It was ugly, and they have it on video. I'm telling you because it's hard for him to talk about."

Liza's guts clenched. This couldn't be good, but what got her more was Justice's deep concern. "I'll do my best, but someone needs to tell me."

He nodded. "Simon was married a few years ago."

Stunned, she dropped her hand. "He was? That's not in anything I've read."

"Not many people knew. It was before I met him, and a short marriage. Just a few months."

"What happened?" How bad was this? God, don't let Simon have done something awful.

"Simon was trying to make it as a solo artist at the time, which meant he was traveling and performing all over the country. He came home after a gig and discovered her dead. Suicide."

"He found her?" Justice had said that, but she couldn't imagine the shock and horror of discovering someone you love like that.

He strode to the window set into the top half of the back door, his back rigid beneath his T-shirt. The tension was so acute she could actually see the outline of his muscles through the cotton fabric. "If this comes out, it's going to rip a hole in him. Ace, the front man for Jagged Sin, said on tape that she'd done it to get away from him. The show hasn't aired it yet, but we think they will use that footage. It's too sensational not to."

An accusation like that would rock social media. It had the potential to make a lot of fans hate Simon, and by association, the band. Liza was still trying to get her head around the whole situation. "Why would Ace do that?" It was so cruel.

"He hates Simon. They have a history, kind of a feud. The show loves that shit. They feed it every chance they get. Until now, Simon ignored Ace. But this..." He shook his head.

This was exactly the reason she wanted to be a publicist, to help people manage these kinds of horrible, underhanded attacks. The brutal cyber trolls and cruel gossips who twisted facts to feed their sick needs. Her inexperience chafed at her, but she was all they had. Think. "Okay, I need to talk to Simon. The best thing we can do is get out in front of this story, getting control of the narrative before someone else does." That was pretty much Publicity 101.

Justice pivoted, frustration bleeding off him. "I don't know if he'll do it. Or even if he *can* do it."

"That's why you told me instead of him." She took a breath. They needed her to step up and be a publicist. She'd find a way to do this. "It's my job to handle this. I'll talk to Simon and see what he's willing to do. I'll also see if I can get anything out of Nikki. She's Jagged Sin's publicist. Frankly, Ace spouting off something like this could backfire on him in a big way, so she may want to stop that footage from getting out too."

His shoulders relaxed slightly. "That's something."

"Let me worry about this, Justice."

He crossed to her. "You're a surprise, Liza. All that happened this morning, and then the producer dropped the news that we weren't getting an experienced publicist."

Now it made sense why he was angry when she walked in. Trying to ease him, she said, "Instead you got a student whose only experience is taking selfies."

His mouth quirked. "And who doesn't even like rock stars."

That pulled a smile from her. "I may be changing my mind on that." Realizing how that might sound, she flushed and added, "I mean as a friend or coworker. Not..."

"Like a groupie?"

The teasing note in his voice broke the tension and relieved her. "Exactly." She'd never get so caught up in a man or band that she lost sight of everything else that mattered.

Justice grabbed a couple water bottles, returned to the dining room and dropped into his seat at the end of the table. "Are you cold? I can shut the front door."

"No, why?" She fiddled with her phone, ignoring her sandwich.

"You haven't taken your sweater off." He'd left the door open to keep her from feeling trapped. He'd been surprised by her reluctance to come in, then felt like an ass. He'd gotten too used to groupies seeking him out, pushing to get inside his hotel rooms. Been awhile since he'd encountered a woman with a little more self-preservation instincts.

But the sweater bugged him.

She shrugged. "I'm fine."

"You look different with your hair down." Her wild curls of rich brown streaked with red entranced him. The urge to touch it grew by the minute.

She jerked her gaze up from the phone, one hand touching a lock. "It's a pain. I didn't have time to straighten it."

Her green eyes magnified by her glasses were stunning. Why hadn't he noticed them earlier? "I like your wild hair."

She smirked. "You would. Did you use your fingers to comb that?"

Yep, she definitely wasn't a groupie trying to get into his bed. "That was a compliment, Glasner. You're supposed to say thank you, not insult me."

"Wild hair is a compliment?"

Oh yeah. One look at that riotous hair paired with her challenging green eyes and his blood heated. Liza was different, an interesting mix of confidence and caution. Like that sweater. He wanted it off her, wanted to break through her wariness to find out who she was. "Not good enough for you? I'll try again. You look pretty tonight. The green in your shirt brings out your eyes, your hair makes me want to touch it and your smart mouth..." Justice stared at her full lips slicked with a soft pink that had him thinking about kissing her.

She stiffened, her shoulders jacking to her ears.

His caution kicked in. *Too far.* "...is funny and annoying."

She let out a breath. "*Annoying.* Wow, I am touched by your charming compliment, rock star."

"What? I said you're pretty."

"Save it, Cade. I'm not interested in your feeble attempts at compliments or whatever you call this." She waved her fork between them, then scooped up some pasta salad and slid it in her mouth.

Justice had to force his stare from her lips. What was up with him tonight? Maybe it was that she'd made her disinterest in him so clear? "Your turn, Glasner." He took another bite of his sandwich, amazed at how much fun he was having.

"For what?"

"Compliment. You think I'm so bad at it? Dazzle me with your talent."

Her mouth curved into a sensual smile. "Fishing for flattery? Seriously?"

"Yep."

Setting her fork down, she hit him with the full force of her regard. "Let's see. You're talented, but you know that. Everyone tells you how great your voice is."

The battle to keep a grin off his face was real.

"There must be something else about you worthy of flattery." Her eyebrows drew tighter behind her glasses. "Oh, I know. That blue jay on your chest is magnificent, almost ethereal yet striking. Your other ink is cool, but that... Yeah. Nice tat."

"Huh. You managed to get a good look in a short time." Given that she'd worn the expression of a woman ready to bolt when he opened the door, he was pleased. "You like me." Teasing her was too much fun.

"I tolerate you." Liza pushed up the sleeves of her sweater, then sighed and took it off.

Justice sucked in a breath. Her hair fell around shoulders bared by a clingy tank top. He'd known she had some curves, but damn. A flush ripped through him, heating right down to his bones. Not wanting to make her uncomfortable, he grabbed his bottle of water and swallowed a long drink. *Don't stare.* She'd finally relaxed. He didn't want to change that.

Scooping up her phone, she said, "I'm bringing up your promo schedule so we can talk about how to feature the other band members. Okay, for the Indie

Rock Broadcast interview, I had this idea for River. It's a little crazy..."

"How crazy?" *Stop thinking about her boobs, you horny bastard.* Hell, the top was fairly modest, not like actual cleavage was showing. He focused on the wide silver watch around her left wrist.

"I have access to your website, so I was reading through your fan mail, and I found one that's from a girl named Cassie Simmons who was in a serious accident and had to miss her senior year in high school to recover. She talks about how River playing his bass guitar helped her through it."

Relieved to have something else to think about, he answered, "That's great, but how do you want to use it?"

Her eyes shined behind her glasses. "This girl really connects with River. We could have River read this letter during the interview, then call the girl and talk to her. I think it would mean a lot to her, lift her spirits and help her to see her hero cares. As a bonus, it'll focus a little attention on River."

"You've been thinking about this. And working on it. How many emails have you read?" He was impressed that she'd taken the band's concerns seriously.

She shrugged. "Dozens. I'll put them in a file for you guys if you want to see them."

"We take turns answering fan mail."

She nodded. "I'll tag it if the fan mentions one of you specifically. But do you think River will agree?"

"Hell yes. He'll be all over that."

After grabbing a quick bite of her sandwich, she asked, "Who among you all would be the best at building sandcastles?"

That was unexpected. "Lynx."

"Perfect, with all his tats and attitude, this will work." She scrolled. "Here it is. All three of the bands will be performing at the Sandcastle Contest and Concert a week from Saturday. So, what if we get some kids to enter, and they are trying to build a sandcastle. But, you know, their castle isn't looking good. Lynx goes to help them. We'll get pictures, do some live tweeting...that will be gold."

Actually, yeah it would be. And easy. "I can arrange that with Drake and some kids from the Fighters to Mentors program. Lynx's great with those kids. He's a natural at that kind of thing."

"Good. I'll get in touch with the Indie Rock Broadcast guys and get that call arranged for River." She made note on her phone, her fingers flying over the digital keypad. "But what's Fighters to Mentors? And who is Drake?"

"Put the phone down, and I'll tell you." He wanted her focus on him.

She fiddled with her glasses. "Do you always need undivided attention?"

His mouth twitched at her snark. "Maybe I just want to know something about you. If you don't like rock stars—" oh he so wasn't letting her forget that, "— why are you interested in working with them?"

"I'm not, at least not long term. But this is great experience, and I need the intern job. There are other jobs in publicity and marketing aside from rock."

He shook his head. "Nope. You're too interested in our music, understand our sound. You like rock." Her comments about River's bass playing were perceptive and spot-on.

She sipped her water. "I grew up on rock music until I was fourteen years old. I can't even count the concerts and backstages I've been to. Seen the inside of a few tour buses. So yeah, I like the music, but not the life."

Her eyes slid away from his, and he didn't like it. Justice caught her hand. "How did you see all that until you were fourteen?"

She swallowed. "It doesn't matter. It was a long time ago."

Was it? Because something haunted her green eyes. "How old are you?"

"Twenty. I turn twenty-one this summer."

"Not that long ago."

"I don't talk about it." She pulled her hand away and picked up her sandwich.

She'd shut down. As in he could almost see the wall come down and her eyes go flat. She huddled back in the chair and shoved the food around on her plate. What was she hiding?

Not your problem. They only had to work together for three weeks. Let it go. He gave her space to regroup while focusing on his own food for a few minutes. But damn, it bugged him. How could a twenty-year-old be such a strange combination of innocence and experience? Taking her sweater off had seemed like a big deal, but she grew up around rock and tour buses? She'd have been exposed to some wild behavior. The silence got to him. "I'm twenty-four. In case you were wondering."

"I wasn't."

"Ouch."

Her lips twitched. "I know how old you are, Rock Ego. I did my research, remember?"

Ha, he was making progress. "Where're you from?" That sounded safe enough.

"Santa Barbara."

Curiosity propelled him to ask, "There's a UC school there. Wouldn't that have been closer to home?"

Picking up her fork, she toyed with her pasta salad. "Too close to home. Look, if you want to know badly enough, spend an hour on Google. You'll find it eventually."

The sudden vulnerability in her voice cut him. "Hey, we all have shit. I'm not trying..." Lie. Total lie, he'd been fishing. "Okay, I was digging around, wasn't I?"

That earned him a smile. "Not even subtly."

"No more digging."

She eyed him. "You're going to look it up, aren't you?"

He hated the tension bouncing off her in near-tangible waves. "How about we make a deal."

"What kind of deal?"

"I'll hold off snooping for a few days to give you a chance to tell me." He'd seen the way she cared about the fan, Cassie. He'd felt her need to give that girl encouragement like she empathized somehow. That brought out his protectiveness.

She narrowed her eyes. "Are you lying? Like you'll look it up the second I'm gone?"

He laughed at that. "Baby, I'd look it up right in front of your face if I was going to do it. We already covered the part where I'm not subtle."

"I almost believe you." Her shoulders lowered a fraction as she took a bite of the pasta salad. "So you were going to tell me about Fighters to Mentors?"

"It's a program of current and former UFC fighters who mentor troubled boys, usually underprivileged or foster kids. Drake Vaughn, a former UFC fighter, is the founder."

"You were in the program?"

"Yep. The day I was released from juvie, Drake was there with my grandmother to pick me up. She knew him from the small diner she owned. After that,

Drake stepped in as a surrogate-father type. My mother had bailed, my father...couldn't be there. But my grandmother..." he paused a second, grief digging in, "...she refused to give up on me." A fact Drake had pointed out to him.

She touched his hand. "Did your grandmother support your music?"

Easy question. "One hundred percent. She said music spoke to me the same way her flowers and cooking spoke to her."

Liza smiled so hard her eyes sparkled. "What about all those chickens in the kitchen? Did they speak to her?"

Justice laughed. "Doubtful. If they were smart, they shut up. That woman made the best fried chicken in the universe. I'm pretty sure all those chickens were afraid of her."

"She sounds pretty awesome. My grandmother has a serious disdain for anything fried."

That offhand comment intrigued him. "She's missing out. Nothing like fried chicken and mashed potatoes."

Liza rolled her eyes. "Shh, mashed potatoes are a sin. But for a special treat, there's always mashed cauliflower with a smidge of nonfat Greek yogurt and broth."

He gaped at her. "Your grandmother made that for you?"

"Yep."

"Did you eat it?"

"Sure. It wasn't bad tasting. But it's not mashed potatoes."

He couldn't resist probing with, "Can I ask if you lived with your grandmother? Or is that prying too?"

"At fourteen, I moved in with my aunt and uncle. All of them are into health food."

"And they forced you into eating it too?" Why had she lived with her aunt and uncle? What happened to her parents? A million questions raced in his mind.

"Forced? No. If I'd complained, they'd have made me something different. But I just ate what they gave me. I tried very hard not to cause them trouble." A grin splashed across her face. "However I hid a stash of candy in my room. Other girls babysat for money. I did it for free junk food and soda. To this day I keep candy stashes in my apartment."

Such the contradiction, and damn that smile—he couldn't resist it. "Do you have any of that candy on you now?"

She glanced at her camera bag, then said, "Don't be ridiculous."

Busted. He jumped up, skirted around her and grabbed the bag. He started fishing through the pockets until... "Ha!" He pulled out a package. Half a bag of mini Reese's Peanut Butter Cups. "You actually carry a stash of candy."

Her face turned bright red, and she glared at him. "What do you care?"

He prowled up to her. "Are you going to share?" This close, he got a nose full of her warm peach scent.

She tilted her head back. "Why should I?"

"Because you like me?"

"Not right now." She snatched the bag from his hand.

He let go of the candy and dropped his hand on the table. Leaning closer, he said, "Please? I fed you dinner."

"Sandwiches? You think a turkey sandwich is worthy of my peanut butter cups?"

The disbelief riding her voice made him grin. "You ate it."

Sticking her nose up at him, she clutched the treats.

"I was being polite. Unlike you. It was rude to look in my camera bag. That does not deserve any peanut butter cups."

True. But he hadn't been able to resist discovering if she really had a stash of candy. There was something so innocent yet secretive in her, he'd wanted to be a part of it. "You're not going to share?"

She bit her bottom lip, then gave him a sly smile. "If I share with you, then you have to answer five interview questions before we go to the club tonight."

He pretended to consider her words, while thinking that for one unguarded moment, he'd just seen the real Liza Glasner. "Okay."

She lifted her chin. "From your chair, not standing over me."

It took effort to push back and put distance between them. This girl was getting under his skin in a big way. Dropping into his chair, he leaned back and stretched his legs out. "Shoot."

"Favorite classic rock song."

"'Kashmir' by Led Zeppelin, 'Sweet Emotion' Aerosmith, 'Wanted Dead or Alive' Bon Jovi."

Liza opened the bag and tossed him a couple mini peanut butter cups.

He unwrapped one and popped it in his mouth, pleased with himself.

"That was a warm-up question. Now I want the truth—the one song that truly means the most to you. And why."

Halfway through unwrapping the second treat, he froze and slowly lifted his gaze. "That's two questions."

"I see you have solid math skills. You agreed to answer."

Shit, she was good. "'Comfortably Numb' by Pink Floyd." That was the easy part.

"Why?"

Dragging in a breath, he tried to figure out how to frame it. "The simple answer is that I know what it's like to try to escape pain with drugs." It wasn't a secret that he'd done drugs. Typical dumbass kid. Although that dumbass shit got serious the day he tagged along with friends to steal beer from a convenience store. He regretted that decision with every fiber of his being.

She set her arms on the table, her bag of candy cradled between them. "That doesn't answer the question. What does the song mean to you?"

He wanted to close his eyes, block out the sweetness of her face. But she had him hooked. "Because the world only wants the hero, not the man. Once you're broken, once you come home wounded and too fucking real, they'll drug you up or shove you out the door." Anger brewed in his guts. The military had done that to his dad. His old man had been used to being in charge, a leader, the one everyone looked up to. Then he came home wounded, traumatized and unable to return to any semblance of a normal life. Justice had been like everyone else.

Impatient. Frustrated. Selfish.

All those years of being a hero meant nothing when his dad couldn't get a job, couldn't function, and his own son was embarrassed. To Liza he said, "No matter how strong you are, life can break you." Like his dad.

She didn't move except to blink, slow and soft sweeps of her lashes that did nothing to dim the intensity breeding in that gaze. "Will it break you?"

"Question number four. No. Nothing will break me or get in the way of what I want." He craved the limelight, the power. That was so much better than the helplessness of searching and searching for his missing father and seeing all those broken people that no one cared about pushed into the shadows.

"What's your goal?"

He leaned closer, sliding into those eyes so green they belonged on a witch, not this mortal woman. "Fame. Our band is going all the way to a platinum, number-one-selling record and Grammy wins." He'd prove he was worth something. He wasn't that fuckup whose own mother washed her hands of him and whose father would rather live on the streets than with him.

One day, Justice and his band would be famous enough that even his father would hear them and finally come home. His father would forgive him and let him help, just like his grandmother had begged him to do before she died.

Chapter 3

FAME. LIZA WAS STILL REELING when the cab pulled up in front of Screech's Nightclub. Justice's answer shouldn't have surprised her. Experience had taught her that rock stars were entitled fame-chasers who would destroy anything in their way. That's what she didn't like about them, why she didn't want to make them her career.

Except Justice had shown her another side when he spoke of his grandmother with unabashed love and respect. He cared about his friend Simon, wanting Liza to help. Yet he expressed his goal with such coldness. No, that was wrong. Not cold.

Heat. Rage. A need so vibrant, her skin had prickled and her heart pounded in response. Both of them had forgotten the candy by then.

She'd had to fight the impulse to run, to get the hell out of there and protect herself from becoming one of his casualties. Except if she did that, then she'd forfeit the internship and have to go home. Back to the house where she had to be perfect to atone for both herself and her mother.

"Liza?"

Damn, she'd been so lost in her head, she wasn't paying attention. Justice had paid the driver, gotten out and held the door.

Sliding out, she looped her camera case over her shoulder and tried to keep up in her heels. "Still can't believe I let you talk me into taking a cab with you. I could have driven us then you take a cab home later."

His hand closed around hers, warm and solid. "This is the Gaslamp Quarter. There's only street parking or a public lot."

She glanced around at all the cars lining the roads. Yeah, parking would be a bitch, and walking to a public lot late at night in the dark wasn't smart.

"Come on, let's go have some fun."

Right, fun. Except the memories... Liza pressed her palm against the vulnerability dancing in her soft belly. She should have brought her sweater, but no, she'd played the big bad publicist and stowed it in her car.

She twisted her head in time to watch the cab pull away. Her escape. Gone.

"Problem?" Justice loomed at her shoulder, concern in his eyes.

Okay, she had this. It was a nightclub, just a club. She'd gone dancing with her roommate and had fun. Going into Screech's wasn't anything different than that. Piece of cake.

Lifting her chin, she said, "World peace. Pollution. Global warming. Child hunger. Homeless animals. Also wildfires. Take your pick."

The corners of his eyes crinkled, and amusement chased out the concern. "Anything else?"

Yeah, the way he looked at her as if trying to solve a puzzle. "Quit stalling, Cade. You've got hot groupies waiting to grope you." She took a step.

His hand wrapped around her arm, his fingers

warm and firm against her bare skin. Moving around her, he filled her vision with his wavy hair, hard face and see-too-much eyes. "You look beautiful. Especially when you do that."

People walked past them, but Justice captured her attention and wouldn't let go. "Do what?" What did he see in her?

"Fight off whatever it is that scares you. It's seriously hot. The timid uncertainty vanishes and your confidence shines through. The green in your eyes shimmers, and I know something snarky or random will come out of your mouth."

"We barely know each other." She didn't want to feel this fascination with him.

"You like me, Glasner." He tugged her toward the club.

She really should pull her arm away. He'd release her, she was sure of it. But his grasp felt safe and comforting as she headed into something she wasn't sure she was ready for. "Not everyone likes you, Cade."

"You do." He opened the door to a small lobby where two security guards stood in front of another set of doors.

"You don't know that."

He nodded to the security guards. "Sure I do. You shared your peanut butter cups with me. You so like me."

Before she could respond, they passed a second set of doors into another world. A Red Hot Chili Peppers song pumped through the building that was once a saloon. People dressed from beach casual to rocker hard clustered in groups, slamming drinks and laughing.

Justice's hand stayed on her arm, an anchor as she absorbed the energy of loud music and fun, similar to the places she'd gone to dance and hang out. Steadier, she tugged her arm free to reach for her camera. As she released it from the case, realization dawned on her—Justice had known what he was doing by holding her arm, teasing her, getting her into the club and past her fear, a fear he probably didn't understand but helped her navigate anyway.

Confusion swirled, creating too many uncomfortable emotions. Needing to focus on something besides her fears and disturbing fascination with Justice, she lifted her camera and took shots of the wanted posters featuring rock stars on the walls. Clever. The weapons wall had various guitars mounted. A huge banner over the stage read *Dueling Grounds*. Liza grabbed a shot of that then looked around. She spotted Savaged Illusions' drummer and bassist, Lynx and River, talking to a group of girls by the bar. Where were the remaining two band members, Gray and Simon?

"Justice." A man cut through the throng. Middle-aged, he wore jeans with a leather vest over a shirt, very little hair on top of his head, but he sported a cliché ponytail. "Great to see you." The man thumped Justice on the back.

She grabbed a shot of the two men, one up and coming in the scene with someone who clearly was part of the old guard. She clicked off more shots to tweet out as little vignettes about the front man of Savaged Illusions.

"Screech, thanks, man."

Liza narrowed her eyes. "Screech Rizo from the Hell Blades?" They'd been hot for a short time back in the nineties.

The man beamed. "I don't care if Justice told you that, I'm going to pretend you recognize me."

"I do. Well, the name helped. And all the memorabilia." She held out her hand. "My mom had your music on all the time." *Damn, shut up.* As a rule, she didn't bring up her mom. "Do you play anymore?" His band had broken up by the time the nineties came to a close.

"Hell yeah. Whole point of the club. I can play anytime I want, and I don't have to go on tour. These bones are too old for that life."

She grinned and gestured to the stage. "Hope I get a chance to hear you before I leave."

"Hey, it's our social director." Lynx strode up, followed by River buried in a crowd of women. One girl had a striped dress, dark leggings and thigh-high boots. A blonde had wrapped her hips in a tiny skirt and a tight shirt with platform heels. A couple wore jeans like Liza, but theirs were expensively distressed. They belonged in this club.

She forced a smile. "Lynx, River. Justice is..." she glanced over to see a girl pushing a drink into his hand, "...there."

"Oh." One of the girls shot up her hand and waved. "Gray. Over here."

Liza followed the girl's gaze to Gray, who was talking to a woman with shoulder-length blonde hair and wearing a copper dress that stood out with its tailored elegance.

"That's Christine Castle of Conquest Band Management."

Startled by the voice next to her, she turned to Simon, who had his ass perched on a table and his legs stretched out as he sipped a dark-looking drink. Scotch?

"Have you been there the whole time?" Thinking of what Justice had told her, she debated what to say to him. This wasn't really the place to talk.

"Just walked up and saw you watching them." He lifted his drink. "I was at the bar."

There was something slightly unsettling about him. On stage, he was a full-bore monster, powering into his guitar riffs, using his entire body to create his own style that made him stand out.

Offstage, a different Simon showed—this serious, controlled man. He looked older, more mysterious. Although in the club lighting, she saw the amber shading in his brown eyes. They did sort of resemble a lion's eyes, especially with their predator intensity. "Is she here to check you guys out? You don't have a manager, right?" If they had, wouldn't their manager have been in on the whole student-social-media-publicist thing?

"No. Those sharks smell money with the possible Tangent contract."

She snapped a few photos of Gray and Christine, then slid out her phone to make some notes. "Wouldn't it be smart to have one?"

"Depends." He sipped his drink. "Bad one'll screw us worse than a good one'll help." Grim determination stole any lingering softness in the man. "No unscrupulous asshole is going to get their claws into our band. I've seen what destroys groups—bad managers, drugs and women. I'll protect us from it all."

Liza nearly took a step back at the icy warning in Simon's tone. *Nope, stand your ground.* She had to get all the band's trust, and backing away would make her look weak. "Or bad publicity." Her mouth dried, but she forced herself to add, "Justice told me."

"I'm aware."

The two words came out sharp and cold. "I'll see what I can find out from *Court of Rock* producers and Nikki. We'll meet tomorrow and plan a strategy."

His gaze didn't flicker. "You and I won't need to plan a strategy if my wife's name gets dragged through the mud."

She frowned. In the couple minutes she'd talked to him, she believed him too smart to think they didn't need a strategy. "Then what will we need?"

"Bail money." He pushed off the table and strode over to join Gray and Christine.

Liza shivered. Was it that coldness, maybe even violence, that drove his wife to suicide? Or was he that way because of it?

Liza moved around, getting pictures of the band members chatting with various people. She spotted Lynx and started his way when the music cut out and the sound of a microphone crackled.

Everyone turned to the stage where Screech stood. "Friends, welcome to the club. Tonight is a very special private party to celebrate one of our own. They began playing here for me a couple years ago, and now they're appearing on the popular reality show *Court of Rock*."

Screams and applause exploded in the room.

"Come on, guys, get up here. Everyone wants to see you."

Liza wove through the crowd and tables, getting shots as Screech introduced each man and they spoke a few words. Simon riled them up, Gray thanked them all for their support, River made them laugh, and Lynx tossed a few drum sticks out into the crowd. She backed up, trying to get a clear shot of people jostling to catch the sticks.

"Liza?"

Lowering her camera, she groaned at the familiar voice. Seriously? Here? Four men huddled around a table drinking, but she homed in on her former boyfriend. "Dillion." The way he'd dumped her still stung.

"What the hell are you doing here?" His dark gaze rolled over her and zeroed in on her breasts. "Looking like that."

She started to hunch her shoulders and caught herself. "Like what? Happy to be rid of you?" It took everything she had to resist dumping his beer over his head and walking away. He wasn't worth the energy.

She made it one step when he latched a hand around her biceps. Pivoting, she said, "Let go."

"Come on, Liza. I miss you."

"Then go cozy up with your fiancée." The one that Daddy had lined up in the wings, and she'd known nothing about it.

His fingers tightened on the flesh of her upper arm. "I didn't have a choice. If you'd just been patient, maybe I could have—"

"No. I'm no man's dirty little secret." Pulling her arm free, she walked away with her shoulders up and back straight. Refusing to let Dillion affect her night or how she did her job, she focused on the stage. Justice had finished up whatever he'd said and handed the mic back to Screech.

The aging rocker said, "Technically Savaged Illusions isn't supposed to perform as a band outside approved events while in the battle to win *Court of Rock*."

After the groans of disappointment receded, Screech went on, "But no one says they can't participate individually in some of our fun later. So buy the boys some drinks and get them all loosened up. Right now, the house band is coming out to cover your favorite songs. Time to party!"

The guys were immediately surrounded as they came down the stairs. Crowds pushed and edged Liza back as she got shots of the excited fans clustering around the band. Eventually the knot broke up as people streamed to the dance floor. River, Lynx and Simon headed out there, creating a sudden rush of women.

Taking a break, Liza ordered a soda, carefully watching as it was served from the fountain. After that, she found a safe place by a table in the corner but stayed on her feet to watch the dance floor. Frantic energy radiated as the house band played a hard, edgy beat. Sexy girls swayed and gyrated. Deep in her stomach, longing spread.

The song changed, and sentiment rushed her, dragging her back to her childhood. On a good day, when her mom hadn't been drunk and desperate, they'd cranked up the tunes and danced. God, her mom had been beautiful then, her hair straighter and with more red than Liza's, and she'd danced with total abandon. The sound of her laughter echoed in Liza's head. An ache opened in her chest. She missed those happy times with her mom.

"You didn't give me a real chance."

Liza clamped her lips tight at the intruding voice. She faced Dillion. "I don't have to give you anything."

"I never meant you to be a dirty little secret. I told you I'd work on my dad."

Annoyance washed over her. What was Dillion's problem? They were done. She could have understood his reason for breaking up, but not what came after. "That's the way it sounded when you made your offer."

He shoved his too-long hair—his one rebellion against his father—out of his face. "I was upset. Dance with me. I'll explain."

47

Unable to resist, she asked, "In public? What if it gets back to your dad?" Yep, still pissed. Not about the breakup—she'd only dated him a couple months and hadn't been in love with him. She'd liked him at first, thinking he was ambitious and interesting. But soon she realized his father's ambition drove him, not his own.

His smooth face darkened. "Don't be a bitch. You're the one who hid who you really are."

There was a smidge of truth in that. "You hid a fiancée."

"We weren't engaged then."

"But you are now." What was she doing? None of this mattered anymore. "You know what? I don't care. I'm not interested in seeing you, talking to you or dancing with you."

"You heard her. Beat it now before I toss you out on your ass." Justice loomed behind her ex, radiating menace.

Dillion stepped to the side. "Hey, man, Liza and I go way back. We're just talking."

"Now you're just getting the fuck away from her."

Her ex gaped at her. "What is he, your new boyfriend? You're dating a musician?" Narrowing his eyes, he added, "You slumming like your mom now?"

A ripple went through Justice, and he visibly swelled with anger.

Liza grabbed Justice's arm. His muscles bulged rock hard beneath her hand. "It's okay. I've got this."

More people moved in closer, including Lynx and Simon. Crap. All too aware of the band's rep for getting into bar fights, she had to get control here. "Dillion, go back to your friends."

He shook his head. "My father was right about you." He stalked off.

Justice reached a hand up as if to touch her, then dropped it. "You okay?"

Too many people stared at her. Simon, Gray, River, Screech, and others she didn't know crowded in. *Quiet, Liza. Don't give them anything more to talk about. Ignore them.* The words bounced and echoed, the memory of her aunt marching alongside of her, head down, shame and anger shrouding them as reporters shouted and cameras flashed.

Justice's hand squeezed hers, mooring her to the present.

Raising her gaze to his, she answered, "Absolutely fine."

"Good, then let's dance." He tugged on her hand.

"Wait, my camera." She scooped the case off the table.

"No problem." Screech stepped up. "I'll lock it in my office if you like."

Handing off the camera, she studied Justice's profile and wondered, "You guys were all surrounded by fans a few minutes ago. What brought you over to my table?"

A tic bounced in his jaw for a second before he answered, "You."

Her hand tingled from contact with his warm fingers. This wasn't good. She couldn't like him that way. The smart thing to do would be to call a cab and go home.

Instead, almost a half hour later, her feet hurt, her throat was parched, and she was having so much fun. The house band was pretty good, covering kickass rock songs that beat deep in her blood. She danced with Justice, then Lynx snagged her, River, Simon and Gray. Their friends got in on it.

Her head ached from laughing. Girls piled onto the floor, many of them friendly, teasing the guys, pulling

Liza into a dance line with them as the band covered Beyoncé's "Put a Ring on It." It took her half the song to figure out the steps, but it was a blast. No one recognized her. She was just one of the crowd, a girl out having fun.

The band switched to the power ballad "Lips of an Angel."

She turned to escape the dance floor and stumbled into Justice. Startled, she tried to shift back.

His arms folded around her, hard bands of muscles easing her against his chest. He smelled like a freshly oiled guitar, a combination of vanilla and cedar, mixed with the earthier musk that was all Justice and much too sexy. The scents invoked memories of outdoor concerts on warm summer nights, and throngs of people on their feet and dancing. As a child, she'd lost herself in the music and joy, unbridled by the fears that haunted her now. But as she swayed with Justice, it wasn't nostalgia that sparked the longing tugging at her insides, but the man holding her. This had to be a bad idea, yet she didn't want to move.

As the song wound down Justice tilted her head up, his eyes molten beneath the club lights.

Her stomach shivered. With his arm around her back and their bodies pressed together, tension simmered between them. His gaze slid to her mouth.

A thread of desire fluttered, delicate and tentative. It should scare her, worry her, but in this moment, Liza savored it, allowing herself to feel attraction without someone telling her it would lead to disaster. She wouldn't act on it, but she could experience the pleasure without guilt.

"There's something about you, Liza Glasner."

His voice sank inside her, fanning the flickers of desire. "Like what?"

He shook his head. "Not sure. Maybe it's your hair." He traced a finger over a wave. "Or your smart mouth. It conflicts with that tight-control thing you have going on. Which is the real you? It's like you keep trying to hide part of yourself, but she's fighting to get out."

He took her breath away, seeing so much more than anyone else. How? Why? "I'm not that interesting."

"Liar."

His voice dropped to a growl that rumbled through her nerve endings. She was saved from answering when the song died away and Screech took the mic.

"Time to play a little Screech Stumper. No cheating. The first one who shouts out a title or lyrics buys a round of drinks for the members of Savaged Illusions. Now let's get someone up here and see if he or she can sing the Screech Stumper."

Baffled, she asked Justice, "What's that?"

"The band plays a few notes of a song, and the volunteer has to start singing within the first eight seconds. If he can sing the first four lines of three songs in a row, he wins a free drink."

"Awesome." She loved it.

"Want to try?"

"Me? No." She huffed out a laugh. "I'm not a singer."

"Chicken."

The first person on stage managed to get a Green Day and a Foreigner song but was stumped on a Bob Dylan tune. As she came off the stage, some guy bought her a drink. Four or five volunteers later, River took the stage. He easily sang the lines of songs from Def Leppard, Fleetwood Mac and the Eagles. Then he challenged Gray, and he passed it off to Lynx and ultimately Justice.

Liza clapped and shoved at his shoulder. "You're

up. Go, go, go." She was having a blast and didn't want it to end.

He turned his gaze on her. "I'll win. I always win." Justice bounded up the steps and took the mic. "Hit it."

Screech and the band played the first notes of "Still the Same" by Bob Seger. Without missing a beat, Justice launched into the song.

The crowd hushed.

Liza stared at the man. In seconds, he'd transformed from the guy she'd had dinner with, laughed and danced with into...

A star.

His voice pealed out, covering the song with power and emotion that made her feel it so deep in her chest, she had to sway to it. There was no room for thinking, not when the music took up all her headspace. The house band kept playing past the first four lines, and Justice sang the entire song.

The crowd clapped loud and enthusiastically. He sang two more songs, both harder metal rock, and he owned the stage, prowling and jumping as he powered into the lyrics.

Beautiful energy flooded the room when Justice performed.

Finally, he stopped and waited out the applause to say, "It's great to be home. Thank you all for coming tonight." Rotating, he faced the piano. "And thank you, Screech, for giving us our chance at this very club and for hosting this party tonight." Returning his attention to the audience, he said, "Okay, guys, now help me all talk Screech into playing 'Reaper's Child.'"

"Reaper! Reaper!" people shouted.

The houselights dimmed, and a spotlight shone on Screech as he began playing the song that had rocketed his band to fame. The notes rang out with a haunting echo of death.

Liza moved up closer to the stage, drawn by the memories. She'd tell her mom all about her experience of seeing Screech perform live the next time she visited. She watched intently, trying to memorize the way he leaned into the mic and sang with fiery anger as the song built to the rage against fate.

Two arms settled around her from behind, and a drink appeared in front of her face. "Thought you might like a frozen margarita," Justice said into her ear.

Liza froze and looked down. A male hand wrapped around a glass unleashed a barrage of memories. Fear shot up her throat. A sense of helpless vulnerability attacked her. In seconds, a whirring noise in her brain drowned out the music. She was trapped.

Cornered.

Unable to escape with the man behind her, arms caging her, darkness closing in on her. Panic jacked her heart. Her pulsed pounded, adding to the noise in her head. Sweat prickled her back.

No. Get control. Now. "No, thank you." Her voice sounded thin and tinny. Far away.

"Come on, taste it."

His cajoling tone rubbed like coarse sandpaper. "No." The word rasped her throat as if it was coated in broken glass. She didn't know how to escape. Where was the door? Was the room tilting?

"It's a virgin margarita. You haven't drank alcohol all night, so I assumed you'd rather not. And since you're underage, I don't want to get Screech into trouble."

Her stare riveted on the drink. Lime colored, not strawberry pink, but she wouldn't touch it. Couldn't.

Just the thought of it made her nauseated. Shaky and scared. So scared. She remembered feeling the darkness rolling in like a swarm, stealing her consciousness. Tears burned her eyes.

Focus. You're in a nightclub, not a bedroom.

With a herculean effort, she turned and concentrated. "I said no." Loud and firm. "I don't take drinks from men. Not unless it's in a sealed bottle or can."

Justice reared back, eyebrows arching in shock. "All right." He took a step away and set the drink down. "Do you want me to get you a water or can of soda?"

She shook her head and pivoted, gripping the edge of the stage. *Leave, get out.* She'd overreacted. Were people looking at her? Was he? Why couldn't she just be normal?

It all crushed down on her, a terrible weight pressing on her lungs. Justice had won the drink and got it for her. He was being nice, maybe flirting, and she'd lost her shit like a crazy chick. But the sight of the frozen concoction and his coaxing voice...

Bitter, metallic fear filled her mouth again. She lowered her head, looking at the floor. Polished wood of some kind. *Breathe, nice and slow. You're in control. Listen to the music. Calm down.*

She concentrated on Screech's playing and the rough timbre of his voice as he sang. Her heart rate lowered, and her stomach settled.

Time to leave before Justice demanded to know what the hell her problem was.

He moved up next to her, close enough that his rigid biceps pressed into her arm. "Was it that asshole bothering you earlier?"

She jerked her head up. "What?"

"The one who put something in your drink." The knuckles of his fingers turned white. "Was it him?"

She closed her eyes. "No." What would he think if he knew the truth? The shame crowded in. She wanted to grab that drink, slam it against the stage until she held the jagged shard of glass, and shove that into her skin, deep enough to hurt. Over and over until the physical pain burned out the agony of her memories. She fought the impulse, struggled to—

Justice's warm hand covered hers for a second, then gently pried her fingers off the lip of the stage.

Startled, she searched his face.

"If you need someone to hold on to, I'm right here." He tugged her to his front, tucking her between his arms.

"Justice..."

"This isn't me flirting with you. Getting the drink for you, yeah that was."

"Then what's this?" She really didn't understand. And why had she felt trapped when he had held out that drink, but now his solid warmth soothed the fear? As if he protected her from all the harsh stares and judgments that had been her world for years?

He settled his chin on her head. "Being a friend."

She shouldn't do this, but his warmth was a comfort she craved. All those nights she'd slept in a locked bathroom, lights blazing because the darkness scared the fuck out of her. A fear so overwhelming she sometimes cut her skin to escape. Being thrust back into the rock world had reopened old wounds. She'd known it would and that she could handle it.

What she hadn't expected was this.

A friend.

Chapter 4

AS JUSTICE STEERED LIZA FROM Screech's office, where she'd picked up her camera bag, toward the front of the club, he tried to keep his eyes off her ass.

She'd been drugged. Was it recently in a club like this? Damn it, he hated not knowing.

Dragging his gaze from her, he caught Dillion watching them with a sullen expression. What a prick. He'd heard the guy say he hadn't meant for Liza to be his dirty little secret, whatever the fuck that meant. Good thing Liza said it wasn't him who spiked her drink or that asshole would be eating out of a tube for the rest of his life.

Yeah, good plan, get arrested, then forfeit the win on Court of Rock *for a girl you just met. Stellar, Cade. Just stellar.*

Right, bad plan. He'd gone through a streak of drinking in bars on tour and ending up in fights. In the last year, he'd cleaned up his act.

They headed out into the cool night. He ushered Liza into the waiting taxi and gave the driver his address.

"You didn't have to leave with me," Liza said.

"Wrong. I saw the way you were casing my house

earlier tonight. I'm not letting you steal those flowered plates and chicken decorations while I'm groping groupies." No way would he let her get in a taxi by herself at one a.m. Especially now, after he'd seen her reaction to that drink.

The dim lighting caught the barest tilt of her lips. "Damn, busted."

As the cab took off, she dug her phone out of her camera bag and frowned.

"Something wrong?"

"No, just a few texts from my roommate, Emily, making sure I'm okay." She wrote out a rapid message and sent it.

"She worries about you?"

"We check in. Safety thing."

She'd taken steps to stay secure by not accepting drinks from men in bars and confirming she was okay with a friend. "Give her my number."

She looked up. "Why?"

"You'll be with me a lot, right? If she can't reach you, she can reach me." He'd begun to feel protective in his house, but after that scene in the club, he'd gone downright caveman. She'd been hurt somehow, but what really got him was the way she'd stood her ground despite the terror in her eyes. No compromise. She'd been clear—she was not taking that drink.

"You know, Cade, you're pretty recognizable from being on *Court of Rock*. You might not want to give out your number to just anyone."

He grinned at her, amazed at how quickly she'd recovered. "Is your roommate a crazy stalker type?"

"I'd say she's more protective than stalkerish. Usually."

The affection in Liza's voice told him enough. "I'll risk it. Give her my number."

She did and slid her phone away. "Thanks."

"So what's the deal with your ex? Looks like he wants you back."

She shook her head. "Not in the way you mean. We dated a couple months. He didn't pry a lot into my past, and I was relieved. But then his father, who's a state senator up in Sacramento and paying for Dillion's education, got wind of our dating. Either searched the Internet or did a background check." Turning away, she leaned toward the window. "His father found out my mother's in prison, which led him to finding out who I am, and he insisted that Dillion stop seeing me."

In prison. Given what Liza had told him earlier today, her mom had been there since Liza was fourteen. Six, almost seven years so far, which meant her crime had been serious. But what did Liza mean about who she was?

He opened his mouth, then shut it on his questions about her mom. Liza had pressed herself into the corner of the cab, her eyes fixed on the window. She fiddled with her wide watch, absently scratching the skin of her inner wrist.

She looked so damned alone and vulnerable.

He knew too well what that felt like. His mom had abandoned him to rot in jail, and Justice'd had no way to reach his dad who was trapped in a mental prison of his own. He'd never felt so deserted and powerless, so stripped of all defenses as he had then. If his own parents hadn't wanted him, why would the world? It was one of things he loved about performing. When he sang onstage or met with fans, they wanted him and in some cases, even fought over him. The attention fed that lonely, scared boy in him and gave him a real sense of power. Now he was driven to attain a level of fame that would guarantee he'd never be that helpless again.

But seeing Liza tucked in her corner yanked at the pit of his belly. He wrapped his hand around hers and caressed her fingers to get them to relax. "You'll tell me when you're ready." He could see how hard it was to talk about her mom, so he circled back to their original subject. "What's this about him having a fiancée?"

"That's part two of Daddy's demand. Once he broke up with me, he proposed to the girl Daddy had all picked out."

"What a pussy. You're over him, right?"

"Oh yeah. And he made sure of it by what he did after he broke up with me."

There was more? He rubbed his thumb over her wrist. "Do you want to tell me?"

"He wanted us to still have sex. He explained he couldn't be seen in places where his father would get wind of it, and he'd have to go home to see his fiancée to keep the peace, but he'd shoot me a text when he was free."

Un-fucking-believable. "I should have hit him. Hell, I should have pounded his face into the floor for that."

Her hand tensed. "No fighting. It's not your problem. Besides, I can handle Dillion. He's mad because he lost his plaything."

Swallowing his anger, he released her hand, put his arm around her and tugged her against his side. "You told him to go fuck himself, yeah?"

"Absolutely," she said as the cab pulled up in front of his house.

Justice paid and walked Liza to her car. A low-grade dread settled in his gut—he wasn't ready for her to leave. This girl fascinated him too damn much. Watching her power through her fears tonight had grabbed hold of him and wouldn't let go.

Realizing they'd stopped walking, he got out of his own head and frowned at the ancient Toyota Corolla. "Is this thing safe?"

"It's fine. I need to get it in for an oil change. Of course they'll tell me I need seven more things, and I never know if they're telling the truth or up-selling, because cars... I can put gas in, and that's it."

Justice blinked at the onslaught of words. Ironic that he had to pry information out of her for most stuff, but this she spilled out. Amused, he asked, "Cars make you nervous?"

She eyed him. "Do I look like an engineer to you?"

Oh yeah, she'd recovered. "Hmm, you're wearing glasses, does that count? But I don't see a pocket protector so..." He was fighting like hell not to drop his gaze to her boobs. He'd watched her all night, which fucked with his original plan to blow off some steam in a night of hard sex. Instead, this girl had him by the balls. But she wasn't looking for a hookup.

"I'm a communications major, not a mechanical engineer. However, I'm proficient enough at math to know I can't afford anything but the oil change. So I'll give them the starving-college-student spiel, then they'll ignore me to help customers who they have a better chance at up-selling. Good times." She took a breath. "And I have no idea why I'm telling you all this."

Because she felt the connection and attraction too. He'd known it when she leaned back against him after confirming that someone had drugged her. Slowly her muscles had relaxed, her body soft and pliant in his arms, the peach scent of her hair making him ache to turn her around and kiss her. He'd leashed the impulse. As much as he wanted to taste her mouth and a hell of a lot more, a victorious pleasure had warmed him at winning a little of her trust. "Tell you what, after practice tomorrow, bring your car over and I'll change your oil."

She stared at him. "You don't have to do that. I'll get it taken care of. I was just venting."

He believed her. She appeared very capable, but changing the oil on an older car wasn't a big deal for him, and it'd give him an excuse to hang out with her. Alone, not with the other guys around. He'd shared her enough tonight. To make her an offer she'd feel comfortable with, he said, "How about I do it in exchange for you helping me in the yard?"

Interest flickered in her eyes. "Helping how?"

He hadn't thought it through that far. "I don't know. Help me hire a gardener?"

She laughed. "How about I weed, prune and feed the roses, and take a look at everything else?"

Reaching for her car door, he smiled at her enthusiasm. "You really do like gardening, don't you?"

"It's fun, unlike cars."

"We need to work on your idea of fun."

She tilted her head. "I had fun tonight."

Did she have any idea how sweet and pretty she looked standing there in the soft moonlight? "Are you surprised?"

"Yeah. You're not what I expected, Justice."

The words slid out of her in a confessed whisper and stripped the lid off his desire. It made him want to touch and kiss her, but he only allowed himself to stroke her cheek. "Same here. I'm attracted to you. More with each passing moment. Go home, Liza. Or this is going to move faster than you're ready for."

"I don't know..."

"I know someone drugged you and likely hurt you." A wave of fury burned his veins at that thought. "I can tell you straight up, right now, I want you in my bed. But I'm not going to push you into something you're not ready for."

Her eyes widened. "Wow, you really aren't subtle."

"Nope. If you say no, it's no. Just like you told me tonight you wouldn't take a drink from me or any man. Got it?"

She studied him for a few seconds before answering, "Yes."

A minute later as he watched her drive off, he had to wonder what the fuck he was doing. He was home in San Diego to win *Court of Rock*.

Not to get involved with a girl who had *complicated* written all over her.

What happened when five perfectionists practiced together?

Liza watched the answer as Simon and River got in each other's faces, arguing about a bass solo versus guitar. An hour ago another argument had broken out about the correct way to say *Scaramouche* in "Bohemian Rhapsody."

In another moment, they'd be laughing, or one telling the other they'd done something stellar.

Finally the practice ended, and it was time for Liza to talk to Simon. Ignoring her anxiety, she went up on the stage. "Guys, I need you for a minute."

Simon glanced at his phone. "Make it quick. I want to be out of here before the next band arrives."

Which would be Jagged Sin. "Well, first." She couldn't hold back her excitement as she held up her phone. "Have you seen your Facebook page? You already have almost four hundred more likes. All your engagement numbers are rising. I posted pictures from practice yesterday, plus at Screech's last night."

Justice took her phone and scrolled. "Damn, she's right."

"Good shot of me." Lynx glanced over Justice's shoulder. "My arms are buff around that blonde."

Simon asked, "What's the Savage Shout-out tag on the pictures?"

"That's one of my ideas. I started with last night's party at Screech's. I linked to Screech's Facebook page too, so people there could see you, and your fans can see the nightclub page." While all of them studied their phones, she went on, "I outlined my plans and sent you all emails. I have your schedules. For this week, you only have the *USS Midway* aircraft carrier museum event on Saturday. Starting Monday you have a big week with some morning shows, the meet and greet autograph sessions at the school, the Indie Rock Broadcast interview, and I want to add in some shoots around town called Savage Shout-outs. We'll go to various places and send a shout-out on social media from the location and use that tag."

"Great cross promotion," Simon said.

"Good." That was the easy part. She steeled herself for the next item. "I talked to the *Court of Rock* promotions department. The new promo packages will be released Monday night during prime time, even though the show itself is on hiatus for the week. They want to really build up the anticipation for the final two shows after the break." It was Thursday now, so that gave them a few days to prepare, if Simon cooperated. That was a huge if.

The man raised his head slowly, eyes like frozen amber. "Are they including what Ace said about my wife?"

"I don't know." The words hung there like an ax

about to fall. "We need to be proactive and get ahead of the story."

He stayed as still as a concrete pillar. "How?"

Wiping her slick palms on her pants, she said, "You have to tell the world first."

"No." He spun and stalked to the stairs.

Damn it. Liza chased after him and grabbed his arm. Desperation to make him understand beat so hard, she spilled out, "Do you care about her memory, Simon? Because let me tell you, if it comes out in an accusation that you were the reason she took her life, then it's going to be ugly, and not just for you. For her...people don't care if she's a victim, they'll rip her apart and judge her. Think they know what she felt and thought, and crucify her for being weak or foolish. They'll find every detail of her life and spread it like a bad case of stomach flu. You don't know." Closing her eyes, she swallowed hard.

Don't talk about it, Liza. You're making it worse. People are judging you. Us. Just keep your head down and stay quiet. The pain and despair that had beat at her constantly was a horrible pressure in her chest. Liza hadn't been able to escape the emotional pain, not even in sleep. Every day it had built and built with no relief. And she was hushed anytime she tried to express herself, leaving her afraid if she did, she'd be thrown out of the only family she had remaining. She remembered the unrelenting emotional pain of being silenced and judged, and how it had driven her to cutting herself in a desperate attempt to make it stop.

She shook it off and pulled herself together to do her job of helping Simon defend his wife's memory. "She can't speak for herself now. Give her a voice before someone else does it. If you care about her, stand for her. Because if you don't, you're handing Ace and *Court of Rock* a loaded gun, and you don't know where, when or how they'll fire it."

Weighty stares pinged against her back, but she kept her gaze on Simon, willing him to hear her and understand. Unless he was so damned cold he really didn't care. She held her breath, praying there was a beating heart under that ice.

The angry chill around him cracked, and he closed his eyes. "What do you want me to do?"

Relief eased her shoulder muscles. "The band has an interview with the local morning show on Monday. If you talk about it then, you'll get ahead of any promo packages. But we have to keep it top secret. I'll have an information packet from the show by this weekend, and we'll figure out how you can reveal her story with the most respect." She touched his arm again. "I'll help you prepare."

"Fine. I hope you're right. It's bad enough I let her down in life." Simon headed down the stairs, with Lynx, River and Gray behind him.

Justice laid a hand on her shoulder. "Let's clear out before Jagged Assholes show up for their practice."

Snapping out of her thoughts, she grabbed her messenger bag, and the two of them walked out. Once outside, she noted the other band members had already left. "They didn't waste any time getting out of here."

Justice paused by the taillights of her car. He was a few spaces over. "Only way to avoid bloodshed. We're trying to keep Simon and Ace separated." Leaning his guitar against her bumper, he said, "See you at the house? I picked up some oil for your car this morning, so we're all set."

Did he have to look so hot? Liza couldn't get the memory of dancing with him out of her head. The way he'd looked, his scent, and his arms holding her close. The feeling of Justice was too addictive. She'd barely slept last night thinking about him. Half of her screamed, *Run. Don't get involved. He's a fame-chaser.*

The other half couldn't resist the magnetic pull of Justice. Even now, with the two of them standing a couple feet apart, his energy crackled over her, almost like a force field.

He made her feel alive, not shoved into a silent corner.

"You're thinking too hard. It's just an oil change, not a date."

Except he'd told her last night exactly what he wanted from her, and damned if she wasn't tempted. Getting involved with a rock star was dangerous to her. For three years, she'd had anonymity. Her whole experience with Dillion had threatened that when his dad investigated her. She'd been terrified he'd tell everyone who she was. Taking this job threatened it too, but she'd assumed she'd keep a low profile, and who would know? Yet she'd already told Justice that her mom was in prison. *Don't do it. Just don't.* "I—"

Brakes squealed and an engine roared. Liza spun, barely catching a glimpse of the massive chrome grill before Justice slammed into her. Lifting her off the ground, he lunged several feet, shoved her back against her car and pinned her there.

"Next time I won't miss," a voice shouted.

Her heart thumped, and her ears buzzed. Stunned, she tried to figure out what just happened. Tilting her head back, she got a close-up view of Justice's rigid jaw and cold eyes glaring to the right. "Justice?"

He shifted his gaze to her. "Did I hurt you?"

He eased her onto her feet but stayed pressed against her.

Uh...she didn't think so. "No, I just... What happened?"

"Ace and his drummer, Mick, gunned their truck right for us then swerved. Bastards."

Liza couldn't look away from Justice to see where Ace and Mick were now. With his body pressed against hers, his chest crushing her breasts, his breath fanning her face, flutters skimmed her belly. All her vivid awareness shifted from the threat of danger to the man who captivated her. She saw the second Justice felt it too. His gaze slid to her mouth. Would he kiss her? The moment stretched out, the air thickening.

Justice stepped back, opened her door and held it. "Lock your car. I'll see you at my house."

"But—"

He leaned down. "I don't want them following you home and harassing you."

"Would they do that?"

Tension threaded his gaze. "They want to win, and they can't do it on talent alone. If they scare you off and claim our publicist quit, that makes us look bad, and we lose votes. They're assholes, Liza. Stay clear of them."

She glanced over to see the two men standing by their truck watching them. Cold dread dripped down her spine. What would Jagged Sin do if they found out who she was?

For that matter, what would Justice do?

Justice changed the oil, washed, and detailed Liza's car, trying to burn off the anger.

And lust. Desire. A throbbing need that left him aching to kiss her.

It was bad enough Ace had gunned the truck toward him. But once the moment had passed, Justice had become powerfully aware of her soft curves pressed against his body and her full lips enticing him mercilessly.

Christ. He'd damn near kissed her right there in front of Ace and Mick. He didn't want them using her. The girl made him lose his head.

Taking the chicken out of the hot oil, he put it on a rack to drain and got to work mashing the potatoes with butter. A soft sound caught his attention. Turning, he took in the view of Liza. After spending two hours working in his yard, her face was flushed, her eyes sparking behind her glasses. She'd cleaned up and changed out of the shorts and T-shirt she'd gardened in, putting on the jeans and shirt she'd worn to practice, sans the sweater.

"Expecting company?" Liza asked. "I'll clear out."

He narrowed his eyes. "It's for you. Stay."

She walked in to peer at the food he had cooking on the stove. "Fried chicken and real mashed potatoes. How can I say no to that?"

He smiled, pleasure mixing in with his growing urge to touch her. Unable to totally resist, he settled his hand on her back. "Say yes."

She glanced over her shoulder at him, her pretty eyes teasing. "Won't that make it a date?"

He pressed in closer. Her scent of peaches and sunshine wafted off her, making him hungry for more than dinner. "I hope so."

Tension twanged in her muscles beneath his hand. "Justice, maybe it's better if we keep things professional between us."

"Too late. We both know it." Reliving that moment in the parking lot, he added, "You wanted me to kiss you today."

"So much. Doesn't make it smart though."

Her honesty sucked the air from his lungs. Despite desire lashing him, he focused on her meaning. "Is this about your secret?"

Worry clouded her gaze. "Yes."

"I didn't look for it online." Oh he'd wanted to, but he'd found he wanted something else more—her trust. He hoped she'd get comfortable enough to tell him why her mother was in prison, and whatever else she hid. "Let's eat."

She opened her mouth in surprise, obviously expecting him to push her for answers.

It took all he had to remove his hand from her to grab plates and fill them. "Can you get some drinks from the fridge? I bought some flavored teas in sealed bottles, thought you might like those. Or there's water or milk."

"Tea sounds good." She took the drinks to the dining room.

He followed, carrying the loaded plates and a small ceramic pitcher.

Liza settled in the same seat she'd sat in the night before. "A chicken-shaped gravy boat?"

Her husky laughter tugged low in his stomach. "It's my grandma's. I gave that to her." The pitcher was brown with yellow tail feathers fashioned into a handle to match the ruff on its head. His grandmother had used it for anything pourable.

"It's, um..." she eyed it critically through her glasses, then met his gaze, "...perfect."

Damn. Warmth flooded him. "Eat." They dug in.

"This is amazing." She held up a thigh. "The chicken

is crispy and tender, so good. Your grandmother's recipe?"

"Yep. I spent a lot of my days at the diner while growing up. My mom worked, so I hung out there. Brought my friends over, it was pretty cool." He took a second, then said, "I spent most of my childhood there or here in this house."

"It's a great house." She took another bite of chicken. "Are you going to keep it?"

He wiped his hands, the old anxiety sliding in. "Yes."

She lifted her head, her eyes on his. "For the memories?"

"For my dad. This is his home. If he ever wants to come back...it needs to be here." Worry and helpless anger rippled beneath his skin.

She settled a hand on his forearm. "Back from where?"

Her gentle touch helped. "Former Marine. A hero injured in the line of duty. Now he's just another homeless vet somewhere out on the streets, and I can't find him." Shit, he hated this. "He has a home, damn it. I keep his room at the end of the hall exactly as he left it with a few extra supplies."

She stroked his arm. "That's awful. You must be so worried."

The truth tumbled out. "That's why I had to sleep before you got here yesterday—I'd spent the night out on the streets looking for him." He rubbed a hand over his face. "I swore to my grandmother I'd take care of him. But he just..." It ate at him. He should be out there searching now, except it was futile. Lynx was right, his dad didn't want to be found.

"Maybe he doesn't realize you're trying to find him."

He snorted, bitterness and anger clumping in an all-too-familiar stew. "Bullshit. He knows. It's his choice. He'd rather live on the streets than with his own son." *Shut up. Jesus. The girl doesn't want to hear it.* Hell, Justice didn't want to believe it. He shook it off.

"Are you going out searching tonight? I could help you look. Do you have a picture of him?"

"You'd do that?" Sure, Drake and Lynx had helped him attempt to track his dad. This was different. No way in hell would he let her go into homeless camps in the middle of the night, but that she'd offered touched him.

"Yes. Maybe we'd have better luck together, and you won't be alone." Sympathy filled her eyes. "No one should be alone like that, or homeless. No one."

The fierceness in that statement told him she knew what it was like to be alone. With her mom in prison and her ending up living with her aunt, it made him wonder. "Have you been homeless?"

She looked away. "No. I was in protective custody for a while but..." She stared down at the remains of her dinner.

God. What the hell had happened to her? "What, Liza? Just tell me."

Her gaze slid to his, pools of worry and uncertainty. "You can't tell anyone. If people find out, I don't have anywhere to go."

He caught her wrist, tugging her hand to him. Her fingers were cold and stiff. "You can trust me." Didn't she see that yet?

She blinked at him. "I like it now when you don't know. I want to be this girl, the boring, average, slightly chunky college girl. Not her."

Chunky? Oh hell no. Liza wasn't thin, but she was

hot. And when she relaxed enough to take off her sweater, her confidence showed through, adding another layer of sexiness. But that wasn't the point here. "Not who, Liza?"

"The girl who ruined a rock star and forced him to flee the country. The girl who half the country thinks is some kind of slut who got what she deserved."

Jesus. His whole body iced. Thoughts clashed and bounced in his head. He only knew of one rock star who'd fled the country for a crime besides tax evasion.

"Gene Hayes?" The full impact slammed into him. Dropping her hand, he jerked back in his chair. "You're the girl Hayes was accused of..." Oh fuck. *Raping. Drugging and raping.* The most sensational story of the decade.

"Yes. My name then was Elizabeth Ranger. I took my mom's maiden name, Glasner, after the trial."

Gene Hayes's trial had been a huge media event, bigger than O.J. and Michael Jackson. After all, how many times does a father take his underage daughter to a rock star's house, knowing she'd be drugged and raped? Then the mother showed up and killed the dad, after which the rock star ran and hid? Hayes was found, arrested and tried...then ran again. Her mom, as Justice remembered it, took a plea deal for second-degree murder of Liza's dad rather than go to trial.

Liza sat still, naked vulnerability in her eyes magnified by her glasses. He didn't know what to say to her. It was all so crazy. His shock spread like a blanket of confusion, slowing his thoughts. Was he getting his facts straight? Or somehow mixing up her story with another infamous one? Gene Hayes, and her parents, Amber and Eddie Ranger. He couldn't quite get his head around Liza being at the center of that nightmare.

"You mean Gene Hayes? The rock star who had everything. His second album had just dropped and went to number one out of the gate. Then he lost it all... That was you?" Oh hell, that sounded like he was blaming her. "I—"

Her frozen state shattered as she shot up from her chair. "Yep. He was a rock god and I ruined him. I'll leave before I ruin you too."

Chapter 5

WHAT HAD SHE DONE? BUZZING cranked up in her head. Pain crushed her chest, like a fist shoved in deep. Liza's world careened out of control.

Justice could destroy the life she'd carefully built. Why had she told him? Don't talk about it, Liza. You're making it worse. People are judging you. Us. Just keep your head down and stay quiet. She was a fool. Stupid.

Maybe she should just go home for the summer. Give up and accept she was ruined. That she deserved to live in silent shame, always atoning for her bad decisions and the pain she'd caused everyone. For forcing her aunt and uncle to upend their lives to finish raising her, the niece they hadn't wanted but couldn't turn away and live with the guilt.

Tears burned her eyes. Her throat constricted. Pain battered her relentlessly, and God, she wanted to make it stop. Just make it all stop.

Especially the way Justice stared at her, his eyes filled with something she couldn't name. Disgust? Hate? Revulsion?

Unable to bear it, she whirled, snatched her purse off the couch and hurried to the door. Blinking furiously, she cleared her vision. Would he tell people? Did he hate her? She reached for the knob, desperate to—

"Liza, don't go. Christ, I'm sorry."

She froze, his voice piercing the harsh noise in her head. The one that made her frantic to escape her own mind.

"Please." He edged into her line of vision, pressing his shoulder against the wall by the door. Concern flickered in his gaze. "I'm sorry. I made it sound like I was defending him." He smashed his lips together. "Defending a rapist. I'm an asshole."

"I shouldn't have told you." She shifted her stare to the door. "I'll go. If you want me to resign as your student publicist, I will." What choice did she have? "Please don't tell anyone. Except for Emily and now Dillion, no one here knows. If they find out..." She'd have nothing. As it was, she'd have to spend the summer in Santa Barbara. But she could come back to finish her degree in the fall.

"I'm not going to tell anyone." He reached a hand toward her.

Liza flinched. Memories erupted of microphones shoved in her face, people screaming at her, hands grabbing her arms and clothes. Her heart pounded, and spots danced in front of her eyes.

She wished she could make it all stop—the shame, the worry that someone would find out, her own anxiety issues, and now this. She'd blurted out the truth of who she was, and it would change how he saw her.

"I'm not going to hurt you." Misery and regret thickened his voice.

Humiliation pushed in on her. She was acting crazy, hell she was crazy. "I know. It's a reflex. Sorry."

"Damn it, you don't have a goddamned thing to be sorry for. I'm the one who fucked up here, and now you're afraid of me." He clenched his jaw. "Look, I know you want to get away from me, I get it. But you're too upset to drive. Call your roommate. She'll come get you, right?"

"I'm not afraid of you." She wasn't. "Not physically. I shouldn't have told you. But I wanted to kiss you. Before we got to that point, I wanted you to know who I really am and still like me." Shut up, what was she doing? Could she humiliate herself any more here? How many times had she been told her feelings didn't matter? It was her actions, always her actions. "It was stupid to tell you." Time to pull herself together. "I'm okay now. I'll drive carefully." She turned the knob.

His warm, firm hand settled over hers. "Liza, hey, look at me."

She lifted her eyes to his.

"Not stupid. Let go of the door and come here." He tugged her into his arms.

Stunned, she leaned against his chest, desperate to soak up his warmth. She relished the feel of his heart beating a steady thump, assuring her that he cared enough to come after her and stop her from leaving. The sensation of being comforted filled her throat. He couldn't know how much she longed for this. All those years she'd been so damned alone and wishing for this kind of solace.

"Justice." Don't cry. Hold it together.

He pressed his cheek against the top of her head. "Just take your time and breathe. You're safe."

Liza burrowed against his chest, her arms settling around him. Her level of trust ripped out his damned heart. He didn't deserve it after he'd been a complete asshole.

He flinched internally, remembering what he'd said to her: Hayes had everything. His second album had just dropped and went to number one out of the gate. Then he lost it all... That was you?

What the fuck was wrong with him? She'd told him her worst secret, and he'd acted like she was at fault, not the rapist.

"People believe I seduced him in some kind of blackmail scheme. That I was a groupie whore like my mother."

"That's bullshit. Utter bullshit." He tugged her head back to look into her eyes. "You were a kid, Liza. And you were drugged. None of it was your fault."

The relief in her eyes almost undid him.

"Will you stay?" He couldn't stop her from leaving, but he really didn't want her driving.

Feeling steadier, she answered, "For a bit."

There she was, the girl who fought back her fears. He guided her around the coffee table to the couch. Once she set her purse down and they were seated, he took her hand. "What I said about Hayes, that was just shock. What I meant to say was that he threw away a career because he was a damned pervert. I'm sorry that you were his victim."

She turned her face to him. "You know the truth about me now. You hold all the cards. If you want me to resign—"

"What does that mean, I hold the cards?" He tried to follow her thinking.

She licked her lips, then said, "You can tell people who I am. The other guys in the band. I'll do what you want. Please. If you don't tell anyone, I'll go away."

Her worry ate into him. She truly feared being

revealed, slamming home the risk she'd taken to tell him. He had to treat that carefully. "I won't tell anyone. Especially not Ace. I don't want you to quit, Liza."

She let out a breath. "Okay. Then we'll work together and keep things strictly professional."

He studied her pale, strained face. Her eyes were huge and troubled with worries that no college girl should have to endure. He'd seen her sexy confidence mixed with flashes of stark vulnerability. How had she survived the whole nightmare to become this smart, snarky, brave girl?

"Is that what you want? Because a minute ago you told me you wanted to kiss me. And, honey, that hasn't changed for me. I want you." More than before she'd told him her past. Not because of who she was, but because she'd trusted him with it. And she hadn't left him when he'd let his mouth get in front of his brain.

It wasn't the first time he'd fucked up with his mouth. His vicious words had driven his dad to the streets, choosing that life over his horrible son.

Liza's eyes widened. "You do? I mean, I like you, I'm attracted, but for almost seven years, all I've tried to do is stay out of the limelight."

"And I'm seeking it out."

She looked down at their joined hands. "I have so much to lose. My family, my anonymity. All for a fling with a rock star."

Fling? Not likely with the hot possession burning his chest. He focused on her family comment. "What's the deal with your family?"

Her mouth tensed. "They don't know I'm doing this contest or the possible internship. I didn't dare tell them. My aunt and uncle took me in and kept me from going into the system. But they blamed my mom—she hooked up with my dad, dropped out of college, married him, had me, after which he left her. Her life continued to spiral out of control. She followed whichever rock bands caught her attention, drinking, doing drugs, partying and getting arrested. We lived in some bad places. She'd started to clean up and had a steady job, but her family didn't believe her. My Aunt Mari, the one who took me in?"

He nodded, trying to follow.

"She's my mom's sister, but Mari wouldn't speak to her. She'd call me on my birthdays and Christmas, and visit me if I was staying at my grandmother's. But she never forgave my mom for screwing up so badly and refused to talk to her."

"That's who you lived with?" She sounded like a bitch.

"Yeah, along with her husband, Spence, and my two cousins. After it all happened and my mom was arrested, I was released from the hospital to a foster home. Mari only agreed to take me if I'd shape up and be good. And I tried, I did."

Justice could feel the desperation, the words just spewing from her as she tried to sum up years in a few sentences. "Good how?"

"No outbursts. No screaming at reporters. Taking responsibility. No more bad decisions and reckless behavior." Her fists clenched, and she dropped her gaze. "Quiet. I was supposed to be quiet, not talk about certain things."

His guts twisted. Liza had been brutalized, and she was supposed to be quiet? He opened his mouth, but she lifted her chin, a spark flickering in her eyes.

"After I won the scholarship and went away to college, it was such a relief. I could breathe and relax." She rubbed her chest, as if soothing some pain. "And then I found communications, a way to have a voice."

He stared down at this girl, stunned. She'd been abused, then silenced, and yet look at her now. She'd found her own power. "You weren't allowed to talk about the rape?"

She flinched at the word, then recovered. "Or my mom in prison. I wasn't supposed to even talk about my visits with her. I had to hide all my pictures of her or the two of us." She fisted her hand on her thigh, the knuckles turning white. "Anything from my life before I went to live with my aunt and uncle, it was gone. Like the girl I was then was silenced, forced into a box and shut away."

He only had to remember his own anger as a teenager, anger at his dad for being injured, his mom for emotionally leaving long before she had physically, to realize how awful that had to be for Liza. "What did you do? Were you getting therapy?"

"I had a court-ordered counselor, but I wasn't looking to make trouble for anyone. I didn't have anywhere else to go, and my aunt and uncle weren't cruel. They took me in, made sure I had school clothes, celebrated birthdays and Christmas, and when I did well in school, they were proud. But they had this fear too. They didn't want to see any of my mom in me. They needed me to prove to the world that it was just my mom who'd gone bad. And that they were good people for stepping in to raise me."

Yeah, well, sounded like they were uptight assholes to him.

"But then I came here to San Diego and discovered the power of targeted, effective communication. I want to be a publicist and help people to defend themselves against public attacks or control their own story. I don't know exactly how, but I'll figure it out."

Damn. "The things you told Simon about giving his wife a voice. They're because you were silenced."

"Yes. I don't know why his wife made that choice, but if Simon really cares, then he needs to be the one to tell her story. Not let the vultures twist it, because they will."

She cared so much. Passion turned her eyes to green fire. "You have no idea what you're doing to me." He leaned down, brushing his lips over hers. "You won't be silent with me. Ever."

Her lips parted, eyes glazing slightly. "It wasn't supposed to be like this."

"Like what?" He touched her face, gliding his fingers over her jaw. "Use that voice."

Her face warmed with color, the strain easing. "You. I wasn't supposed to want you so much I'd risk it all to find out what this is between us."

Hot pleasure skated through him. How she could be this brave, he didn't know. He understood now what the stakes were for her. But she was here, and for this moment, she was his. "It's going to be okay, Liza. No one has to know your past. We'll see each other and not make a big deal of it publically. I won't hide you, I'm not doing that, but we won't give anyone a reason to look any deeper."

He'd protect her. She trusted him, and he'd damn well make sure that trust wasn't misplaced.

Liza desperately wanted to believe him because right now her want outweighed her brain. She'd told Justice the truth, and he still saw her as the whole woman, not just the girl at the heart of the scandal of the century.

But was the risk worth it?

Easy answer. One look into his eyes, seeing the sincerity, and the way he'd treated her—yes. She'd lived on the sidelines for long enough. "So we're doing this?"

His eyes crinkled. Shifting, he put his arm around her, drawing her close to him. "Oh we're doing it, but not tonight. Not before we talk about what you went through so I understand your triggers, what scares you and what you need."

His bluntness shocked her. Few people discussed the whole nightmare so frankly. A cool sense of relief swept through her. She didn't have to pretend or act like it didn't happen. It made her feel less freakish that she could talk about it. "I was drugged, so I don't remember the actual rape. I woke up in the hospital sick, vomiting, people telling me things, cops asking questions." The room had been cold. That sensation stayed with her. The bone-chilling cold, followed by flashes of icy heat, frigid sweat covering her as her stomach heaved. She hadn't known where she was, what was happening. Her brain was fogged, everything hurt, and she wanted her mom. "My mom wasn't there. I didn't understand why. I kept begging them to get my mom, please, just get my mom."

"Shit."

She jerked her gaze up. Justice's face had gone hard and mean. Okay, she'd gone too far. "Sorry, I—"

"Don't you fucking dare apologize. Yeah, hearing it makes me pissed and ready to kill the bastard who hurt you. And the people who took your mom away when you needed her. I don't care who she killed that night—she should have been there until you got your bearings. So we're setting the rules, right here, right now. Those are my feelings, and we don't silence those. Not mine and not yours, got me?"

Never had she been lectured and loved it so much.

"Yes." Her courage notched up. "Since I don't remember the actual assault, my problems aren't really with sex. I've had sex, maybe not great sex, but I'm working on getting there. But I can't go to sleep around anyone else, especially men. So I don't do overnights and that kind of thing. As for what I do remember, I'm not ready to tell you all of it." She held her breath, waiting to see his reaction. She'd been as truthful as she knew how, including the part about maybe not having great sex. Would he think her too much work? Not worth it?

He rubbed the bare skin of her arm. "So let's talk about something else."

She relaxed, some deep tension easing. "Like what?"

"Something I'm curious about. Were you always called Liza? You said you changed your name, but Liza is a nickname for Elizabeth, right?"

"No. My mom called me Beth, or Elizabeth when she was pissed. Most everyone did—called me Beth, I mean. Elizabeth Ranger was somewhat recognizable, even though most of the media didn't use my name since I was a minor. After the trial, my aunt and grandmother wanted it changed to attract less attention. Liza is what they picked, and I did what they asked. Glasner is my mom's maiden name, and fewer people knew that. So I became Liza Glasner."

"Beth." He uttered it slowly, as if savoring the single syllable. "I like it, the softer side of you. It's pretty."

"Soft?" She refused to think about her thighs straining her jeans, the price of using candy as one of her comforts. Although writing her secret stories, creating entire worlds that she controlled and her characters could say anything she wanted them to, helped her cope the most.

He pressed his fingers beneath her chin, tilting it up. His blue eyes homed in on hers, fierce and steely. "Soft in all the right places. Beth fits you, at least who you are right here with me."

The intimacy in his gaze went deeper than sexual, stirring ashes of the girl she'd been. It made her long to reach out and try, to push herself to see who she could really be. Although, she'd reached for a dream once, and that had led to her rape, her dad's murder, mom in prison and Liza bearing the endless shame.

All the emotions of the night were almost too much. She instinctively pulled back, needing to get a handle on herself. Tugging her chin from his hold, she twisted her watch, staring down at the big piece of jewelry covering her ugly scars. "It's just a name."

"Your name. It's yours, Beth. No one else gets to take it from you."

Involuntarily, she looked up. He'd shifted, leaning back and giving her a couple inches of space. But his words...he got it. So much of her childhood and identity had been removed or hidden, as if shame were attached to it. She swallowed, ready to shift the spotlight off her. "Where'd you get your name?"

A thin smile ghosted over his lips. "My dad chose it. Justice is one of the fourteen leadership traits that earns a Marine respect."

"Lot of pressure for a kid to live up to." A military dad and a name like that must have set up a lot of expectations. "Did he want you to go into the Marines?"

"Probably." He leaned forward, scooping the remote off the coffee table. "Want to watch a movie?"

Diversion tactic, but they'd both had enough emotional minefields tonight, or at least she had. "Sure."

He switched the TV to Netflix and handed her the remote. "Pick something. I'll put away the leftovers and get some popcorn." Justice left the room.

She made a selection, then waited a couple minutes, but Justice didn't return. Unable to just sit there, she headed into the kitchen to find him loading the dishwasher. He glanced up. "Regular or cheese-flavored popcorn?"

Gathering up the pans, she took them to the sink. "Cheese. Go do that while I wash these."

He glanced down at her. "Bossy."

She smiled sweetly, enjoying the lighter moment. "You'd rather wash the pans?"

"Cheese popcorn coming right up." He headed to the pantry.

Liza found the soap and got to work scrubbing the pans to the sound of the popping corn.

"What movie did you pick?"

He'd been so nice to her, she should tell him the truth. Yet when she opened her mouth, she couldn't help answering with, "The Notebook."

She heard the thunk of a bowl hitting the counter. Liza focused on rinsing the first pan and tried not to laugh. She'd had a hunch he'd object. It really wasn't a guy movie.

"You better be joking." The microwave opened and closed, and a few seconds later the scent of popcorn and cheese flooded the room.

"What? It's awesome. Have you seen it? I love that movie." She scrubbed the skillet, keeping her head low and hair covering her face.

"I'm calling bullshit." His low voice sounded behind her, so close the cadence shivered inside her chest. His warmth spread out along her back. Her skin came alive, prickling with awareness. Her belly fluttered with a sweet sensation, a combination of fun and desire.

"Okay, fine, I was kidding. I picked Twilight." She turned her head, doing her best to look innocent. "It's my most favorite movie ever. I love men who sparkle."

"Such a little liar."

"Am not. Men who sparkle are hot."

A low laugh spilled out. "Now I know you're lying."

"You don't know that."

"Oh I know. You like me, and I don't sparkle. You like your men raw, honest, maybe a little rough. But sparkle? Not even that pussy Dillion sparkled." Justice ran his hands down her arms, skating over her bare skin to the insides of her elbows.

Pleasure rushed through her, and her breath caught. She clutched the edges of the pan. Dillion never made her feel playful desire. Because you never dated men you really liked, but ones you thought you could control. Lifting her chin, she met Justice's gaze.

"You're tempting me," Justice said. "Too damned much."

That growl thrilled her and scared her a little. "Justice..."

Before she could form the thought, he caught her shoulders and turned her.

Warm soapy water flew from her hands. "You're getting water everywhere."

He framed her face with his palms. "Don't care. Now tell me. Want me to back off?"

Her heart thumped. "Shrek. The movie I chose."

Amusement flashed in his eyes. "That I believe and approve of. Shrek's cool."

"And no."

"Don't stop? I'm going to kiss you, Beth. Is that what you want?" He leaned closer.

Her mouth dried. The microwave dinged a distant, faraway noise that barely registered while Justice filled her world, his hands on her face keeping her anchored. Putting her palms on his shoulders, she could feel the coiled tension through the cotton of his T-shirt, indicative of the control he exerted over himself. What would happen when he let go of that? "Kiss me."

Justice wrapped an arm around her, tugged her into his body and brushed her hair behind her ear. Intensity rippled between them. "Be sure, baby. I'm not holding back. I crave you too much to pretend this is anything but the kiss of a man who wants you."

God, he didn't treat her as a freak. "I'm sure."

His mouth curved. "We'll stop with a kiss. You already told me you're not ready for more."

She shivered, completely believing him. He'd sent her home last night with nearly the same words. He brushed his full lips over hers.

The kiss was sweet and pleasant, but not hot. Was he holding back despite what he said?

Justice shifted, gathering her hair in his hand and tilting her head back. He trailed his mouth over her jaw, down the tender skin of her throat.

Wet fire licked her flesh. Shivers danced, tingles shot to her nipples. She clutched his arms, aware of his strength. Now she understood—he'd been giving her a few seconds to adjust. To feel him, trust him.

He took her mouth, sliding his tongue in. He tasted of dinner, heat and all male. He feasted on her in a maddeningly slow and sexy assault that ramped up her hunger to taste and explore. Liza went up on her toes, dueling her tongue with his, her own aggression startling her.

His hand glided down her back, cupping her ass.

Against her belly his erection pressed thick and hard.

Her blood thundered. Need twisted low in her pelvis, making her gasp. She gripped his shoulders, desperate to taste and feel more of him.

He broke the kiss, burying his face in her hair, and whispered, "Beth. What are you doing to me?" He cradled her face to his chest.

His heart thumped against her cheek through the cotton of his shirt. "I don't know."

He tugged her head back. "I didn't expect it to get out of control so fast. You're just so damned perfect." He drew a deep breath.

She glanced away, staring at the wall by the backyard door where a set of four tiles with chickens and roosters hung. She wasn't perfect, and her issues bothered her. In the past, she'd chosen weak men who let her set the terms. It wasn't going to be like that with Justice. Not that he'd pushed, but rather he evoked her own desire to be wilder, to just let go. And that scared her. "Those chickens are staring at us."

"You afraid of chickens?" Sliding his hand up her back and beneath her hair, he wrapped his warm fingers around her nape.

"Nope." She liked them, and loved how warm and lived-in this kitchen felt. Homey. Safe. That made her brave enough to tell him the truth. "I might be a little, tiny bit afraid of this, of how you make me feel."

"And how's that?"

"Out of control. Needy." She licked her lips. "I want to keep kissing you and not think anymore."

He dragged his thumb along the curve of her neck. "Good." Leaning down, he pressed his mouth to hers. "When you want it bad enough that it hurts, when you can't bear not having me inside you, then you'll be ready." Pulling back, he released her. "But that's not tonight. Unfortunately." He took another long breath and walked stiffly to the microwave. "Grab some drinks, and I'll get the popcorn."

Feeling slightly off balance, she blurted out, "That's your plan?"

After getting the popcorn and some napkins, he looked over his shoulder. "What?"

"Make me wait?" She wasn't sure why it threw her. "Is this some kind of tease thing?" Justice didn't seem like the type to hold back.

Picking up the bowl, he crossed the kitchen and stared into her eyes. "I'm not teasing. I want your trust. All of it. I've never really cared before. If a girl wanted to fuck, and I was attracted? It was on. Clothes off, dick covered, and I fucked her."

She almost stepped back at the raw honesty. Almost. She'd asked him, so she'd stand there and hear the answer.

"You're not that girl. I don't know exactly what you are yet, but you matter. And right now being back in this town, fighting to win Court of Rock, is consuming me. My band? They're everything to me. I need them, but when it comes down to the end—it's going to be on me. If I screw up, I'll lose it for us. That pressure rides me like a rash day and night, sucking the ability to breathe out of my lungs." He paused and added, "I can't let them down."

The admission surprised and touched her. She was seeing the human side of the rock star.

"And being here in this house? I love this house, but part of me hates it at the same time. Every time I see the closed door to my dad's room, I know I've failed to keep my promise to my grandma to find him and bring him home. And it pisses me off, an icy-hot rage that's right there, crouched in my mind, ready to spring." His fingers around the plastic bowl whitened. "I'm not good enough for my dad."

Rage? Frustration? Hurt? She put her hand on his arm, trying to ease the pain in him.

"And then there's you. Every time you look at me, trust me, I'm a freaking god. You make me feel that. So this? Waiting for you to be ready to let go?"

Liza held her breath and tilted toward him.

"Worth every second it takes. I'm not teasing or playing mind games. I'm giving us time to figure out what we're doing here. Now grab a couple waters, and we'll watch the movie." He walked out to the living room.

Liza stood in the kitchen beneath the gaze of the chickens. Oh she was in trouble here.

She might fall for a rock star. And fall hard.

Chapter 6

LIZA'S PHONE KEPT VIBRATING ON top of her messenger bag in the theater seat next to her. On stage the band was finishing up practice while ignoring the newly installed stationary cameras catching raw footage. She stayed out of camera range even when taking pictures or videos to post to social media.

Scooping up her phone, she glanced at a series of the texts from Aunt Mari asking variations of, *Have you heard back on the internship? What's the name of the company?*

Annoyance had her squeezing the phone. Same questions every few days. Quickly she typed back, *Not yet. I won't hear for another two weeks. Will let you know.*

Setting her cell down, she returned to her laptop and filling out the information package for the morning show interview coming up on Monday. They had asked for a biography of each band member and an outline of discussion points so the interviewer could prep over the weekend.

Her phone vibrated once more. A glance at the screen told her it was her aunt again, and she ignored it. She switched to her notes from the meeting she'd had with Simon this morning. Could she tout that one of the band members was going to break their silence on their past or something like that?

Tempting, but she knew the answer—no. They didn't want to give any advance warning that might clue in Ace and let him release the story first. Simon was somewhat grudgingly trusting her, and she wouldn't let him or the band down. Liza stared at the screen, thinking...

Her phone vibrated over and over. Shifting her gaze, she saw it was a phone call this time. Aunt Mari wasn't giving up, and it wasn't right of Liza to ignore the woman who'd done so much for her. After shoving her computer into the bag, she slung it over her shoulder. The guys were finished for the day and talking on the stage. Grabbing her phone, she answered with, "Hang on a second, Mari." She slipped out a side door to the backstage area.

"Sorry," she said into the phone. "How are you?" She kept an eye out for the Jagged Sin guys. They had the next practice time.

"It's you I'm worried about. It's not like you to hide something. Why is it taking so long to hear on this internship? And why won't you tell me the company?"

Crap. Tension tightened the back of her neck. For weeks she'd informed her aunt she was applying for several internships, which was true. Then she'd said it was down to one. "I told you, it's a big company in Los Angeles. I'd only intern over the summer, mostly getting coffee, making copies, monitoring social media accounts, that kind of thing."

"What if they find out who you are?"

She gripped the phone, squeezing her eyes shut. Her throat ached with the words: *I'm more than that one night. More than one bad decision.* But Liza didn't lash out or lose her temper. Her aunt and uncle had done too much for her. "It won't matter. I'll just be doing grunt work, not dealing with the clients." Before her aunt could lecture her on how it did matter, she added, "I have to get to a meeting. Please don't worry."

"Liza, wait."

She repressed a sigh. "What?"

"Just promise me you're staying out of trouble. Not drawing attention to yourself, drinking or dating the wrong kind of boys."

Wrong kind of guy? Like Justice? Lead singer of a rock band, covered in tats, had a record...

Guilt plopped his fat, ugly ass down on her chest. Nothing like dating a reality TV star to not call attention to herself. "Everything is fine here. I'll call you next week." She hung up and dropped her forehead against the wall. What was she doing? Walking a tightrope over an alligator pit while slathered in yummy chicken guts.

One wrong step and she'd tumble down into a pit of snapping jaws.

"A meeting, huh?"

Startled, Liza spun around. Justice stared back, one eyebrow lifted in silent challenge.

"Uh...what are you doing?"

"Looking for you. I saw you rush out. Annoying phone call?"

How much had he heard? "My aunt." The pressure built in her chest, and before she could think, she blurted out, "She's worried I'm drawing the wrong kind of attention, getting drunk, and/or dating the wrong kind of guys."

Justice leaned in. "Like me?"

Her mouth dried as his scent washed over her. His jaw was covered in sexy stubble, his eyes challenging.

"Exactly like you." Yep, she was teetering over the alligator pit. Tension popped and sizzled between them.

"Get a move on, J. Sloane's waiting for us at the gym." Lynx stopped by them. "Hi, Liza, thought you left."

"Nope. Who's Sloane? Some kind of personal trainer?" They had those at the gym, right? Not like she'd know. Going to the gym sounded a lot like going to the doctor's, only more painful and exhausting.

Lynx laughed. "Not quite. Sloane Michaels is a UFC Heavyweight Champion. We're going to spar and work out with him."

Liza jerked her gaze to Justice. "You're what? UFC? That's, uh, like fighting? He's a fighter?"

"Does that worry you?" Justice asked.

"Of course it does. The next *Court of Rock* show is a week from Monday. What the hell do you think you're doing sparring with some fighter? What if you hurt your hands? Your ribs? Your voice?" Furious, she glared at both of them. "No."

Lynx swiveled his head to Justice. "Did our little publicist just forbid us?"

Justice folded his arms over his chest. "That's what I heard."

"Huh. She's cute. See you there?"

"Yep."

Lynx sauntered off.

"Hey." Liza yelled after him. "You can't fight. What if you hurt your hands? How will you drum then?"

Lynx strode back to her. "Even with two broken hands, I'd be on that stage giving it my all. Nothing is going to hold me back." Then he turned and vanished around a corner.

Liza whipped around to glare at Justice. "And you?"

"Relax, Beth. We've both trained with Sloane for

years. So did River. We were all in the Fighters to Mentors program together. Sloane's better than us, but he's not going to hurt us."

"What if he does accidently? And what kind of moron gets into a ring or whatever with a professional fighter?"

"You're looking at him—if it's Sloane." He slapped his hand on the wall and lowered his face to hers. "That's what makes me bad, sweetheart. The wrong choice for you according to your aunt. I'll take the risk. And that's exactly what you want, why you're drawn to me. Because you want to take the risk too."

He hit that so dead center, it took her breath away. For years she'd been flying under the radar, afraid to let anyone know who she was or see the real her. She plucked at the oversized sweater she wore. Again. "I think you're right."

He opened his mouth, when the sound of feet coming down the stairs and laughing voices announced the rest of the band making their way offstage. Grabbing her hand, he yanked open a door, tugged her in and closed it.

The automatic overhead lights went on, revealing one side with a long row of mirrors and tables. The other side had individual curtained stalls. At the end was a sofa and a couple chairs. "Dressing room."

Justice walked her back to the first mirror. "Yep. The perfect place to take off your sweater." He eased her messenger bag from her shoulder and set it on the table. "Or leave it on."

She couldn't quite get a handle on him. "Are you commanding or suggesting?"

"Your choice." He caught her chin in a gentle hold. "It's always your choice. You're perfectly capable of telling me to fuck off."

Her mouth dried, and flutters danced low in her belly from the way he said that, completely confident she would speak up. "Or kneeing you in the balls." A smile spread over her face. "I took a class."

"On kneeing balls? Is that required for your communications degree?"

"Self-defense. I consider it a backup form of communication. But nope, not required for my degree. Just my safety."

"You just got sexier."

"Seriously?" He liked that about her?

"Oh yeah. Confidence is hot." His gaze dropped. "I'm desperate to kiss you until I'm so hard I can't walk and you're so wet..."

"What? So wet that what?" She'd really asked that? But she wanted to know. She'd never felt this hot wash of exciting desire edged with danger. Justice was taking her into a world that had been forbidden to her since she was fourteen. And she wanted to go, more than she'd ever realized.

His eyes glittered. "You beg me to make it better."

Excitement pounded through her, throbbing at every pulse point until her skin ached for him to touch her, her lips tingled and her nipples tightened. "Will you?"

"Hell yeah, but not until you're ready. And definitely not here where someone else might hear your cries when you come. Only me, Beth." He stepped back. "Do you want to take off the sweater?"

Any shred of fear, of needing the barrier, vanished. Justice had seen her without her sweaters. She stripped it off.

Jesus, the girl was going to kill him. Liza had her hair in a ponytail, very little makeup and her dark-rimmed glasses perched on her straight nose. He suspected she thought it made her invisible.

Not fucking likely. Not with those green eyes and that smart mouth.

But when she took the sweater off?

His guts clenched, and his blood ran hot. Fire licked down his spine. She had on an oversized coral T-shirt that draped over her breasts and down her front. He barely noted the shirt was longer in back than front. She had on dark leggings or whatever they were called.

His skin prickled as his blood rushed to his dick. Closing the distance, he sank his fingers into her hair, finding the band and easing it out. Her wild, silky locks fell free, curling around his hands. The sensation rippled straight to his cock.

She looked up, her eyes shimmering with a combination of wary innocence and brazen need. The effect punched him low and hard. *Trust, Cade. She trusts you. Don't screw this up.*

Some distant voice tried to warn him to walk away, to leave this girl alone.

But one look at her full lips with that light coating of gloss and he was lost. He fisted his hand deep in her fire-licked locks and kissed her. God, the first tentative touch of her tongue to his undid him. Sweeping her up, he planted her ass on the makeup table and pushed her thighs open. Tilting her head, he dove into her mouth until all his awareness centered on his blood pounding and Beth.

His Beth. Soft, hot and his.

She broke the kiss, leaning her head back and exposing her throat.

Taking that as an invitation, he kissed over her satiny skin to her pulse point. He kept going, tugging the neckline of her shirt down to the swell of her breast. Pale flesh spilled over a black bra.

Justice sucked in a breath, fighting his primal need to touch and taste, to possess this girl with the big tits, smart mouth and way-too-vulnerable heart. "You're sexy as fuck." Unable to resist, he cupped her breast over her bra, thumbing that hard nipple while kissing the mound.

Greed snapped at him. He wanted to strip her naked, lay her on this table and lick her everywhere.

When she shuddered, he drew down her bra, her flesh spilling free. The dark-tipped nipple the color of ripe raspberries enticed him mercilessly. Closing his lips over that rigid tip, he sucked.

Liza shuddered, her fingers digging into his hair. "Justice."

The hot need coating her voice rammed into him. Right on the edge of mad lust, he pulled back.

Had to. Now. Or he'd go too far, too fast. Releasing her, he yanked his head up, dragging in air. In the mirror he caught sight of his face. Flushed, eyes too bright. Nearly wild.

She did this to him.

"You stopped."

Get ahold of yourself. He tugged her bra cup and shirt up, then framed her face with his palms. His cock ached like a mother. But when he saw the unfocused trust in her eyes and shameless desire coloring her skin, it was worth it. He dropped his forehead to hers. "Not here. Screw my workout. Let's go to dinner. I'll take you anywhere you want, then we'll go to my house. Or yours." Wherever she was more comfortable.

"I can't."

The hard catch in her voice concerned him. Was she apprehensive? Or frustrated? Pulling back a little to see her eyes, he asked, "Not ready?" He could handle that. "Then let's go to dinner and do something fun." He just wanted to be with her.

"No. I mean, I don't know if I'm ready. I was a minute ago." Her smile tilted. "But I really do have a meeting for a group project. We only have another week to get it done."

Disappointment rolled over him, but he banked it. She had a life, they both did. "Tomorrow night we have the *USS Midway* event. Go with me."

"I'll be there. I have a pass in my packet from Tangent and *Court of Rock*."

She wasn't getting this. "Together. I'll pick you up, and make sure you get home." Safely. Now that he knew her past, a fierce protectiveness had taken hold of him.

"A date."

"Yes. We won't make a big thing of it at the event and draw too much attention to you." He got that she didn't want any undo notice focused on her. "But we'll be there together."

Her gaze searched his, and finally she smiled. "It's a date, rock star."

"Wait, what did I do?" Liza cried, reaching through the cell bars of the brig on the *USS Midway*. "Come on, guys, let me out."

Simon crossed his arms. "Nope." He laughed as River took a dozen pictures with her camera.

Gray had her phone, which she'd foolishly unlocked and handed to him, thinking he'd take a fun picture of her in the brig.

"Don't you dare post those."

Gray lifted her cell up. "Oh look at this cool little FB

app. What do you think, guys? Does it go to our little publicist's personal account? Or our band page?"

"Gray." He wouldn't, would he? "I don't post my picture on social media." She'd wanted to be part of the college crowd, so she used avatars and kept it all low profile so she could follow her friends without calling too much attention to herself.

Lynx frowned at her. "Why not? You look hot in that dress."

Liza rattled the door, trying not to let that compliment get to her. "Not everyone wants to flex their tatted biceps every time they see a camera. Now let go." She glared at the drummer who held it shut.

"Simon, hold this," Lynx said. "I'm going to go get some bread and water. That'll make a great picture."

Simon grabbed hold of the door, and Lynx trotted off.

"Justice, are you just going to stand there?" Liza demanded.

"Of course not." He spun round. "Lynx, make sure Beth's water is in a sealed bottle." He shifted to Gray. "Don't post the pics. We'll just hold them as blackmail to keep our publicist in line." Returning to her, he grinned. "You're welcome."

"Works for me." Gray took more pics.

"Jerk. You're all jerks." She would not laugh, nope. She didn't mind being the target of their teasing, it made her feel like part of the group. But what touched her the most was the way Justice slid in the reminder that he had her back by insisting they bring a sealed bottle of water for her and telling them not to post any pictures. Yeah, he was watching out for her. It made her feel protected and happy.

"Beg us some more," River said. "I've got the camera set to video now."

She would not. Instead she stuck her nose up in the air. "Don't you think imprisoning me is a little bit of an overreaction? I only made a suggestion."

Gray lowered her phone. "That I fall overboard and the other guys jump in to rescue me."

Okay, yeah, now that she heard it repeated back to her, it was a little over the top. She was saved from having to think up an answer by the crowd coming down the hall.

"Wendy," a male voice cried. "This isn't funny."

"Oh it so is."

Lynx bounded in with some kind of basket and a few bottles of water, followed by a bunch of girls and a guy.

Liza eyed the Fury Run band members tugging their publicist with them, and urging him into the brig with her. She sighed. "Hey, Karl, they harassing you too?"

He shoved his hair back out of his face. "Your drummer suggested it." Karl crossed his arms over his skinny chest and glared at Wendy. "I'm using a wide angle next time I take a picture of you. Your ass will look like a truck."

The lead singer tossed her bright pink hair. "Can we beat them with a hose or something? Oh I know." She reached into the basket Lynx held and lobbed a dinner roll at them.

Karl caught it and took a bite. Once done, he grinned at Liza. "First thing she said to me when I met her was, 'Don't make my ass look big.'"

Liza laughed. "Rock egos, what can you do?" She, Karl and the third liaison, Nikki, were fast becoming competitive friends. Karl wasn't the least bit afraid of the Fury Run chicks. Nikki was having a harder time building a relationship with her band. Liza had seen her a couple times tonight, and the girl looked exasperated.

"We can leave them down here. No one will find them 'til Monday." Wendy flashed an evil grin their way. "Except the rats."

River took a few more shots with Liza's camera, then lowered it. "So what did yours do?"

Wendy gestured toward the cell. "He got an idea by seeing what your publicist is doing by utilizing your band name with Savage Shout-outs, etc."

"It turned out awesome." Karl grabbed the bars. "Stop complaining."

River tilted his head. "If it's good, what's the problem? Liza's promos have been a huge success for us."

"He made us actually *run*, over and over, in several locations, all the while shouting, 'Show them how Fury Runs, ladies.'" Wendy rubbed her thighs through her tight leather pants. "My legs are screaming."

Justice barked a laugh, creating a domino effect until they were all cracking up. Simon let go of the door long enough for Liza to nudge Karl, and the two of them made their escape from the brig. Liza managed to reclaim her phone and camera.

Once they reached the hangar deck where most of the party was going on, Justice snaked an arm around her shoulders and hung back. "Let's go to the flight deck and take a walk. Hardly anyone's up there."

Justice looked hot in slim-fit dark pants, a metallic-colored slouch T-shirt and long dark coat. Trendy with a slightly formal touch. His hair was doing its usual sex-messy thing, and his dark, scruffed jaw added that rocker edge.

"I don't trust the man who threw me in the brig."

Grinning, he said, "You shouldn't, I fully intend to—"

Female voices cut him off.

"It's him! Justice!" A group of women rushed up, surrounding him.

Liza didn't let the interruption get to her. It'd been like this all night with fans suddenly converging, and it's what they were there for. "I'm going to use the restroom." Once he nodded that he'd heard her, she headed into a hallway and found the ladies' restroom. When she was washing her hands, another girl came out of a stall. "Nikki?" Her blond hair was falling out of the pretty twist, and her lipstick was all chewed off. "You okay?"

"Yeah, I just needed a break."

"From?"

"Ace and his crew. They seem to think I'm their personal servant, running me ragged. 'Get a beer, I need more potatoes, go tell that chick to come over here.' What am I, a publicist or a pimp?" She grabbed a wad of paper towels and dried her hands.

Heading out together, Liza said, "You look more red carpet than pimp-like in that dress." The sleeveless navy dress with the mesh panels had an understated nautical theme and looked fantastic on Nikki.

That got a smile out of her. "Thanks. How's it going for you?"

"I had to break out of the brig." Liza told her the story as they walked back to Justice. Simon and River had joined in to pose for pictures. The crowd of women was thinning out.

"I'd better go find my guys. See you later." Nikki waved and left.

"What were you two talking about?"

The cold voice prickled. Swinging around, she faced Simon. "Nikki? I was telling her about being thrown in the brig."

"Just be careful. Anything you say can get back to

Ace and his band of assholes." He walked away.

"Sheesh, someone's having mood swings," she muttered. Fifteen minutes ago, he was teasing and laughing.

"It's not you," Justice said, obviously finished with the fans. Taking her hand, he led her toward another set of stairs. "He's edgy from being on the same ship as Ace. Ever since that showdown the other day, Simon's developed a hair-trigger around the guy. He'll be better after the show on Monday."

"Whatever. Not letting Simon get to me tonight." She'd been having too much fun. All the bands had performed a song, they'd had a decent dinner, and she'd mingled with lots of people. No one knew who she was. To them, she was just Liza, and she loved the freedom. But best of all was the feel of Justice's hand holding hers.

Up on the flight deck, they strolled around the planes and nodded to the security guards keeping any partiers away from the aircraft. They headed to the railing, looking out at the slices of moonlight on the dark water.

For a few seconds they stood there watching before she became aware of Justice's gaze on her. "What?"

"You look beautiful tonight. All damned night, I've watched you. Every time you laughed, it jolted straight to my cock. I wanted to yank you against me and kiss the hell out of you, show the entire ship that you're mine." He clenched his jaw, his eyes glinting. "I've never had this possessiveness over a woman."

Energy crackled between them, a connection so magnetic she leaned into him. For years, Liza had felt like a burden forced on her aunt and uncle. The outside world judged her without even knowing her. But Justice did know her, and he wanted her. That sensation poured into the loneliest part of Liza, making her feel sexy, worthy and a little bit wary. She wanted to feel this, but not lose her head.

"Lust. This is just lust, right?" She needed something to tell herself, to hold on to. She wasn't going to throw her life away or become her mom. "It'll burn itself out." Not destroy her.

His gaze scorched into hers. "That what it feels like to you? Like a couple orgasms will cure this attraction?" He fingered a lock of her hair. "Or will it whet your appetite for more?"

The way he stroked her hair caused sparks to skim her arms. "I don't know." She closed her eyes. "I shouldn't trust this."

"You were comfortable enough with me to shower and dress at my house before the event. We both know you wouldn't do that if you had doubts that you can trust me. That's the key here, Beth. You trust me."

She snapped her eyes open, and Justice filled her vision. He was so solid and sexy, like one of the heroes she wrote about late at night when she couldn't sleep. A fantasy, and yet Justice was real and he was right that she felt safe with him. But it was all moving so fast, she lightened the moment with teasing. "My power was out. Do you know what this hair looks like if I don't tame it?" She gestured to her smooth locks. "I needed electricity. Plus I didn't want to take a cold shower." Her power had gone out earlier this afternoon. When she'd called Justice to tell him she'd have to get ready at her roommate's boyfriend's house, he'd suggested she make it easier and use his house.

"If your power is still out, you can stay at my place." He held up a hand. "In the guestroom. Which has to be better than your roommate's boyfriend's couch."

Her mouth dried. Could she do that? "I don't know."

"Up to you if you want to stay or leave. But if it makes it easier for you, let's take sex off the table tonight. No expectations. But I will kiss you." He leaned down, sealing his mouth over hers.

The fire that had simmered since his kiss yesterday erupted into a blaze. She rose on her toes and kissed him back. Time slid away as heat ramped up between them. Unable to resist, she tunneled her fingers in his hair and sank her tongue into his mouth. She tasted the tang of Justice, and it made her hungrier. Needier.

Lifting his head, he brushed his thumb over her bottom lip. "Maybe we should nix kissing too. I want you too damned much to exert control. And you're wearing this dress with the skirt sliding around your legs all night in a wicked temptation." He took a breath. "No kissing once we're home."

He made her feel sexy. Adventurous. Everything in her craved more. "What if I want it on the table?"

"Kissing?"

Nerves shimmered, heightening the anticipation. "And sex. With you." She didn't want to be careful anymore.

Heat flared in his eyes, and he skimmed his knuckles along her cheek. "Depends."

"On what?"

"Whether you still feel this way when we get back to my house."

She sucked in a breath. There it was again, his reassurance that she could say no. Be safe. "Do you have condoms at your house? I'm not on birth control, and I don't want to take chances."

A tremor ran through his body. "A whole goddamned box."

He made her feel brave enough to say, "Show me."

Chapter 7

FORTY-FIVE MINUTES LATER, JUSTICE ushered her into his house and tossed his coat on the couch. "Before you say anything, I want to show you something."

Following him around the couch to the hallway, she swallowed her nerves and tried for a little humor. "Is this condom show-and-tell time?"

"No." He stopped inside the first room on the right, across from the hallway bathroom. Flipping on a light, he said, "Extra bedroom. You can stay in here if you want to with zero expectations. If you close the door, I won't come in."

Liza took in the average-sized bedroom. Carpeted floors, a double bed covered in a dark green comforter and stacked high with pillows. A dresser, nightstand and small bookshelf filled out the room.

Justice crossed to the bathroom, then returned and set her overnight bag on the bed. "Just wanted you to know it's here. Your choice." He walked out, leaving her standing there.

Alone in the room, she surveyed it. The bed would be more comfortable than Ben's couch in his one-bedroom condo, but the implications... She'd known this man less than a week. Yet it felt like more. So much more. She couldn't believe how hard he worked to make her feel safe. In control. He'd given her a safe zone.

No one had ever done that.

She returned to the front of the house and found him leaning against the rear of the couch, waiting for her. It was late, after midnight, yet he looked relaxed and sexy. She went to him. "You know what I want?"

"Chocolate?"

He did know her. "More than that."

"What?"

Liza closed the last few steps. "You. Us." Pausing, she added, "When you kiss me, I stop thinking. That's what I want." He quieted the constant anxiety riding her that sometimes built to unbearable levels.

Heat leapt into his gaze. Slipping a hand beneath her hair, he tugged her between his thighs and glided his thumb over the fluttering pulse at her throat. "You do the same to me. Every time I touch you and you respond—" his fingers on her nape pulled her closer, "—my control slips, and something primal takes over. The need to possess you. Not just fuck you, but possess a part of you no one else has, the part you'll only give me."

Tremors of desire made her ache. She wanted to be the woman who drove him to that. "Don't stop this time."

A ripple went through him. He surged up, swinging her around and perching her butt on the back of the couch. Keeping an arm around her waist, he settled his other hand on her knee. "Beth." He brushed his mouth over hers.

She parted her lips on the sweetly fervent way he said her name.

Diving in, he deepened the kiss, his tongue gliding against hers. Hot thrills charged over her skin, her nipples tightening until she moaned. This man unleashed a side of her that she'd never experienced.

Justice shifted, sliding his hand up and down her thigh, all the while kissing her, his mouth growing more demanding. She clung to him, never wanting it to end.

Discovering this untamed sexiness in her own body inflamed her desire. And she didn't want to lose it now. Sinking further into the kiss, she explored him. His taste was wild and edgy. She licked and sucked, desperate for more.

Justice groaned. "This dress drove me out of my mind tonight. It swished around your legs, never quite letting me see." Gripping the material, he eased it up her thighs.

"See what?"

His gaze burned into hers. "Your panties covering your hot little pussy."

Liza hissed, shock and heat colliding. No one said those things to her, not like this.

A wolfishly smug grin pulled at his lips. "Told you, baby. I'm not holding back, and neither are you." The dress slid higher. "Until you ask me to stop."

An ache ignited between her legs, centering on her clit. "No stopping. Not now."

She barely got the words out before he covered her mouth with his in a possessive, fierce kiss. He grazed his fingers along her inner thigh and over her panties.

He brushed against her aching clit.

Liza jerked her head back as fiery pleasure shot from that sensitive bud and coiled into a knot of vital need in her belly. The urge to chase the sensation, to experience it over and over, dragged a moan from her.

"It's been too long." She didn't think, the words just tumbling out.

He kissed her ear. "Jesus, I can feel how hot and wet you are through your panties. So perfect."

He didn't judge, and that propelled her excitement. Ready to make him feel as fevered as she did, she cupped him through his pants. "I feel you too. Hard and thick." She rubbed along his length, and when he jolted in response, she loved it.

She writhed, trying to get closer to him, half embarrassed, half desperate for Justice to touch her and ease the throbbing ache in her clit. Some tiny voice in her head whispered, *This isn't you. You don't do this.*

But she was doing this, wanted it, could feel her orgasm gathering. "Justice, I'm..."

"Don't think, Beth. Just feel." Reclaiming her mouth, he shoved her panties aside and circled her clit with glorious friction. Helpless beneath the passion roiling in her, she rocked against him. While his tongue mated with hers, the savage demand of his fingers stroked her bud, rocketing her higher, making her frantic for release. She stiffened, so close to climaxing but unable to quite let go...

He broke the kiss. "Do you know how hot you are? Sexy? Your eyes are burning with green fire." He slid one finger inside her, invading her with more sensations, and rubbed his palm against her clit. "It's yours, Beth. Your orgasm. Take it. Own it."

His command broke through any barriers she had left, and Liza lost control. Holding on to his shoulders, she ground on his hand, beautiful tension ratcheting up and up, stealing her ability to think or breathe, only to feel. Just as her arousal climbed to unbearable, pleasure exploded in a wild climax.

Strong arms wrapped around her. "I've got you." He crooned soft words in her ear as he carried her...somewhere.

Justice set her on her feet by his bed. His body was so tight, he damn near shook like a teenager about to get laid for the first time. He'd never seen anything like her going after her own orgasm. He'd been tempted to shove his jeans down, rip her panties aside and bury his cock deep inside her. Ride that sweet wave with her.

Feel her owning it.

Christ, she undid him.

Quickly he grabbed a couple condoms out of the nightstand then returned to Beth.

She shivered, growing cold. Unsure? He reached for her, pulling her against him. Wrapping all that hair around his hand, he eased her head back to see her eyes. "What do you need?" *Please don't let it be to stop.*

But he would if she wasn't ready.

"I just...maybe leave the light on?"

Ah. The dark made her uneasy. He snapped on the light to flood the room, chasing out shadows, and returned to her. "Done. I want to see you. But if you're not ready..." It fucking killed him to say it, but Beth was worth waiting for. She'd been in a situation she couldn't control before and rendered helpless. He wouldn't push her for more than she could handle. "We'll stop."

One second of hesitation lurked in her eyes behind her glasses. Then she stepped back.

Regret clawed at him. Fisting his hands, he clamped his jaw to keep from begging. This was her choice.

When she unzipped her dress and let it drift down her body, his heart kicked. Bare shoulders, black bra cupping her luscious breasts. He hissed in a breath, his cock engorging.

The dress inched farther, revealing her belly. No six-pack, just a creamy, soft stomach. Black panties. She kicked the dress away and released her bra.

Her breasts bounced free, and holy fuck. She was stacked, high and big enough to overflow his hands, with dark, stiff nipples. His heart rate shot up, and his cock throbbed. He leaned down, taking one peak into his mouth.

Beth moaned, her hands sliding into his hair. Hell yeah. She was with him now, not worrying about anything but the pleasure he gave her. He switched sides, taking the other nipple in his mouth, sucking her, gliding his hands over the swells of her hips.

Catching her panties, he crouched and eased them down.

His heart pounded at her warm, musky scent. The sight of her glistening pussy and swollen clit peeking out from damp curls fueled his pride. He'd done that to her, pushed her fast and hard to drive out any thoughts, leaving only pleasure.

Now she had him on his knees, and he couldn't resist. He buried his face in her folds. Her taste surrounded him, igniting his hunger. His control cracked, and he gripped her hips, anchoring her to his face as he licked and sucked, pushed by a primal urge to make her come again. Hard. Right there, where he could taste her release.

She hissed, her fingers tangling in his hair as he licked her. So fucking good. His cock surged against his pants, balls tight and hungry as he licked and sucked.

Beth's fingers dug into his scalp as she writhed. "Justice."

Her thick, husky voice cut through the madness pushing him to keep tonguing her. Tugging back, he looked up. She was so stunning his heart swelled. Beth was full in all the best places, rounded hips, tucked-in waist and heavy breasts. But it was the color in her face, the need and slight unease magnified in her eyes, that called to him. Rising, he caught her face between his palms.

"Right here," he reassured her. He didn't think she was panicking, it was more like she needed to touch him. "Just you and me, sweetheart. Tell me what you want."

"Not to be the only one naked."

The vulnerability in that statement slammed him. Letting him strip her last defense away with her panties...she needed more reassurance. "Anything you want." He yanked off his shirt and tossed it, then shed everything else, his cock thick and hard for her.

Her gaze drifted over him, color darkening her cheekbones. She touched his chest and skimmed her fingers lightly along his stomach.

Her touch was so delicate he leaned into her, his nerves leaping and chasing the teasing sensation. Heat chills followed, and Justice gritted his teeth to stand still and let Beth explore. When she circled her fingers around his cock, he growled a fierce note of pleasure. Her thumb brushed the moist tip, dragging him up to his toes as he pumped into her fist.

"Beth." He clasped her wrist, tugging her to him. "I need to be inside you." He swallowed as she wrapped her arms around him, pressing all that softness against his burning skin.

"The first time will be fast and hard." He heard the demand in his voice. Couldn't help it. He eased her down onto the bed, covering her with his body, kissing her and bumping into her glasses.

Liza reached up to remove them.

Justice caught her hand, kissed her palm, then asked, "Can you see?"

"Not up close, but I can feel." She parted her thighs, rubbing her warm, slick cleft along his rigid cock.

He clamped his jaw to resist the powerful urge to surge up inside her. "Keep them on. I want you to know who you're with every second."

He wanted her to feel safe.

Liza understood what he was doing, making sure she didn't feel too vulnerable, like not being able to see. A deep warmth spread through her, drawing her into him and the experience. "I don't need them, not when you're touching me." She took them off and set them on the bedside table. Justice's sharp features fuzzed, but she could tell it was him. "Hurry."

"Demanding, aren't you?" He pushed back on his knees, ripped open a small package and rolled on a condom.

Her heart pounded. Even without her glasses, he looked like a sex god. His messy hair fell around him, wide shoulders, tatted arms, and his washboard stomach. She lowered her gaze to his latex-covered cock—long, thick and bobbing with excitement.

For her. This man wanted her—the real her. "Can't handle the pressure, rock star?"

He dropped down over her, his hard body surrounding her. "I can't handle how badly I want you. It's killing me." He lined up his cock, pushing in.

Her breath caught as his shaft penetrated her.

He squeezed his eyes shut. His jaw bulged as he

stopped. "You're so tight. Don't want to hurt you."

Oh no. Not after he'd made her come right there in his living room, then stripped her and kissed her all the way down between her legs. Now he was holding back? Wrapping her legs around him, she ran her hands along his powerful back to his sculpted ass. Gripping him, she tilted up, trying to get him deeper.

Justice snapped his eyes open. "Don't."

She squinted to bring his image into full focus. "Or what? I want to feel you buried inside me."

His arms bulged; she could actually feel them thickening where he braced them on either side of her face. Then he leaned down, his eyes burning into hers. "Or I'll lose control and fuck you like your mine. Hard. Until you're writhing and begging to come. And you will come. None of this holding-back bullshit." He dragged in an audible breath. "Now be still and give me a goddamned minute if you want gentle."

The control he exerted over himself was evident in every muscle. Even his stomach pressed to hers rippled with the tension of holding back. The realization bolted a spasm of pure sexual lightning through her. She didn't need her glasses to feel his searing gaze on her or the energy coursing between them. Her nipples tightened, and an ardent yearning to be completely filled seized her. The frantic compulsion was more than physical, it was an emotional urge to be so totally connected to Justice that he'd leave a permanent imprint on her.

"Screw gentle, I want you." She arched her hips up, forcing his cock deeper.

He hovered there a second longer, as if measuring her. His cock pulsed halfway inside her, as impatient as she was. Liza rocked and squeezed, determined to have as much of Justice as she could take.

His control snapped. He surged in, sheathing himself to the hilt, stretching and penetrating her until she gasped with the too-full, and yet not enough, sensation.

A dark laugh spilled from him. "Look at you," he growled out. "Writhing like a wild thing, so hot I can't stop. Can't get enough." He braced himself over her and thrust hard.

Liza bowed as he hit a pleasure spot that tore a cry from her. Every time he pulled out, her internal walls spasmed, as if they could hold on to him. A primal fear that he'd leave her wanting, hurting with this unbearable need.

He powered into her, his cock hot and steel-like, driving her higher. Her belly constricted. She planted her heels and tilted her pelvis up, meeting every thrust, her fingers clamping on his shoulders. "Please."

His eyes burned. Shifting to one arm, he slid his hand down her belly and thumbed her clit while slamming into her until all her sensors fired at once. Crazed noises spilled from her throat. Desperate panting echoed in her ears.

"That's it, Beth. Let go."

The pressure detonated at the sound of his voice. She exploded, sucked into a pleasure vortex.

He pounded into her, stiffened and came. His cock pulsed hard and wild deep inside her while his chest heaved, his entire body bucking.

Finally they both settled, and Justice leaned down, kissed her, and then brushed her damp hair from her face. "You okay?"

Liza swallowed at the way he studied her while his cock still throbbed inside her body. He'd given her the thing she hadn't realized she craved so badly, an intimate connection that made her feel cherished beyond physical satisfaction. A little overwhelmed, she opted for an understated answer. "A smidge better than okay, I think."

He laughed. "Yeah? Well, you damn near blew my mind. I'll be right back." He pulled out of her, rolled off the bed and headed through a door. She presumed a bathroom.

As soon as the door closed, anxiety nibbled into her contentment. She scooped her glasses off the nightstand and put them on. The whole room came into focus, and with it a dose of reality. She'd slept with a rock star. And now she thought it was more than sex?

Oh God.

Her chest tightened, and the old scars on her wrist itched as panic built. All the names she'd been called, *slut, whore, Lolita,* pounded her head. The glare of the spotlight, the shame...

What was she doing here? Was she going to become her mom and repeat all her mistakes? Think that Justice wanted her for more than sex?

She had to get out of here now.

Justice came out of the bathroom to find Liza tugging on her panties.

"Going someplace?" Not if he could help it. He fought the primal urge to scoop her up and plop her back in his bed.

"I thought I'd leave."

He frowned, wondering where that had come from. She'd been fine a minute ago. Striding to her, he took hold of her wrist. "Regrets, Beth?" He loved calling her that, a name she didn't share with everyone.

Her gaze focused on him. "Not regret. I'm not sure how to do this."

Her uncertainty crawled into him. "Us?"

"This is just sex, right? Because I've never had sex like that, not..." She looked down, twisting her watch. "I don't want to be my mother, mistaking sex for a relationship. I'll go home."

No way was he letting her leave like this, upset and feeling used and uncared for. Justice curled his fingers around her arm and pulled her to him. "Not just sex. This was never just sex." Not from the first second she'd walked into their practice wearing that ugly brown sweater and overflowing attitude. She'd stood up to him and taken control.

So seeing her vulnerable and lost as if he couldn't be bothered with her once he'd gotten his rocks off? He couldn't bear it. "Don't leave. Please. I know you can't sleep in bed with me." He hated that, but it didn't take a genius to figure out she was afraid of what would happen when she was asleep. That asshole drugged her, then when she was helpless to fight him off, raped her. She needed to feel safe. "Sleep in the other room. You can brace the door with a chair or wedge something under it and no one can get in. Tomorrow I'll get you a lock for it so you have a place when you stay over."

Liza jerked her head up, shock making her blink. "How do you understand so well?"

"Because you're not the only one who's fucked up. If you leave me, I'll be alone in this house, haunted by guilt and anger. I'll go looking. I won't be able to stop myself. I'll go out on the streets, searching for the man who doesn't want to see his son. But when you're here, that compulsion dims. You share your troubles and let me help, and that makes me feel better and worthy in a way I haven't for a long time." He didn't know how else to explain it. She let him touch her, hold her. Give her so much pleasure it clearly scared the hell out of her.

She closed her eyes, swallowing, while twisting her watch. "I'll stay."

Relief cascaded in cool waves, quieting the inner turmoil clawing at him. Two things usually did that, music and sex. And now Beth.

His gaze caught on her watch, and he noticed that her pale skin had reddened at the edge of the metal band. He covered her fidgeting fingers in concern. Had he grabbed her wrist during sex and dug that woven mesh band into her flesh?

"Did I do this?" He soothed the spot with the pad of his finger.

Her eyes snapped open. "Do what?"

"This irritated spot. Did I accidently press on the band? Here let me take it off and see—"

"No." She tugged her wrist from his hold.

He drew back, startled. "Okay." He wouldn't touch her watch if it bothered her. But why was that a big deal? "Was it a gift? From your mom or something?" Before she went to prison?

She compressed her lips, as if deciding. "Not a gift exactly. My aunt bought it for me." With a deliberate inhalation, she released the hidden catch. "To hide these." Liza slipped the watch off and turned her arm to show him the inside of her wrist.

What the fuck? Two white, jagged scars slashed the delicate skin in a bumpy, uneven V shape. Icy shock dropped over him like a blanket. He couldn't tear his stare from them. "These aren't knife cuts. What happened?" Could Hayes have done this to her? Or had she... "Oh Christ, did you—?" A vortex opened up, trying to suck him in. "You tried to kill yourself?"

She snapped her wrist down. "An accident." With

her back rigid, she snatched up her dress, bra and shoes, then strode out of the room.

What just happened? Was she leaving? His muscles fired with adrenaline, the need to go after her pushing him. Quickly, he stepped into his shorts, and he followed her, fearing she'd rush out into the night.

He only made it out the doorway of his bedroom when he caught sight of Beth. She'd turned left down the hall and vanished into the room he'd told her to use, and softly closed the door.

She'd shut him out, but she hadn't left the house.

He turned his attention to his dad's room directly across from his bedroom. That door was closed too, although no one was inside it. But once in a while he found things in there disturbed, telling him that his dad had come in and out when Justice wasn't home.

Each time it hurt. His father wouldn't see him, talk to him or let him help.

When he'd seen those scars on Beth's wrist, all he could think was she'd tried to leave too. Permanently. Would she do it again? What had he gotten himself into?

All his brain cells screamed to go check on her, to make sure she stayed. But that door and his promise stood between them. If he broke his word now, how would she ever believe him?

Fighting his instincts, he returned to his bedroom, snatched up his guitar and sat on the bed. He didn't think, just played and sang, pouring his frustration and worry into the music. He'd played two songs and was on the third, when her voice broke in.

"'Something to Believe In' by Poison. That's one of my mom's favorite songs. I grew up listening to it."

Liza—his Beth—leaned a shoulder against the doorjamb of his room, clutching her laptop to her chest with one arm. Hanging from her fingers was a bag of M&M's.

"You didn't leave."

She came in, rounding the bed to settle next to him against the pillows, and set the computer on her thighs. "You didn't follow me."

The feel of her next to him eased his tension. She'd pulled on a coral tank top, and her mahogany hair was around her shoulders—a perfect picture in his bed. "Wanted to. But I promised." And meant it. "You're not wearing the watch." That she'd come to his room and left her wrist bare, exposing the scars that she normally hid, told him she was ready to talk about it.

Beth lowered her gaze and fiddled with the bag of M&M's. "For a while, when I got too scared, usually at night, I'd lock myself in the bathroom and sometimes...I cut."

"Yourself?" Stupid question, he'd seen the scars on her wrist.

She closed her eyes. "Usually my thighs. The pain was a release, something else to focus on to block out the internal fear. I couldn't sleep, sometimes for days."

Cold, sick dread spread in him. Another indication that this girl was dealing with some deep psychological issues.

Like his father.

Not the same thing, since Liza was here with him, and she hadn't run off. Focusing on her, he asked, "So your wrist?" Had she done that to herself?

"It happened the night the court announced that Hayes had fled the country. Gleeful protesters filled the street in front of our house with huge signs that said, *Run, Hayes, Run! She asked for it! Recant! Hayes is the Real Victim!* And they screamed things like *lying whore*, *slut*, even *cunt*. My little cousins, Kristen and Rafe, could hear it too. We had security, but on that day...the crowd couldn't be stopped." The bag crinkled beneath Liza's fingers.

He desperately wanted to pull her onto his lap and shield her from her memories. But she was trying to share with him, and he needed to let her do it. "And?"

"My aunt and uncle had Rafe and Kristen in the family room with them at the back of the house where they wouldn't hear it as much. But my bedroom was at the front. I could hear it all. Every word." She lifted her eyes to him. "It wouldn't stop, the voices screaming over and over, filling every part of my head until I was drowning in their hatred. I wanted to shriek back, but I wasn't allowed to. It wasn't just my aunt who told me that, but the DA's office and everyone who worked with me to help prepare me for trial. They told me to only speak in the courtroom, or to my therapist, and even that, they warned, could be risky. What if the therapist's notes got out? Or someone broke into her office? It happens."

Had they realized what they were doing to this girl? A victim? Justice knew all too well that many ambitious people didn't give a shit. Oh they said they did, until it came down to a choice of their goals over the other person's welfare. The military trotted his dad out as a hero until he became an embarrassment suffering severe PTSD, then they abandoned him. And Liza? She was their star witness whom they silenced to protect their case. Bastards. "That's wrong. You know it is."

"Maybe. But they pointed out that if I spoke out and hurt the case, Hayes would do it again to some other girl. I couldn't live with that."

He fisted his hands against the urge to punch the pricks who'd put that on her. Worse, they'd done it when she hadn't had a mom or dad around to protect her. He honestly couldn't tell if her aunt meant to protect her, or what. "So what did you do?"

"I tried to stay quiet, but it was building in me. All the words I couldn't say became a painful buzzing in my head, constantly there, pressing against my brain. I just wanted it to stop. I wanted it all to stop."

Had anyone even seen the signs that she was cracking under the strain? He prompted her with, "So what happened?"

She braced her wrist on her laptop, staring at it. "I lost control. Broke a drinking glass and started cutting my wrist. The sharp, hot pain made everything else go away. I sat there on the floor of my room, pushing that jagged piece of glass in. Then I picked up a second one and pushed it in."

Christ. He could picture it, young Beth—Elizabeth then—alone in her room, hurting so much she jammed broken glass into her wrist. Would she do it again now? "What stopped you?"

"My aunt when she came in to check on me." She looked over at him, her eyes unfocused. "She screamed at me. I can still hear the crunch of glass as she stepped on it to kneel down, her hands shaking me. 'What have you done? Elizabeth, you can't do this.' But it kept bleeding. My uncle came in, and he called an ambulance.

"While we waited, Mari calmed down and said, 'It has to be an accident. Do you hear me, Elizabeth? Tell them you broke the glass accidentally. If the hospital thinks that you tried to hurt yourself, they'll take you away, put you in an institution or group home. They might even take Rafe and Kristen away, fearing we're unfit. You can't ever tell anyone. And you can't do this ever again. Ever. No cutting.'"

Justice narrowed his eyes, rage nearly blinding him. "She knew you had been cutting? And did nothing?"

"Guessed. Bloody tissue in the trash, that kind of thing. And before you jump all over them, thinking they didn't care, they did. But we were all living in a pressure cooker. Mari had a sister in prison for murder, an infamous niece at the center of a media circus trial, her house surrounded by protesters, and just going to the grocery store or mailbox was almost impossible. Her life, all our lives, was this house of cards, and she kept trying to shut out the smallest breeze that would cave it in. She was trying to hold it all together and shield her kids."

"You needed help. You should have told someone."

"Really?" she snapped back. "And then what? Get them in trouble for not reporting it? Be taken away? They had legal guardianship, but they were subjected to social worker visits and their family scrutinized. Even the media spotlighted them. After all, Amber Ranger is Mari's sister. Are they alike? They were raised together. Why would I make it worse for them? And then end up living in some home where I was even less wanted?"

"Shit. I just hate it. It's wrong." He'd had his grandmother fighting for him, and later, Drake too. Then he'd had friends. Who had Beth had? An aunt and a whole legal system that kept silencing her. "So you hid your scars?"

"Yep. The ones on my thighs are barely noticeable. Few people ever see those."

He jerked, realizing now why... "That's why you stopped me when I was licking you." He'd been so into her, he hadn't noticed any scars.

A blush stained her skin.

Putting his arm around her, he tugged her chin up and waited. She'd answer when she was ready.

"That was most of the reason. And it was just overwhelming. Sex isn't like this for me. I don't lose control. That's part of cutting. I have control over something."

"Two conversations here. First, on sex, you don't need control when you're in my bed. All you need are words to tell me when something crosses your line. You did that."

"It's not a permanent line."

"You want my mouth on you, sweetheart?" Damned if his cock didn't totally get into the idea. But not right now, they had a conversation to finish.

"I liked it."

He fought a grin. He'd tasted exactly how much she liked it. "I'd love to talk about spreading your legs and licking you, but I need to know." His stomach clenched. "Do you still cut?"

"No. At my next visit with my mom, she saw the bandages. I told her it was an accident, but she knew." Liza closed her eyes. "She said, 'Don't leave me, Beth. I can bear living in here. I can bear anything but losing you. Please, baby, don't leave me. I wish I'd gotten there sooner, saved you before that bastard ever drugged or touched you. Find a way to survive. Please.'"

Justice pushed the computer off her lap and pulled her into his arms. He didn't say anything. Couldn't. He'd been so furious that she had no one, but she had—her mom.

"I realized then exactly what she'd sacrificed for me," she said softly. "My father was dead, so he didn't matter, but I wasn't going to let Hayes take any more from us." She looked up at him. "I found a way to get through the nights."

Her glasses were slightly askew from him pressing her face against his chest, and she was damned beautiful. Adjusting her glasses, he asked, "How?"

"When I got scared, I escaped into my own world by writing. They started out as short stories, and now I'm writing books. It's my secret place where no one else can go. And I control everything."

That was a hell of a lot better than cutting. "You've never told anyone?"

"I mentioned I like to write to my mom, but not that I'm writing books." She smiled at him. "Until now."

Her trust had his chest puffing up. "I'm glad you told me."

Her expression dimmed. "I'm not sure what we're doing here. I don't want people to know who I am, and you..."

Worry bit into his earlier pride. "I want the whole world to know me and our band. I have to make it. I have to." His mom had told him he was nothing, a screwup. His dad couldn't be around him and chose the streets over him. The only one who'd believed in him had been his grandmother. He couldn't let her down.

If he didn't make it, he was a loser. Not good enough for his grandmother.

Or anyone.

"What are we doing then?" she asked. "We want different things. I wanted you to understand, I don't know what I can handle. And you...you can't be held back from your dream."

He couldn't bear the idea of her walking out now. "We'll figure it out. Give me a chance. Give us a chance." She'd come to him, told him her secrets, that had to mean something. "Do you want to be with me enough to try? Or do you want to call it quits?" She had to want their relationship too.

Had to want him enough to stay. He'd find a way to protect her. But right now, he waited for her answer, every beat of his heart growing more painful.

It'd been hard enough when she'd walked out of his room earlier. He didn't want to lose her.

Finally she said, "I want you. For as long as it lasts."

He leaned down and kissed her, tasting the woman he was already starting to care about and need.

Too damn much.

Chapter 8

MONDAY MORNING, LIZA STOOD IN the wings of the morning show set, desperately trying not to fidget. Had she made the right call pushing Simon to talk about his dead wife?

Or would it backfire?

Time to find out. She focused on the five members of Savaged Illusions sitting on the half-moon-shaped red couch with the show host, Missy, in the center. On her right were Gray, Lynx and River, on her left, Justice and Simon. They were all doing pretty well, although Gray was quiet on the end, the other four personalities overshadowing his calmer demeanor.

Missy moved to the final question. "All the women want to know—are any of you guys in a relationship with some lucky girl?"

River shouted out, "Dozens! Love you all, ladies!"

The audience laughed.

Missy focused to her left. "What about you, Simon? Is there a special woman for you?"

Liza's heart slammed up her throat. This was it.

She had to be right, because if she was wrong, she didn't think Simon would forgive her. And he was important to Justice, so she couldn't let him down.

Simon slowly leaned forward, settling his elbows on his thighs. He dropped his head for a beat, then raised his chin, his eyes on the camera. "Just one. My late wife. Her name was Julie."

The audience reacted with stuttered sounds of shock.

Chill bumps rippled down Liza's arms. Despite knowing he'd talk about his wife, the way he said it was a gut punch. So real, everyone in the room could feel Simon's love and loss.

Missy rose and motioned for Justice to slide over on the couch. The show's host sat next to Simon. "What happened?"

The camera tightened in on the two of them.

Simon turned to Missy. "We were both ambitious and driven. Julie was an actress and dancer, and she'd gotten a callback for a made-for-TV movie. She was so excited. I was supposed to be there, but I got a gig. At the time I was pursuing a solo artist career." Simon shifted his gaze to the audience. "She asked me to come home just for that night, you know? In case they gave her bad news. My wife had anxiety issues, but this was my chance too. I was opening for a huge name. So I told Julie I'd call as soon as I could, and I headed off to Vegas."

The entire room held their breath, waiting for Simon to go on. Liza was impressed with the morning show host; she didn't jump in to fill his pause. She seemed to have excellent instincts, or she was just as caught up in the story as everyone else.

Simon shifted on the seat, as if the memory dug at him. "That night I called her, there was no answer. So I performed my opening set. When I finished, I called Julie again, and still no answer. No messages or texts.

I started to get pissed. I left a couple messages telling her to stop being a drama queen."

Liza squeezed her eyes shut. Oh God. Poor Simon.

"I was angry," he went on, his voice heavy with brutal regret. "But I had to go home and check on her. I got to our apartment about four a.m. So early...and too late. Too damned late." He dropped his head. "She was dead from an overdose. I found her on the couch. She'd written all over her body in black marker, *Too Fat. Casting director told me to my face, Too Fat.* Everywhere I looked on my beautiful girl were the ugly words: *Too Fat.*"

Simon pulled his gaze up. "Part of me died that day. I won't love again. Can't. All I have now is my music."

Missy said softly, "I think I can speak for the audience here in the studio and at home, we're all heartbroken by the cruelty your wife suffered and by your loss."

Simon slowly nodded. "Thank you. Julie didn't have to die. I'll never forgive myself for not being there when she needed me. But there's a bigger responsibility here. Words matter. I don't care how big and powerful a person is, they don't get a free pass. Words matter. And on that day four years ago, thoughtlessly cruel and needlessly vicious words killed my wife."

Missy turned to the camera. "We'll be right back after these messages."

Staff swarmed the set, removing mic packs and ushering the guys out the door. Liza hurried out into the long hallway and caught up to Simon. Touching his arm, she said, "Oh, Simon, I'm so sorry. But you did something important today, telling the world that words matter." Liza's throat tightened in sympathy for that woman. She knew what it felt like when vicious words played over and over in your head, until the only thing that existed was the truth of those words. The need to just make them stop, to end the pain. But Simon had stood up for Julie, told the world his wife hadn't deserved that. "Your love for her showed."

He stared down at her, his jaw slicing from side to side, fury and pain rolling off him. "Don't sugarcoat it. I used my wife's death to win. That's who I am." He strode out.

A hand settled on her shoulder.

She turned to see Justice staring after Simon.

"I'd hoped he'd feel better. He did the right thing by getting control of the story before Ace or *Court of Rock* uses it for their own gain." Liza added, "And he sent a powerful message that words matter and we all need to be responsible for the things we say."

Justice rubbed his thumb over her shoulder. "He knows that, or he wouldn't have done it. He's not mad at you, but he can't forgive himself."

She didn't have an answer for that. Almost seven years and she still hadn't forgiven herself for wrecking so many lives. Even knowing the rape itself wasn't her fault, she'd set it all in motion with her bad decisions. Just like Julie's suicide wasn't Simon's fault, but some of his decisions likely made him feel he didn't do enough to be there for her. "Maybe getting it out in the open will help."

As soon as the words were out, she internally cringed. She kept her secrets but asked Simon to reveal his. Hypocrite much?

"Hey, Justice." River strode up them. "We have a meeting in less than an hour."

"I'll catch you guys there, going to walk Liza to her car." Justice shifted his gaze to her. "Where are you parked?"

"Public lot outside."

He took her hand, and they headed out into the bright sunshine.

Curious, she asked, "What meeting do you have?" It wasn't anything she had on the *Court of Rock* schedule for the band.

"With Christine Castle."

It took her a second to place the name. Oh right, that was the woman Liza'd met briefly at Screech's Nightclub. "The business manager."

"Yep. She's very interested in us now that we have a real shot at signing with Tangent. She's driving out here from Los Angeles to meet with us, so she's serious."

"You want to sign with her?" She tugged him toward her little car tucked among all the big SUVs. Stopping, she reached into her purse for her keys.

Justice eased her back against the door, looming over her, body vibrating with a low-grade energy as he stared down at her. "What I want is to kiss you."

Her body answered with her own tremors. Not fear, oh no. Awareness. Anticipation. Why hadn't having sex with him taken the edge off? How could she want him more?

He leaned down, brushing his mouth over hers. His fingers slid into her hair and his tongue into her mouth.

Her belly unknotted, melting the tension she'd been carrying all morning into a pool of warm desire.

He pulled back. "I've wanted to do that since you showed up at the studio this morning looking so damned sexy."

She'd paired a long-sleeved, black-and-cream tunic with black leggings and ankle boots. "Me? You're the one who had the audience screaming when the morning host introduced you." Wait, was that jealousy? Not good. She had to keep some common sense and boundaries. She wasn't her mom, she had her own life.

"Fans are awesome. We couldn't do this without them. But you're the only girl I can't stop thinking about." He touched a tendril of her hair. "I walked you to your car for a reason."

"To kiss me?"

He raised his eyebrows. "I'm always thinking about kissing you. Licking you. Hearing your cries as I thrust into you."

She closed her eyes, sucking in air. The things he did to her—this couldn't be normal.

His palm settled on her cheek. "But also to ask you to go to dinner with me tonight." He hesitated a second, then added, "Out to a restaurant, anywhere you want to go. You can tell me about your book."

"Books. More than one." It was out before she could stop it.

"How many? Never mind. Tell me at dinner."

She studied his face, searching to find what drove him. He didn't have to do this. She'd already agreed to a sexual relationship. "You really want to know about my writing?"

"Hell yeah, I want to know everything about you." He shook his head, as if surprised at himself. "I was jealous of that book on Saturday night. Once you started working on it, you were so absorbed, like you'd been transported to another place."

That's exactly what it felt like, and it's what had kept her going during long nights or bad days. "Why does that make you jealous?"

"Because you went there without me."

Stunned, she hissed in a breath, strange sensations rocking her. "That's..."

"Insane." He nodded, as if confirming his own thoughts. "But true. So tell me about your stories tonight over dinner. Take me with you."

He wanted that? Her writing had always been the one place where she could escape to her secret world and she had full control over everything. While every moment with him Liza took another step out on that high wire over the unknown. He stripped her control, made her want, dream and hope. Self-preservation told her to run back, get to safety.

But when she looked into his eyes and saw the need there, she wanted to keep going. "I'll tell you...oh wait." Disappointment crashed her back to reality. "I can't go out tonight, or this week. I'm working on a group project for my communications class. It's for our final grade. Every free moment will be spent on that until we turn it in on Friday."

"Damn, I won't get you to myself for four more days?"

Temptation rippled. She couldn't blow off her commitments, but maybe she could go over to his house afterward? They'd be finished around ten or eleven and—

And what? Screw him then go home? He'd see her as just a fuck buddy, and worse, she'd view herself as that. Firming her spine, she said, "Yes."

"I get it. So how about Friday night?"

She hesitated. "I kind of have a commitment then too. But, um, you could come along. It's dinner with my roommate, Emily, and her boyfriend, Ben. We meet at Wylie's." Would he want to go?

He didn't even hesitate. "It's a date. I'd like to meet them."

A huge smile erupted on her face. "Emily's bugging me about meeting you."

His eyes crinkled at the edges. "Wants to check me out, huh? Make sure I'm good enough?"

She started to say no, but why lie? "Maybe a little. But she's nice if she likes you."

"And if she doesn't?"

She thought of Emily when she'd found out Dillion broke up with her and made her that ugly offer. "How fast can you run?"

"That bad?"

"I sort of had to hide her car keys to keep her from going after Dillion. I put them in the freezer. By the time she found them, she got sidetracked by ice cream."

He dropped his forehead to hers, laughing. "I think I like her already. Everyone needs a friend like that."

Pleasure warmed her, and she got hotter when he kissed her again.

Liza finally came up for air. "Thought you had a meeting? You know, becoming famous and all?"

Color had darkened his face, and he narrowed his eyes. "You're a dangerous distraction, Glasner." He opened her car door. "Go before we both forget we have places to be."

"Good luck in your meeting. If Christine's what you want in a manager, I hope she'll sign you."

His eyes hardened with ambition. "She's a shark, exactly what we want. She'll make signing us contingent on winning though, to be sure she gets at least some income. This is just a prelim to discuss a potential business plan and strategies. We have to win."

As she drove away, the warmth of Justice's touch faded beneath the memory of his fierce drive. He'd told her what he wanted.

Fame.

He was living in the spotlight. How long did Liza

think she could hang around in that glow and not have it come out who she was? Then it'd all start again, the media scrutiny, the terrible things said about her. Her family would be furious.

She gripped the steering wheel tighter as she headed toward campus.

She didn't want the fame part of Justice, she just wanted the man for as long as it lasted. Because one way or another, fame and stardom would pull him away.

It always did.

She just hoped her life, and that of her family, didn't end up as collateral damage.

Again.

Justice grinned at the group of women in the Beachside Java Shop. For three days, Liza'd had the band doing mini appearances around San Diego in between all their other commitments. Sure it took a lot of effort, but it was paying off with more and more fans showing up each time.

"I'm a huge fan," one of the women said. "We've been voting for you guys since the start of the season."

"We follow the Savage Shout-outs hashtag. I can't believe we were able to catch you guys here," another one added.

Liza buzzed around them, taking pictures with the fans' phones for them and getting a ton of shots with her camera.

"Simon," a third woman spoke softly. "I saw your interview on that morning show. You were so brave and touched a lot of people who've endured bullying."

Focusing all his attention on the dark-haired, slightly plump woman, Simon asked, "Including you?"

She looked down. "Sometimes."

Simon gentled his voice. "What's your name?"

"Jane."

"Liza," Simon called out. "Can you get a shot of us with my friend Jane here to post? Let's show everyone how beautiful she is."

The woman lit up, her smile beaming.

As they all gathered around the woman, Justice couldn't help but stare at Liza as she moved around them, happily taking pictures. Simon hadn't wanted to talk about Julie to random strangers, no matter how well-intentioned. Liza had understood, and she'd suggested that when people approached him and mentioned the interview, he turn the attention away from his deceased wife to the fan. That worked, and it seemed to fill a need in him, one Liza had somehow seen.

It amazed Justice that for a girl who'd been through so much, she managed to still have compassion and empathy.

Or maybe that was what made her care so much. She had her own scars hidden beneath the watch.

Whatever it was, it had him by the balls.

Twenty minutes later, the crush of fans left, and the coffee shop quieted. He spotted Liza out on the deck, bent over her computer working. The bright sunlight highlighted streaks of red in her brown locks.

It was all he could do not to stride out there, wrap her ponytail around his hand and kiss her. Possession burned through him, fisting his hands.

How the hell did he want her more? Usually once he had sex with a woman, his interest faded. He was too focused on his career.

But Liza—his Beth—got under his skin, creating an irresistible need to touch her, feel her. Every night, once he got home and settled into bed, when the house grew too quiet and his mind too loud with the impulse to go look for his dad, he called Liza. Just the sound of her voice calmed that frantic energy always snapping beneath his skin.

God he wanted to get her alone and hear all about the worlds she created.

"Liza was right."

"What?" He yanked his gaze away from the girl consuming his thoughts to Simon.

"About the interview. As a preemptive strike, it took the punch out of that promo package the show's been running for a couple days."

"Hell yeah," Lynx added. "But using that footage was low."

It pissed them all off. A man's dead wife should be off-limits. But that's not how reality TV worked, and Ace was too dumb to realize the show execs didn't care if he won or lost, they only wanted higher ratings. They were manipulating that dimwit as much as anyone else in the remaining three bands.

"Let's hope they don't blindside us with anything else." Justice shifted his gaze back out to the deck.

Like using Liza? Did the show know about her past? Probably not, he decided. They wouldn't care about her. She was just a college kid competing for an internship. They were focused on the talent—the bands—not publicists and college students.

"Dude, is this going to be a problem?" Simon demanded.

Justice jerked his gaze from her for a second time. "What?"

Simon crossed his arms and glared. "You're acting like a chick, staring after the girl. Obviously you two have something going."

"Since when do you care?"

"I don't." His eyes froze, hard-ass Simon making an

appearance. "Unless it gets in the way of our band. We're less than two weeks away from the win, a label contract and signing with the best business manager. Nothing gets in our way now."

Justice snapped upright. "Liza's not in the way. She's busting her butt for us." Simon had just said she was right about the interview, so what had crawled up his ass?

The man shook his head. "You're getting distracted. That's the problem."

His muscles tensed, anxiety roiling in his gut. *We're all uptight*, he reminded himself. The thought did little to calm him, and Justice leaned in. "Bullshit. I've been working my ass off."

For one second, the hard shell Simon wore like skin cracked. Raw pain burned in his eyes. "You can't have it all. I know, I tried. When you have two passions, two things you want and love. One always gets hurt. Or dead."

Christ. He was talking about his wife. Justice had no idea what to say. "It's not the same thing." He and Liza weren't married.

The cracks closed, and Simon said, "Just keep your head in the game. Without your voice, we don't win." He strode out.

"Fuck." Simon was a control freak, but this was over the top even for him. "This isn't the same thing," he said again.

"No?" Lynx asked. "She going to understand that music comes first?"

"She knows the life." Better than a lot of girls would. Automatically, his gaze traveled to her, sitting... "Oh hell no." He broke into a jog, easily weaving around customers and bursting out on the patio. Liza sat at a small table in the corner.

Across from her sat Dillion. Smug asshole had sunglasses covering his eyes and entitlement in his slouch. Justice paused a few feet away. Liza could handle the jackass. Yet the urge to be nearby had him hovering, ready to go Rambo on Dillion's ass if he crossed the line.

"Come on, Liza," her ex whined. "You don't have to be like that. I'm only asking for tickets."

His girl jerked her head up. "No. Why are you still here? Go away."

"Look, I'll pay you, 'kay? I'm in a tight spot here. My fiancée is a fan of that band—"

"Are you kidding me?" Liza's voice pitched up. "I should care what your fiancée likes?"

Dillion tilted his head. "I'll pay you double their face value. My fiancée is coming down to see the show on Monday night, and they're sold out."

"Not my problem."

He smacked his elbows on the table. "You're working for the band, right? I mean I thought you were dating Cade but now realize you're just working for him." His too-thin mouth turned down. "He's got tons of girls throwing themselves at him. Why would he go for you?"

That jerk pole-vaulted right over the line, snapping Justice into action. Two steps and he leaned over Liza, slamming his palm down on the table. "Got a hearing problem, douchebag?"

Liza jumped. He settled his other hand on her shoulder, letting her know it was him. She relaxed.

But Dillion shot to his feet, skidding his chair back. The other customers watched.

Justice didn't care. His attention was on Liza's ex. "She told you no, now get lost."

The man looked around, then back at Liza. "Text

me. Name your price. Just get me the tickets." He spun and hurried out of sight.

Justice focused on Liza. "You okay?"

She stared after Dillion, chewing her lip. "Yeah. Aside from you scaring the hell out of me. I didn't hear you come outside or approach the table."

"I saw him talking to you, came out and stood back since you had it handled."

"And then?" Challenge radiated from her fiery green eyes. "Did I suddenly turn fragile or weak?"

"Nope, he mouthed off. It's a guy thing, baby. Not about you being strong or weak, it's about you being *mine*. No one talks to you like that." The truth rolled right out of his mouth before he weighed the words.

Her soft lips parted as she stared at him. Finally she said, "I should be mad. That's so archaic. And sexy. You were watching me?"

Relief sucked out the last of his anger at her ex. "Always watching you. It's an addiction." While the ire had faded, concern lingered. "How did he know where to find you?"

"Through the Savage Shout-out hashtag. Someone at Screech's club obviously told him I'm working for your band. He figured I'd be here with you guys and he could get me to score him tickets."

"What an asshole." He narrowed his eyes. Taking her chin, he ran his thumb over the lip she was abusing with her teeth. "What's bugging you? Did he make threats?"

"No. I just...I wish he didn't know who I really am. It's hanging over me, I guess. Feels like too many people are learning it."

That pinged him. "Even me? I'm not going to tell anyone."

Her mouth relaxed into a sweet smile. "I chose to tell you. I wanted you to know. Not him."

Damn, that inflated his chest.

Liza added, "I'm surprised he went to the trouble of tracking me down. Would have been easier to text me. It's not like him to go out of his way."

Justice knew why. "Jealousy. At the club he could see I was into you. He's trying to see if I'm still interested."

She frowned. "But he said—"

"I heard. He still wants you, Beth, and that's what has him pissed off. He was forced by Daddy to give you up. He can't stand that someone else has you."

Her eyes took on a gleam. "Not just someone. A rock star."

Her skin flushed with a glow of triumph. Not a damn thing wrong with her enjoying the moment after Dillion had dumped and insulted her. If the jerk didn't have the balls to stand up to his father for Liza, he didn't deserve her. On the other hand, Justice couldn't resist teasing her. "Are you gloating, Glasner? I distinctly remember you saying you don't like rock stars."

Her grin widened. "Maybe you're not a big enough rock star for me to dislike." She patted his arm. "Keep trying though. You might make the cut someday."

Snatching her hand, he leaned in close. "You like me. And you'll keep liking me no matter how famous I get." Simon and Lynx were wrong, there was something real between him and Beth. If they both wanted it, they'd find a way to make it work.

"Think so?"

More with every moment that passed. "Keep using that smart mouth on me, and I'm going to pull you in my lap and prove it. I don't care who's watching."

Each day it got harder to keep things light in public. Beth wanted to keep a low profile, and intellectually he got it. But another part of him clawed with the urge to claim her. Tell the world she was his. He'd never had this insane, animalistic need to mark his territory, not over a girl.

"Keep looking at me like that, and I might let you."

Lust ripped into his belly, his cock engorging right there on the deck of the coffee shop. But it was more than physical, more than scratching the lust-itch. He looked forward to any time they spent together, even if it was just talking and watching a movie. Beth was fast becoming the first person he thought of in the morning and the last person he talked to before he went to sleep. "You have time for dinner after practice before your group meeting? We could grab something quick."

A crease appeared in her forehead. "We're doing pizza and working through dinner and the night. We only have two more days to put the finishing touches on our project and prep for the oral presentation."

This was important to her and her grade. Liza's degree meant a lot to her, a symbol of success where her mom had failed. She needed that and worked hard for it. "You'll do great," he told her. "But you're right, you need to focus."

She flashed him a smile made up of relief and happiness. "What are you doing tonight?"

"Working out."

She wrinkled her nose. "Again? Don't you run most days too?"

"Best way to keep my stamina up onstage." He leaned in, stealing a kiss. "And drain off some of this constant arousal for my hot little publicist."

She sucked in a breath, color spreading on her face.

"After I'm finished at the gym, the band is going to

work on some original songs. We need one for the finale. We're debating between a couple songs."

"Ha, I've seen your *debates*. Might want to skip your workout. You'll need a lot of energy for all that yelling and throwing things. Oh and River stomping out."

"He comes back. Usually." Their creative process was loud, messy and sometimes a tad violent, but it worked for them.

"So what song do you want?"

"One I wrote." A song that meant so much to him. "'Expired Hero.'"

Time stretched out, the sound of the waves and distant chatter of other patrons filling the void. Liza squeezed his arm. "For your dad?"

"About him, for him." He ran a hand through his hair, dogged by the familiar frustration of not being able to find or help his dad.

Her fingers wrapped around his fist on the table, and she leaned closer. "I want to hear more. Will you sing me the song?"

Her touch and voice poured into him, solidifying his need for her. She'd heard all the things he'd told her, and cared enough to remember and understand. It made him want to pull her into his arms, just for the pleasure of holding her close. But they were still in public, so he dialed it back a bit. "Looking for special privileges, sweetheart? You know, from your rock-star boyfriend?"

Her eyes widened. "Boyfriend?"

That made him laugh. "What would you call it?"

She opened her mouth, when her phone beeped. Pulling it out, she released a long sigh. "Crap. I have to leave to get to my class. But I want to hear more about the song and your dad. I could call you tonight if I don't get home too late?"

"It's never too late. Call me." Two more days and he'd get her all to himself. "Give me your phone."

"Why?" She handed it over.

Justice accessed her calendar and reminders, keyed in his own and handed it back to her.

"What did you do?" She scrolled through, then read it. A tender look filled her face.

"A reminder that Friday night, you're mine." That's exactly what he'd written on Friday night.

Mine.

Chapter 9

FRIDAY AFTERNOON LIZA WAS RUNNING late but paused at the backstage door to the auditorium. "Hi, Colin. Everyone behaving today?"

The older security guard held the door for her. "Nah, the shenanigans are starting. Girls trying to sneak in or bribe me, guys telling me they have a date with Wendy or any one of the Fury Run girls." He shook his head. "Keeps things interesting."

She looked back over her shoulder at the group of college-aged kids, mostly girls, huddled around their phones. Turning back, she answered, "You love it."

"Yep. Most of them aren't hurting anyone. Nothing wrong with wanting to see the band you love, maybe get a picture."

"They'd all want a picture with you if they knew all the famous people you've met." He'd talked her ear off a couple times about the roadie jobs he'd had.

Giving her a grin, he eyed the coffee clutched in her hand. "Long day?"

A wave of giddiness filled her. "Good one. Turned in a huge project in one of my classes, did an oral presentation and nailed it."

"Hey, congrats, kiddo."

"Thanks." She almost bounced with excitement. "And tonight I'm going out." On a date with Justice and her friends. She couldn't wait.

Mine.

For two days, whenever she was exhausted, she'd pull up that note on her calendar for Friday night. Such a simple gesture, and yet it felt big to her. Just like their nightly phone calls and texts.

"With Justice?"

She stared at him. "How'd you—?"

The man laughed. "Not much happens around here I don't know about. Have fun, you deserve it. Right now, though, you need to get on up there." He waved to the stairs. "They're already taping the interview."

"Thanks, Colin." She rushed up the steps, her heart rate keeping up with her good mood. Even with all the long nights and stress, she loved it. Loved succeeding in school, competing for the internship and being part of this crazy world. Having new experiences, feeling more confident, more herself.

And Justice?

Anticipation fluttered her belly. They'd go out, then be alone together.

Stop thinking about Justice, and focus on your job.

Right. The Indie Rock Broadcast Interview. She needed to get a few teaser clips from that to post online. She'd done all her prep, including contacting the mother of the girl, Cassie, who'd written the band and singled out River. They were all set up to make the call during the interview, or River could call her after, depending on how things went.

Stepping out of the wings of the stage, she took in the setup. Gray leaned against his piano, almost in the background. She'd have preferred him in the front, but

Gray didn't like attention. But at least standing gave him the appearance of being bigger and more dominant in the band.

Lynx sat on one end of a row of chairs, wearing shorts and flip-flops, one ankle propped on a knee. Justice had spun the next chair around and straddled it, arms stacked on the back. River sprawled beside him, arms crossed, his long hair settling around his shoulders, and finally, Simon had his legs stretched out, rolling a guitar pick between his fingers.

Keith, the interviewer and owner of Indie Rock Broadcast, faced them. With his stiff white-blond hair and arms sleeved in tats, he appeared at ease in the rock world. "Whose idea was it to start a band?"

"Mine," Lynx said. "I wanted to be a drummer in a band since I saw Dave Grohl on a kit in Nirvana. Then I met Justice in juvie, heard him sing, and it clicked."

"Once we got out of juvie, we started looking for others," Justice added. "We found River next."

The bassist nodded. "We had a good sound, but it wasn't enough. Justice is solid on guitar, but we needed a lead guitar player to really cement our savage resonance. Went through..." he eyed Justice, "...three lead guitarists?"

"I believe so. Including that chick, Darla, remember? She was the best of the bunch on the guitar, but her voice didn't work with mine."

River grinned. "She was hot though."

"Shot you down the first ten minutes." Lynx laughed. "Saw right through you."

River ignored Lynx. "I heard Simon in a club. The guy can rip up the strings, you know? Told him he needed to jam with us."

Simon glanced over. "I wasn't interested."

"Few people can say no to me for long." River flashed his killer smile. "Sure enough, he gave in, came by a practice to see what we're about. He picked up his guitar and joined in that day. That's when we knew we had the kickass sound we wanted."

"Quit my other band that night," Simon said.

The host leaned forward. "How'd the other band take it?"

Simon stayed relaxed, his gaze steady. "Why don't you ask Jagged Sin when you interview them?"

"No shit? They were your band?" Keith whistled.

Liza nearly dropped her coffee. The feud, that's what it was about? Simon quit Jagged Sin and joined Savaged Illusions? Why the hell hadn't they told her that? Wait, had she asked? Damn it, they should have told her this. A ripple of foreboding went through her.

She remembered Ace aiming that truck at her and Justice. That guy wasn't right. Who did that? But the man's anger and bitterness had some real roots, and she should have been informed. Liza was going to have to think about how this might change their strategy. She focused on the interview, not wanting to miss any more bombshells she should be aware of.

"That promo with Ace yelling at you that he'll tell the world about your wife..." Keith let it hang for a second. "Is that why you talked about your wife after all these years?"

Simon's jaw clenched. "Yes."

Liza held her breath, her heart beating in her ears as she waited. *Move on*, she silently pleaded with the I.R.B. host. Ace had been posting some ugly comments, claiming Simon had used his dead wife for pity votes and had rage issues. They didn't need to harp on it.

"So, Gray, what about you? How did a classical pianist end up in a rock band?"

Gray shrugged. "I needed a change of scenery."

Too stiff and vague. She clutched her coffee tightly. *Come on, Gray.* The interview was fading out.

Justice caught her eye for one second, then twisted around to face Gray.

"What made you choose rock?"

Gray ran his hand along the piano. "My sister loved rock music. She'd climb up on my lap and beg me to play her favorites. When I played for her, I was happy." Dropping his hand, he looked straight into the camera. "Now it's all I have left of her."

The impact almost knocked Liza back a step. Oh man, when Gray decided to share, he went for the jugular. She'd had no idea he had a sister. What happened to her? Realizing Justice was talking, she focused on him.

"Gray was the last to join the band. He found us, heard us at a gig, approached and offered to play with us."

"These guys." Simon lifted his hands and shook his head. "They had no idea who he was and tried to blow him off."

Gray laughed. "Lynx especially, once he realized my training was classical." Puffing up his chest, he clearly mimicked the drummer, "We're a rock band, not an elevator."

"Elevator music doesn't jive with our sound," Lynx said. "How would I know you could actually play something good?"

Gray raised his eyebrows. "Everything I play is good."

Lynx sighed. "Truth, damn it. Guy's a freaking genius on the keys. Any keys. He could probably play my car keys. Only not while they're in my pocket, cause..."

"Right," Keith said, fighting to keep a straight face.

Liza had to cover her mouth, too many emotions twirling around. This was the Gray she saw in practice—real, confident in his ability and a sneaky sense of humor—like the imitation of Lynx. That was perfect. But she hadn't missed the underlying dynamics. Justice had nudged Gray when the interview sagged, and Gray had revealed something personal to help take the focus off Simon and his wife's suicide. Then the others in the band had immediately closed ranks around Gray to lighten the tone to keep the host from digging in on Gray's sister. Her heart swelled watching them. They screamed and fought amongst themselves then protected one another from any outsiders. These guys really were a family.

"Our publicist, Liza, has had a lot of great ideas and is helping us connect with more fans," Justice said.

Crap, she'd lost track of the questions again. Liza focused as Justice went on.

"In fact, she has a special letter she'd like to share."

The host turned to her. "Hi, Liza, I'm Keith from Indie Rock Broadcast, come join us with the letter."

Wait, what? No. Her pulse rocketed, and her mouth dried. All of a sudden the camera turned to her. Buzzing roared in her ears. Memories danced like shadows, people reaching out to her, shouting questions and demands. Dread spread thick and cloying in her chest.

Realizing they were all staring at her, she took a breath and walked over. All she had to do was hand Justice the phone.

Lynx popped up from his chair. "Sit here."

With no choice, she sat and tried to smile. "Hi, Keith." Now what?

"So you read all the fan mail?"

What? Oh...fan mail. No one was asking her ugly questions, like how she felt when she woke up and learned she'd been raped, her dad murdered and mom arrested. This was a cakewalk. "Yes. I compile it from all the sources, website, social media and email, then bundle it for them." Relaxing a bit, she added, "It's fun to see how much the fans love the guys and their music."

"What about you, Liza? Do you have a favorite savage?"

"Pick me," Lynx said.

River leaned around Justice. "Nah it's me, right, Liza?"

Laughing, she shook her head. "I don't get to play favorites." She worked to keep from looking at Justice. The way he straddled the chair next to her, pressing his warm thigh against hers, was distracting. Okay, time to lead into the letter and get herself out of the interview. "But I can tell you this. Sometimes fans feel a special connection to one band member. In fact, I recently read a letter that really touched my heart." She handed Lynx her coffee and held up her cell phone. "This email is from a young woman who suffered a car accident and..." She turned to look at River. "Actually, I'd like you to read it. I've cleared it with her mother."

Surprise registered in River's expression. "First I heard of this."

"I know. Because I wanted to show everyone exactly how you guys react to your fans." Although her plan had been for Justice to show him on camera, not her. She offered him her phone.

River took it, his eyes quickly scanning the screen. A crease dug in between his dark eyebrows. He began reading:

"Dear Savaged Illusions,

"I love your music so much. My name is Cassie Simmons, and I'm nineteen years old. I'm in my last year of high school. I missed a year after I was in a car accident. The lower half of my right leg was amputated. I'm doing much better now, but sometimes it's just hard. I'm not the same as the kids my age. All my friends graduated and went to college while I'm learning to walk again on a prosthetic leg.

"I know I could have died. I know I'm lucky. It's just sometimes I'm mad. I didn't go to my senior prom, didn't do all the senior stuff. I'm taking the year over, but it's not the same. All my friends moved on without me.

"Your songs capture all that. Especially River on his bass guitar. When he plays, it feels real, like he gets me, like he would understand. I'm trying to learn the bass guitar now. I love it, even if I'm not very good yet. When I'm playing, I feel like all the other stuff doesn't matter so much.

"Anyway, I just wanted to thank you all for your incredible music. One day when I'm a little better on my leg in crowds and can afford it, I hope to see you guys live in concert.

"Your biggest fan, Cassie."

River looked up, his face heavy, eyes somber. "Do you have her number?"

Damn. She hadn't had to lead him at all. "Yes, it's in my contacts. I have two tickets to the final show for her and her mom. Her mom knows."

River smiled. "You knew I'd want to call her."

"Yes." Okay, not when she'd first showed Justice, but after a few practices and events, where she'd gotten to know the guys better, she could have predicted River's reaction. They really did care.

Keith broke in, "How did you know that, Liza?"

She tried to explain it, warming to her subject. "Because the fans are real people to the guys. They get it, they understand their music gives voice to the emotions that we sometimes can't express ourselves. They get that because each of them has lived those very same emotions. They make mistakes too, ones that sometimes cost them. They understand that no one gets through life unscathed. That sometimes it's other forces that lay you out, and other times we do it to ourselves. But either way, they get it. It's what makes their music so authentic."

Keith turned to Justice. "Is that how you view it?"

For one single heartbeat, Justice said nothing as he stared at her, his eyes so intense she could hear a sizzle in the air. Everything in her wanted to lean into him.

Justice broke eye contact and focused his attention on Keith. "That's exactly who we are. And she's right. Anyone with access to Google or YouTube can find out about my past, my dumbass mistakes that landed me in juvie. We're real, and all we want to do is play music. Not only for ourselves, but for the fans."

"Fans like Cassie," River added. "She makes all the struggle worth it."

"In closing, River, is there anything else you'd like to say to Cassie on video before you make the call to her?"

River faced the camera. "Cassie, it would be my pleasure to meet you. I'm hoping you'll be willing to jam with us all a little bit. And..." He paused as he braced his elbows on his thighs. "I'm hoping your first dance on that shiny new leg of yours will be with me."

Keith ended the interview, and Liza sighed in relief that it'd gone so well. River already had the phone to his ear. He got up and headed to the side of the stage, Liza assumed to hear over all the chatter.

So yeah, it had come off even better than she'd hoped. But she'd never planned to be a part of the interview.

What if someone saw it and recognized her? Or told her aunt or grandmother? She still hadn't informed them she was working with a rock band on a reality TV show and competing for an internship at Tangent—a record label.

Justice was drawing her deeper and deeper into his world.

Could she handle it, or was she taking too many risks?

Chapter 10

JUSTICE KNOCKED ON THE DOOR of the second-floor apartment. The building was old with dirty gray walls and cracked floors. This was where Liza lived?

Once the door opened, he forgot about his reservations. She'd smoothed her hair back into a low, sleek ponytail and wore a loose deep-blue shirt and slim jeans with heels.

"Nice," he told her.

"Come on in, and I'll grab my stuff."

He stepped in, closed the door and pulled her against him. Her softness filled his arms, and her sultry peach scent teased, creating an instant ache to have more of her.

All of her.

He released five days of longing into a single kiss.

She opened beneath him as if starved for him. Justice tasted toothpaste and warm heat. Her fingers dug into his arms, and she pressed her breasts to his chest.

Lust fired hard and raw, pulsing in his cock. He had to stop, now, before he forgot that he'd agreed to meet her friends for dinner. Breaking the kiss, he dragged in air. Brushing his thumb over her lip, he said, "So your project, how'd it go? I didn't get time to ask you today."

A real smile lit up her face. "Pretty sure we'll get an A."

It meant so much to her. "Then we'll celebrate your success."

Her happiness dimmed, and she ducked beneath his arms to stand a couple feet away. "Before we go, I need to know something."

She looked serious, making his neck tense. Had he pissed her off about something? "What?"

"Why didn't you, or Simon, tell me he was in Jagged Sin and quit to join your band?"

"I should have," he admitted. He'd seen the shock on her face when Simon said he'd left Ace's band for Savaged Illusions. "When I originally told you, I thought it'd be smarter to lead with Ace's threats and get you fully on our side. My original plan was to share with you about Simon's wife, then wait for you to ask what caused the feud."

Beth winced. "I never asked, and I absolutely should have."

Her swift shift to guilt spurned him to say, "Yes, but I should have told you too. By the time we went to the club, I realized you would do your job even if you didn't like the way Simon left their band. If I'd been smart, I'd have told you that night before you went home, but I got distracted by my attraction to you." That was the flat truth.

She fidgeted with her watch. "I'm getting too reckless. Letting myself be sidetracked by you and not asking the right questions like what Simon and Ace's feud was about."

He didn't get why she was making such big a deal out of it. "That's a mistake, not reckless."

"I joined the interview on camera today, exposing

myself to the public. And worse, my aunt could have seen it. I've been hiding this gig from her, then I went on camera as your publicist."

He could feel her worry building and wanted to kick his own ass. "Shit, I'm sorry. I'm the one that dragged you into it." He was showing her off and hadn't thought about her reasons for wanting to stay out of the limelight. "But why would your aunt see that? Does she follow the rock scene?"

"No." She kept twisting the watch.

Justice hated that he'd caused her this distress. Catching her hand, he tugged her up against him. "I don't think your aunt will see that. I.R.B. has a big following, but it's not mainstream."

She released a breath. "True. I guess I'm overreacting."

He smiled, happy to see her relaxing. "You've worked hard all week on band shit and your school project. That's dedicated, not reckless. You deserve to go out and have some fun." He hadn't met her roommate yet and added, "Is Emily going with us or her boyfriend?"

"No, she met Ben at Wylie's a bit early to hold a table for us. It gets crowded on a Friday night." She shrugged. "Em spends most of her time at his condo anyway."

He glanced around the tiny apartment. Plants, brightly colored pillows and pictures enhanced the shabby space, but it wasn't a great place. "You stay here alone?" Did she get scared? It bothered him. Liza deserved to feel safe.

"I'm fine here, but when I return for the fall quarter, I'll have to figure something else out. Rent a room somewhere."

"You're not going to live with Emily?" He'd

assumed they had something planned for after the summer.

"Em's moving in with Ben. That's another reason this internship will be good if I get it. We've already given notice on the apartment and have to be out in a couple weeks. If I get the internship in L.A. this summer, then I won't have to worry until I come back to San Diego to finish my last quarter. I'll rent a room or something. I'm looking into it. Let me grab my purse." She darted down a hallway.

Curiosity about her family had him prowling until he found some framed pictures on a low shelf beneath the wall-mounted TV. He picked up one of a younger Beth with two other kids on donkeys.

When Beth returned to the living room, he asked, "Who are you with here?"

Crossing to him, she eyed the picture. "My cousins when we went to the Grand Canyon years ago. Kristen is twelve now. She's super smart and already says she wants to be a doctor. And Rafe." She huffed but couldn't hide her grin. "He's nine and loves extreme sports. He's already broken an arm and had stitches in his chin from skateboarding."

She picked up another family photo. "This is my grandmother Wanda sitting in the chair with Rafe and Kristen next to her. Here's my aunt Mari—her full name is Marissa—and my uncle Spence." She shifted her finger to the girl by Mari with the pretty green eyes behind her studious glasses, wearing a cap and gown.

"That's you." Except her smile was a little dimmer than he was used to seeing. "Looks like your high school graduation?"

"Yep."

"What about your mom?" He scanned the photos. "Do you have any of her? Of the two of you?"

She carefully set the picture down. "I have an album with early pictures and a few from my visits to her in prison. I keep it in a drawer in my bedroom."

Hidden. Which made sense in a way. A lot of people would recognize Amber Ranger. And yet... He eyed the graduation and vacation ones again. They told a story of a happy family, but Justice had seen Liza's scars on her wrist.

Silenced and blamed.

A deep protectiveness flared in his chest. This was why she didn't want to be exposed as Elizabeth Ranger, the girl who ruined the rock star.

That she trusted him at all was a freaking miracle.

She turned to look at him. "Ready?"

He'd better be, because this girl was special. "Yep, let's roll."

Twenty minutes later, they headed into Wylie's Cantina. The walls were done in a rich burnt umber and the air laden with the scent of Mexican food that made his stomach growl. The left side of the entrance boasted a crowd with college-aged to young professionals hovering around a bar. The polished wood tables spread over the right side of the restaurant appeared as crowded as the bar. Good thing Liza's roommate got here early.

He caught a few people staring and whispering. Even heard a murmured, "Justice Cade from Savage Illusions." A surge of adrenaline rushed his system. He freaking loved it. Would it ever get old?

He doubted it.

Liza tugged his hand. "Em texted they're on the patio."

Right, they weren't here for him to bask in recognition, but on a date. Tonight was about them. "You come here a lot?" She seemed to know it well.

She glanced back at him. "I work here on school vacations and occasionally when other employees are sick. Right now, I'm off the schedule entirely so I can focus on winning the internship."

She worked on top of everything else? But he supposed that made sense. Beth had mentioned she was at school on a scholarship, and he knew money was tight.

Out on the patio, lights were strung overhead, a fire pit flickered in the middle and tables were placed around it.

"Liza." A girl popped up from the table on the opposite side of the fire pit. A tad shorter than Liza, she had straight blond hair, blue eyes in an oval face and a slender build.

The man with her rose slowly. Tall, brown hair and dark craters beneath eyes that screamed the need for sleep. The man smiled at Liza, then sobered a bit when his gaze landed on Justice. Assessing.

After the introductions, they sat, and he focused on Emily. "Do you work here with Liza too?"

"I used to," Emily answered. "I sucked as a waitress though. Liza cleaned up on tips. Half the time I got stiffed."

Liza laughed. "True."

Emily rolled her eyes. "Now I work part-time for the school clinic. Liza snags me free food, and in exchange, I share with her the gossip on who's knocked up."

Liza choked on her water. "Lies. You never tell me anything interesting or scandalous from work. And I'd like to point out, I bring the food home for *me*. I go take a shower, come out and find you eating it."

"Wylie's food is excellent. How can I smell it and not eat it?"

Despite the teasing, Justice could easily see the affection between the two friends. He jumped into the conversation. "So what do you recommend here?" Justice asked.

"I love the spicy tequila ribs," Liza said.

"She really does," Em agreed. "The fish or shrimp tacos are good too."

"Don't listen to them, Justice. Go for the tamales." Ben picked up a tortilla chip and loaded it with guacamole. "You won't be sorry."

He shrugged. "Tamales sounds good to me." He set his menu down to focus on the man sitting across from him. "So Liza says you're a doctor?"

"Yes. I'm planning to specialize in anesthesiology. I've just started my residency and dream of sleep like other men dream of sex."

Justice choked on his water. Ben wore a button-down shirt, for Christ's sake. He hadn't been expecting that. But he liked the man a hell of a lot more now.

"Because you already get the sex other men dream of," Emily said.

Liza groaned. "You two couldn't behave for five minutes?"

"Fine, I'll tell you about my exciting day as a doctor," Ben announced. "I performed a disimpaction today on a severely distressed woman."

Liza focused on him. "What's that?"

His brown eyes glinted, and his mouth twisted. "An enema."

Justice slapped down his beer, laughing his ass off. "Bet you felt like a real doctor then."

Ben raised his beer. "I was *the shit*."

Justice cracked up and couldn't catch his breath. Finally he turned to find Liza shaking her head.

"And here I was worried we would bore you."

He sobered. "Why?"

Uncertainty slipped into her gaze. "Look around, Justice. This is it, our big night out. Em and I are college students on a tight budget. Ben spends his days in a hospital or classes, while you're on a hit reality show and ready to go big."

Justice took her hand in his. "Right now, I'm not thinking about that. I just want to be here with you, Beth. On our date." Would he ever be bored by her?

Her smile nearly blinded him.

"Beth?" Ben broke in.

Justice froze, realizing he needed to be more careful. She'd hidden who she was for a reason. He opened his mouth to say something.

But Liza jumped in. "Liza is short for Elizabeth."

"Oh. I never thought about it. You're just Liza." Ben dug into another bite of his tamale, clearly satisfied.

"So you're at the nickname stage," Em said. "What do you call Justice?"

Beth's gaze stayed on him. The moment thickened. Usually she called him Rock Star, Rock Ego or some variation. What would she come up with this time?

"Rooster."

He burst out laughing. Ben and Em joined in.

"What?" His girl projected innocence. "He struts, he crows, he's super cocky." She leaned across the table and lowered her voice. "And he has a weird obsession with chickens. Seriously, they're all over his kitchen."

She thought she'd bore him? He couldn't take his gaze off her. Beth glowed from suppressed laughter. So damned beautiful, funny and real. When he was with her, the lonely ache that lived in his chest—the one that raked his insides with his own failures—vanished. Leaving a bright and shiny...what? What was this feeling? The one he really only got when he went onstage? Or back in the days when he walked into his grandmother's diner after school. Or his dad came home from another deployment.

Happiness.

Beth made him happy, along with his music.

Simon's warning ghosted in his head. *You can't have it all. I know, I tried. But you can't have two passions, two things you want and love. One always gets hurt. Or dead.*

No one was going to get hurt. Justice would make sure of it.

Liza came out of the restroom to find Justice waiting. Emily and Ben had left since Ben had to get up early for his shift at the hospital.

"All set?" Justice asked.

"Yep."

He took her hand, and they headed past the bar toward the front of the restaurant. Happiness danced in Liza's stomach. Justice and Ben had cracked themselves up all through dinner and teased her and Emily. The whole night had been easy and fun.

When they neared the door, Justice looked down at her. "I can't wait to get you home."

"Me too." She hesitated a beat, then said, "I have the same sleeping issues at my apartment, and there's not an extra bedroom."

"Don't stress." He halted, tugging her to a stop with him. Longing glinted in his eyes as he laid his palm on her face. "I can leave or sleep on the couch. Or we can go to my house, if you like."

The way he touched and reassured her sank in. She'd never had this sense of being accepted with all her problems. "Let's go to my apartment." She wanted to give him a break too. Justice had told her what it was like for him when she wasn't with him at his house.

If you leave me, I'll be alone in this house, haunted by guilt and anger. I'll go looking, Beth. I won't be able to stop myself. I'll be out on the streets, searching for the man who doesn't want to see his son.

Justice needed her too, and he hadn't been afraid to tell her. They could kick back at her place and give him a break from being reminded of his dad. Then later, they could decide on sleeping arrangements. Although she was aware of people watching Justice and the whispers of recognition, she felt like the center of his world right now. Circling his wrist, feeling the power in him, she said softly, "I want to do wicked things to you in my apartment."

He opened his mouth—

"Justice!" A burst of voices cut him off before he could speak. Several girls rushed up. The first one grabbed his arm. "It's really you. Justice Cade from Savaged Illusions. I vote for you every week. And I go to UCSD. I've been hoping to meet you. Can I get a picture?" She shoved her phone at Liza. "Will you take it?"

Justice stepped back from Liza as a charming grin slid into place. "Do you mind?"

"Now?" She heard the disappointment in her voice and bit her lip in an attempt to stem the sharp wave of resentment. Yeah, they were on a date, but this was his job. If he wanted to win, he had to cultivate every vote he could. And it was her job to help him.

"Liza?" He glanced at the growing crowd, then back to her.

Forcing a smile, she said, "Sure," and took the phone.

Justice put his arm around the slender, dark-haired girl.

Her stomach twisted with a pang of possessiveness at the sight, and something else—fear. Because this was going to be Justice's life as a rock star. He'd always be surrounded by adoring fans, and if she was dating him, she'd always have to share him. Would she even be enough for him, or would the beautiful girls become too much of a temptation?

Was that fear and insecurity part of what drove her mom to drink and do drugs?

This wasn't the time to think about that. Instead, Liza focused on the task. She had no reason to be jealous, and worse, she couldn't let her feelings interfere with her job. Savaged Illusions winning *Court of Rock* was a win for her too since she'd get the internship.

She'd barely taken one picture when another phone was thrust into her hand. "Take mine too."

She dutifully took every picture of all the girls with Justice. But her mind was on her emotions and the niggling of disquiet that had begun popping up. How many times had she seen her mom go apeshit with jealousy over some musician?

I'm not my mom. She could handle this.

This was no different than when they did Savage Shout-outs all over town. In fact, Liza should get her cell out, take a picture then post it with a tag to Wylie's Cantina.

She started to feel more in control of her emotions now that she was thinking like a publicist rather than a jealous chick. This was better.

More girls pushed in, edging Liza back toward the bar area. There had to be fifteen fans squeezing in around him. Justice's voice rose as he said something Liza didn't catch, and laughter broke out.

Another stab of annoyance flashed, and Liza gritted

her teeth. Why was it getting to her tonight when she'd seen Justice mobbed by fans repeatedly? Why did she feel so damned raw and exposed?

Because you're falling for him.

Another girl jostled to get in front of her, tipping Liza off balance.

She tumbled sideways into a couple of men. Ice-cold liquid hit the front of her shirt, making her gasp. Jerking, she managed to stay on her feet, but lurched a few steps the other way until her back hit a wall. Her soaked shirt stuck to her skin, liquid dripping down her legs.

"Shit, sorry." A guy with dark hair, regretful eyes and an empty cup approached her.

The other one laughed. "You got her nice and wet for us. Look at those tits. She could be a stripper."

Liza hunched and crossed her arms, sick anger rippling through her. They were blocking her against a wall. Around them, people talked and laughed. Fear chafed at her muscles.

"Knock it off," the first guy said.

"Hold this." The obnoxious man shoved his beer in the other one's hand, then pulled out a cell phone. Grabbing one of her arms, he tried to take a picture of her boobs.

Liza's temper ignited, and self-preservation kicked in. What was she doing cowering? She wasn't a scared kid anymore. Straightening off the wall, she knocked his hand holding the phone aside and yanked on her arm. "Let go of me." She used a loud, clear voice, exactly as she'd learned in her women's self-defense class.

The first guy said, "Jesus, Hans, get away from her. What are you doing?"

Anger clouded his eyes. "Shut up," the blond

snarled and turned back to her. "You spilled my friend's beer. You owe us at least a picture." He squeezed her arm, his gaze tracking down her wet shirt.

Oh she was done. She kicked him in the shin. Hard.

"Ow! You bitch!" He released her and stumbled back.

Liza rubbed her arm. "Back off," she demanded. "You touch me again, I'll do more than kick you." She wouldn't let anyone scare and intimidate her. And pictures? Hell no.

The man's eyes narrowed, and his face turned dark red. "You and who else?"

"Me."

The man spun, coming face-to-face with a furious Justice.

His eyes were cold steel, his shoulders straining his T-shirt. He stood loose and ready. More people gathered around.

"What's going on here?" Her boss, Wylie, broke through the growing crowd. He swept his gaze over the scene then landed on her. "Liza?"

"She kicked me," the blond man said. "And this prick is threatening me."

She quickly summed up falling into the two men, the first one being nice and the second a jackass.

Wylie rubbed his forehead. "Do you want to press charges?"

The last thing she wanted was to call more attention to herself. "No. I'm fine."

Wylie turned to Hans. "I want you out of my restaurant, and don't return."

The man opened his mouth, glanced around at the throng of onlookers and stormed out.

The first man paused in front of her. "I'm really

sorry about this whole thing. I had no idea he was such a jerk when he drinks."

She forced a smile. "Thanks, but you don't have anything to apologize for. I tripped and fell into you, and you were kind." She appreciated that.

He nodded and left.

"Liza, can I get you anything?" her boss asked.

"I'm okay, Wylie. Thanks."

The manager turned to shoo the rest of the spectators back to their drinks and meals.

Justice loomed in front of her. "Are you really all right?" He touched a red mark on her arm.

She looked down at her soaked shirt clinging obscenely to her breasts. Lifting her gaze, she saw all the people staring at her. Sick memories blazed across her mind. People closing in around her, whispering, shouting, having microphones in her face, some grabbing her arms or clothes. She hunched her shoulders, drawing back, trying to appear smaller. To avoid all that judgment piled on like condemning shovelfuls of dirt on an open grave. *Answer him.* But she couldn't. Her throat felt as though a clump of soil was stuck in it, and buzzing rose in her ears.

Liza used the tricks she'd learned, the ones her therapist helped her work on to testify in court. She blocked out everything but one face, the one that anchored her. Back then, it had been the prosecutor who questioned her.

Tonight?

It was Justice. She zeroed in on him. All she felt from him was concern, not judgment. He'd realized she was in trouble, and found her. The knot in her throat eased. "I want to leave."

He started to speak when a flash went off from someone taking pictures.

Justice's mouth tightened. Without a word, he pulled his shirt off and settled it over her head. He put his arm around her and led her out.

"Thank you."

He bundled her into the seat of his car, and they took off. Once they were on the road, he reached for her hand. "Your apartment or my house? It doesn't matter to me, Beth. I'm not leaving you. Tell me where."

"My place." She had no trouble getting the words out now. It'd be easier to shower at home where she had all her stuff. As her shock, anger and sense of being stared at cleared, something new rooted in her chest. Pride. "I handled the guy."

After turning a corner, he looked over at her. "Damn right you did. I saw you kick him. Nice move. You can handle drunk jerks."

A grin tugged at her mouth. "Yes I can."

He laughed. "Feeling badass?"

Using her other hand to tug the two layers of shirts from her chest, she answered, "A beer-smelling badass."

Justice squeezed her hand. "My favorite kind."

She was doing all kinds of new things, and the world wasn't ending. Nope, she was rising to the challenge. So far, no one had recognized her, and nothing bad had happened.

If she could handle everything else, then surely she could handle falling for Justice.

Because she was falling for him. Hard.

Chapter 11

Justice ushered Beth into her apartment and dropped his keys on a table.

Beth locked the door, then set her purse and phone down. "I'm going to take a shower."

He caught her hand. Tonight had to have scared her. She knew firsthand just how vulnerable someone, especially a woman, could be. "Let me help you. We'll take one together." It'd make him feel better.

She shook her head. "You did enough tonight. I'll be fine just knowing you're here." She glanced at the apartment door.

He could almost smell the sharp scent of fear mixed in the stale beer clinging to her. "I told you, I'm not leaving you alone. I'll be right here."

"Okay." She walked away and turned into a small hallway on the left side of the apartment.

Justice prowled around, edginess growing in him. He wanted to be in there helping Beth and taking care of her. She was bound to have a reaction now that the shock, and a bit of the elation at fighting back, had cleared.

A chill went down his spine. *Beth used to cut.* Would she still do it? What if tonight caused her to relive the memories of being drugged and raped?

A thunk from the bathroom whirled him around. Unable to help it, he strode into the small hallway and faced the closed door. He reached for the knob, then stopped.

Think, man. She'd already been attacked tonight. He shouldn't burst in the bathroom and traumatize her further. Justice knocked. "Beth, you okay?" Two agonizing heartbeats passed.

Something muffled came out.

He frowned, urgency riding his spine. "Beth?"

"The door's unlocked," she called.

Relieved, he strode in and stopped. Beth leaned out of the shower, one hand braced on the vanity, the other holding her watch. "I forgot I had my watch on and knocked off the lotion trying to set it down. Uh, I don't have my glasses on and don't want to drop it on the floor."

He attempted to focus on her words, but all he saw was her bent forward, her face free of makeup or glasses, wet hair hanging around her shoulders and rivulets of water trailing over her breasts. *Don't leer at her, not now.*

He zeroed in on her hand holding out the watch and saw her fingers tremble. That got his mind out of his pants. He took the watch and carefully set it aside. "You look a little shaky."

"Shh, I'm a badass, remember? Don't tell anyone I might have weak moments."

He wrapped his hand around her quivering fingers. "A badass who left the door unlocked and pretended she couldn't set her watch down on the counter to get me in here." She wore that watch all the time, so taking it off before she showered would be automatic. As far as her vision, she could see well enough to function in her own bathroom. He leaned closer, relieved that she didn't instantly deny it, and said, "Now a real badass would demand what she wanted from me."

Vulnerability shimmered in her eyes. "I don't know. I want you in here with me, but I'm scared…"

He flinched back. "Of me?"

"Of us. Of what I feel. Tonight, I wasn't even surprised when you were suddenly there behind that jerk threatening me. Do you know what that felt like? I mean I had it handled—"

He rubbed his thumb over her skin. "You did." It was clearly important to her.

"But I was relieved to see you. I knew I was safe then."

Oh he liked that a hell of a lot. She knew she was safe with *him*. "I'm coming in." Justice shucked his shoes, socks and pants, and climbed into the tub-shower combo.

Beth stood under the spray with her head tilted back and water running rivulets down her lush body. He ran his gaze over every visible inch. No marks or blood, aside from the redness on her arm where the asshole had grabbed her. She hadn't cut.

Her gaze slid to his engorged cock.

Determined, he picked up a bottle and opened the cap. "Ignore my hard-on. My dick might not care that you were accosted tonight, but I do. I'm not in here for sex." He squeezed some shampoo out and began working it into her hair. "Tell me one thing."

"What?"

"Do you have the urge to cut?"

Her eyes widened. "No. I have some of the anxiety right now, but it hasn't built up to the buzzing. You know when there's a sound, like a low-pitched whistle that won't stop?"

"Yes." He eased her back into the spray to rinse out the suds. Done with that, he poured out some conditioner and worked it into her strands. "Like feedback on speakers? That drives me out of my mind." But the sound crews always fixed it, giving him relief. He began to get a sense of how powerless and aggravated Beth must feel when she couldn't make the noise stop, and why she would resort to something self-destructive like cutting.

"That's a good example. Tonight wouldn't trigger that reaction because I fought back. It's when I feel powerless that the buzzing noise ramps up to an unbearable pitch in my head. Cutting stopped it, or at least disrupted it enough to make it bearable. Most of the time if it happens now, I can lose myself in writing and it stops."

"And other times?"

"I fight through it. Snapping a rubber band on my wrist helps, but I rarely reach that level anymore."

He picked up a washcloth but couldn't make himself use it. No fucking way. Another man had laid hands on his Beth. After dumping soap in his palm, he worked up a lather and began with her neck, over her shoulders and arms, then her breasts...

That bastard had humiliated his beautiful girl by leering like her tits were public property. Justice's control slipped another notch, the fury he'd been holding back rising. He'd never had these dueling urges before: to protect and care for her while battling with the need to sexually claim her.

Her hand branded his stomach.

A whip of heat lashed through him. His cock bounced, seeking Beth's touch.

"Your jaw's clenched," she said. "Are you mad because you thought I was cutting?"

He jerked his gaze to hers. "No."

"Are you angry at me for something else?"

That got his attention off his lust. "I'm not upset at you. I'm damn proud of you."

"Then what?"

He could give her the sanitized version, but why? Beth knew she was safe with him. "If I tell you, it'll be the unvarnished truth. Ready for that, baby?"

Her chin shot up. "Bring it."

"That bastard had his hand on you." He gently touched the mark on her biceps. Her skin was so fair she'd have a bruise, and that fed his rage. "I'm pissed at myself for not getting there fast enough to stop him. I'm furious that you were backed into a corner with some asshole scaring you, touching you or even looking at you. I'm edgy as hell, and never have I needed to kiss and fuck a woman the way I do now. Not proud of it," he quickly clarified. "And I'm sure as hell not acting on it, but you drive me to places I've never been. I want to get that other bastard's scent off your skin and memory wiped from you mind, so that you only think, feel, hear and come for me."

Her mouth stayed open.

His brushed her bottom lip with his thumb and repeated, "I won't act on those feelings."

"I was jealous," she blurted out. "Or possessive or something. I didn't want to share you with those fans at the restaurant. I wanted all your attention on me. That's wrong, I'm your publicist." Misery clouded her eyes. "My feelings are swinging around today. I was wildly excited for our date, and yet I'm freaking out. It's too much, I'm losing control."

"You don't need control, not with me. You can be jealous, and mad, and even yell. If you're mad at me, say it. Tell me off." Anything was better than being shut out.

She grazed her fingers lower, brushing over his pubic hair. "I don't lose my temper. I readjust my expectations."

Justice shuddered, his belly tightening with raw need. But he heard her words, and they infuriated him. Beth had been forced to stifle her feelings, hell she'd been compelled to repress part of her personality after her rape. He didn't care that her aunt and uncle had problems, Beth had been the victim and the child— she'd needed love and support, not a demand for silence. "That's utter bullshit. You don't hide your feelings with me."

"Is that right?" She stroked her hand over the head of his cock.

He moved back from her touch, the spray of hot water cascading off his shoulders. Damn near helpless to stop himself, he lowered his hungry gaze over her soft belly to the hair slicked down between her legs. Jesus. Fiery lust rammed into him, taking his cock from hard to one massive throb. He should reach behind him and twist the water to cold, but he couldn't harness enough brainpower to actually do it.

"You told me you found your voice here in San Diego. Use it. You want something from me?" He wasn't going to unleash his needs on her until he was sure it was exactly what she wanted too.

Naked anger sparked in her eyes. "I didn't like the way I felt. It was our date, and those girls were touching you. I wanted to push them off you and kiss you right there in front of everyone. Maybe I'd shove my camera in their hand and demand they take a picture, then I'd post it and show the whole world that you're mine. How's that, Justice? That enough feelings for you?" She closed her eyes. "I know how stupid that sounds. I want you to win and—"

"Don't you dare backtrack now." He stalked her to the shower wall. "Those are your feelings. I want them. Every damned one."

Her stare roamed down his body, then snapped back to his face. A current arced between them. He didn't touch her, yet the connection shivered on the moist air. Need screamed between them. Her nipples hardened, and she raised one hand toward him.

He saw it again, that fucker's hand wrapped around her arm and Beth kicking the shit out of his shin.

"You want me to kiss you? My hands on you?" He slapped a hand on the fiberglass over her head. "The only reason I'm not kissing you in public and making it clear you belong to me is that you want to keep our personal life out of the limelight." He didn't like it either, but he understood. "We're not in public now."

She caressed the thick head of his cock. "Yet you're holding back."

A harsh sound escaped his throat as streaks of heat licked his nerves and brought out his primal instincts.

She gripped his shaft and jacked a slow, torturous path, until he saw spots. "I wanted them to know you're mine."

Swear to God, it almost sounded like she was growling. That pitch burrowed into him and spread a raw, pulsing throb of desire. He loved that she trusted him with her most intimate thoughts.

"But you're not," she added.

Pissed and possessive Beth was hot as Hades and consumed him. "Bullshit. I'm yours right here, right now." He wrapped an arm around her waist, tugged her to him and devoured her mouth. Plunging his tongue in, he tasted and probed, while spreading his hand over the back of her head and holding her in place.

She dug her fingers into his hair and tugged, moaning into his mouth. Her aggression raked over him in provocative waves. She burned for him, and he loved it, loved that she didn't hold back.

He slid his fingers between her legs, parting her folds, which were wet and swollen with her clit exposed. God. Heat and blood roared in his ears. He fought to slow down, to savor her and give her what she needed. For too many years she'd held back parts of herself. But not now, not with him. He feathered touches, discovering the spot that made her whimper. He kept kissing her, melding their mouths and tongues, and eased a finger into her tight sheath.

Beth ripped her mouth away, burying her face in his neck. "Please. More. I need you inside me."

Hooking an arm around her waist, he lifted her. Water rained down on them, steam billowed, and his entire world narrowed to her. "Put your legs around me." He lined up his cockhead to her entrance. The feel of her slick heat made him shudder, and he gripped her tighter. He didn't dare let her go, couldn't. Setting his jaw, he pushed in.

"Say it, Beth. Say I'm yours." He wanted her to claim him, mark him, and never let go.

Her eyes widened, and she pressed her forehead to his. "You're mine. Right here, right now, you're mine."

Seeing that she needed this as much as he did, Justice surged into her. "Damn right." Too desperate to care about anything but them, he held her hips and thrust. Again and again. She clawed at his shoulders, riding the sensation as he drove his cock into her while mating their tongues. Electric pleasure pounded higher and higher.

He yanked his head back, gaze locked on her. "Do it, Beth. Come on my cock." The words ripped out of his chest. He wanted to feel her pussy milking him. "Possess me." A distant warning screamed in his head that something was wrong. For a heartbeat he tried to think.

Beth grabbed his attention as she slapped her shoulders against the wall, hips pumping on his dick, and detonated. Cries spilled from her lips. Her face and chest flushed, and her internal walls spasmed.

"Damn," he snarled out as he clasped her hips harder, riding her. Looking down, he got a full view of his bare cock covered only in her juices, plunging in and out. So fucking hot. His balls drew up as fire lanced down his spine, and he climaxed. He wrapped Beth tight in his arms, holding her against him as the ferocious pleasure slammed him over and over.

Finally, he managed to get a breath, and oxygen hit his brain full force. That earlier niggling warning exploded into clarity. Panic nearly buckled his knees.

I forgot a condom.

The four words screamed in his head as he eased Beth to her feet.

She glanced down at his cock then back up. Her eyes widened as comprehension chased out the afterglow of wild sex. Her lips parted, but nothing came out.

His panic ratcheted up. "Tell me you went on birth control this week." How long would it take to be effective? Were they covered? He grasped desperately at the possibility.

The color drained from her face. She wrapped her arms around herself and shivered. "No. I lost control and didn't think."

"Easy, Beth." Her frantic tone cut into his panic. He

turned the water off, grabbed a towel and wrapped her in it. "We'll..." What?

He was a rock star. It was the only thing he was good at. The only thing that made him worth anything. He sucked at being a son. And look what he'd just done to Liza—fucked her without a condom.

He couldn't be a father.

What had she done? Liza stood in the tiny laundry room located on the first floor. Two machines rocked on the old tile, sounding like they were filled with shoes, not fabric.

Leaning her forehead against the wall painted the same color as overripe bananas, she tried to calm down.

Think.

She'd had unprotected sex. With a rock star.

She'd seen this movie. Read the book. Lived it. The plot twists scared the shit out of her. There wasn't a happy ending—just ask her mom sitting in prison.

Lifting her phone, Liza eyed the text she'd frantically typed but had yet to send. *I screwed up.* Finally she hit send.

Her phone rang.

"What did you do?" Emily demanded. "I left you at the restaurant safe and sound like an hour and a half ago."

It spilled out of her in one breathless sentence. "Fans bombarded Justice, he asked me to take pictures, I got jealous, fell into a guy who dumped his beer on me, another guy tried to take a picture of my wet boobs, I kicked him and had unprotected sex with Justice."

"Damn, girl, you pack a lot of action into a short film. Question."

"What?" Too much anxiety had her bouncing her knees as she stared at lint rolling across the floor.

"Did you have sex with Justice at the restaurant?"

"Of course not. In the shower. I was trying to get the beer off."

"That's a relief."

"Em, I can't get pregnant." She needed help, not commentary on her sex life.

"Three words, genius. Ready?"

"Run like hell?"

She snorted. "Nope, can't outrun pregnancy. Morning-after pill. Be at the clinic at nine a.m. I'm working in the morning, I'll get you in."

Morning-after pill. She could do that. What she couldn't do was have a baby right now.

"You're going on birth control too. Low-dose shot. No arguments."

Relief helped her breathe. "Thanks, Em." She wouldn't argue. She should have done it as soon as she realized there was a possibility of a sexual relationship with Justice. She was normally more careful, but something about Justice made her reckless. *Careless. You were careless with your life and that of a possible child's life. That's not acceptable.*

"You done beating yourself up yet?"

"Not even close." She looked up at the washing machines and dryers. She'd tossed her beer-soaked clothes and Justice's shirt in one of those. She had no idea what was in the other machine, but it was making an ungodly racket.

"You didn't commit a crime, Liza. You both just made a human mistake. Tell him you'll take the morning-after pill and get on birth control."

She sank back against the chair. "I lost control tonight. I didn't even think about a condom." When he talked to her, touched her, even snarled at her, she forgot to be careful. Justice Cade unleashed the wildness in her she'd been suppressing for years. She didn't think of consequences.

She was on the verge of disaster, teetering on a high rope and she'd just dropped her balancing pole.

Was she careening out of control like her mom had?

Justice answered a string of texts on his phone and tried to keep his panic at bay. Liza had shot out of the apartment so fast they hadn't had a chance to talk.

Tossing his phone down, he wandered past the bar into her tiny kitchen. The refrigerator boasted a few yogurts, apples, some cheese, two eggs and Mountain Dews. After shutting that, he scrounged up a glass, filled it with water and drank it.

Nope, still had a gut full of acid.

He couldn't have a kid. Liza would get that, right?

You're a rock star, man. What if she's more like her mother than you think? Come on, Amber Ranger got knocked up and married. What if Beth...?

He shook his head, dislodging the thought. That wasn't Beth. She'd been honest, even telling him who she was. He just needed to get his head together, and they'd sort this out.

A thick cloud of black, choking guilt hovered over him. He'd messed up twice tonight—first by not realizing Beth was in trouble soon enough at the restaurant and then forgetting a condom.

How many chances would she give him?

The door opened, and he was about to get his answer. He clinked the glass down and crossed the tiny apartment to drag her into his arms. He needed to feel her softness against him. His worry calmed. "We'll figure this out. There's a fair chance you're not pregnant."

She stiffened, then pushed out of his arms. After adjusting her glasses, she said, "I already arranged to take care of it. I'm going to the clinic in the morning to get the morning-after pill."

Relief broke up some of the guilt cloud. "Okay, we'll go together after we get up and have some breakfast." How far could he stretch those two eggs? Or maybe he should run out and pick up some more eggs and bacon.

"You don't need to do that. Go home and sleep in. I'll handle this myself and see you at the Sandcastle Contest."

A cold twang vibrated through him. He knew when he was getting his ass booted. "You want me to leave." After they'd agreed to stay the night together. This wasn't about her sleeping issues. She knew he'd crash on the couch. He just wanted her nearby.

Liza dropped her gaze to his chest. "We need to slow down, step back. This is moving too fast. It's not you—"

"It's me you're throwing out." His fuse lit. His adrenaline had gone into overtime since they'd gotten back to her apartment.

"Justice, don't make this harder."

Was she serious? "You want me to make it easy to dump me?"

"I'm not. Damn it, I just need time to think. Take a break." Going to the couch, she sank down as if she were too burdened to stand any longer. "I'm taking too many risks. I didn't even think of a condom." Her eyes lifted to his, wide, pleading and scared.

"So you decided to quit instead of working together to solve problems?"

"Slow down, that's all I'm asking. Take a break, see

how things go." Clutching her phone, she added, "We're getting in too deep."

Crossing to her, he glared down. "Only way I roll. I don't take a break, Liza. I don't slow down. When I want something, I go for it. All in. Unlike you."

Her chin wrenched up. "Meaning?"

She'd started this fight, not him. "Exactly what I said. I want to sing, so I went for it. Every goddamned day I fight and claw, I put myself out there, front and center. Sometimes I win, sometimes I lose, but I'm there. And you." His chest tightened into a vicious knot, damn near choking him. "I wanted you. I went for it. But all you've done is wave caution flags, tell me how bad I am for you." She'd eased that wall of constant loneliness that left him agitated and searching for more every waking second. But she wouldn't battle for the chance to find out what they had together.

"All in? Is that what you're calling it? You told me in the shower I didn't need control. I let go, and now I might be pregnant." She shot to her feet, her face infusing with anger. "I'm doing exactly what my mother did—dating a musician and making stupid decisions."

He curled his fingers into his palms to keep from touching her. The need made his muscles twitch and ache. "When I look at you, I see fire. Passion. When you let go, you fucking burn, your flames jetting into the sky. But you keep banking it, turning that fire into a bare spark. If that's what you want, fine, live your careful life. Be a coward. Keep hiding. Don't tell your family about your real dreams, your passions. Just do what they expect you to do."

"I told them I'm getting a communications degree and going into publicity. They wanted me to be an accountant."

"Crock of shit. You didn't tell them you're working for a rock band and trying to get the internship at Tangent. But that's not the worst. I don't even care that you're hiding me. What really bugs me is that you hide your writing. I saw you sitting on my bed writing your book. You love it the way I love singing. And you hide it, afraid to own it and fight for it. Just like you're afraid to fight for me, for what we could have together."

She drew back. "That's not fair."

"It's the truth. Things got a little scary with me, you're feeling too much, and we forgot a condom. But instead of the two of us figuring it out, you're doing the same thing you've done for years—you hide." He shot his gaze to the shelf that held pictures. "You hide your mom, your writing, and your scars."

"You don't know what it's like. I don't have anyone if my family cuts me out." Tears welled in her eyes.

It tore his damned heart out to see her cry. "You could have had me, Beth. I'm right here. But I'm too human for you." He shoved his hand into his hair. "I screwed up, forgot a condom, stirred up some uncomfortable feelings, and you're done."

Two huge tears spilled over her cheeks. "I'm not blaming you, I'm just..." She trailed off.

It was unbearable to see her hurting and pushing him away at the same time. He strode to the door and turned back to her. Did she have to look so alone? Scared? It pissed him off more. Why couldn't she just trust him? Believe in him? Just give him a fucking chance? "It feels that way to me. I tried to be supportive by wanting to take to you to the clinic, and you tell me to leave. How am I supposed to take that?"

"I don't know what to do. I need to think."

Her insistence on cutting him out set off a fury that

boiled up and erupted from his mouth. "I was sixteen when I was arrested for a dumb robbery. I was a scared boy trying to be tough, sitting there in that holding cell, waiting for someone to come. I knew I'd fucked up. I was in huge trouble. My dad had already left to live on the streets, and my mom... I waited and waited for her."

Liza wiped her eyes. "Did she come?"

"Eventually. I was so relieved that when they brought me into a room to see her, I damn near cried like a pussy." He tried to fight back the words, to just shut up. But as usual his mouth was way ahead of his brain. "I told her I was sorry, so sorry, that I'd be better. I'd shape up, make her proud. Get a job, help her out more. Find my dad and bring him home. Whatever she wanted. But it was too late. It's always too late. Her face turned purple red, and she screamed at me, telling me I was a loser, the reason my father left and she was done with me." He finally slowed the words, dragged in a breath, and added, "Just like you." The last three words scraped up his chest and burned his throat. For one second his gaze locked on hers.

The pull between them was so powerful, it created a physical tug on his muscles to go to her. He wanted to beg, plead for another chance.

But what would happen the next time he screwed up?

He tore his stare away, yanked open the door and left. Ignoring the elevator, he burst through the stairwell door, down two flights and out of the building into the night.

He rubbed his chest, the pain knot morphing into ropes of pure agony twisting together. They'd been together less than two weeks. How the hell could it feel this shitty?

Less than an hour ago, he'd held her in his arms, buried balls-deep, making her cry out in pleasure.

Now he had nothing but his music.

Liza ran to the door, yanked it open and stumbled into the empty hall. Justice was gone, leaving only an echo of his last sentences.

I was a loser, the reason my father left and she was done with me... Just like you.

She closed the door and leaned against it, every cell in her body heavy and sick. He hadn't talked about his mom except to say she'd bailed, while Liza'd prattled on and on about her dramas. Now she understood why Justice didn't seem to hate her mom like much of the rest of the world did. Her mom had gone to prison to protect Liza, while his mom had left him in jail. He'd been a sixteen-year-old boy. As far as Liza knew, he hadn't been in trouble before that. He'd just been a dumb kid.

Now he was a man, and the reality of how deeply she'd hurt him slammed home.

He offered to go to the clinic with you. And don't forget, he backed you up tonight at Wylie's. Gave you a safe place in his house. In a short time, he'd been there for her over and over.

And what had she done? The first bump in the road, she'd tossed him out. Wasn't that why she'd tried to be so good for her aunt and uncle, because she was scared of being thrown out of the family?

Justice was right, she was a coward.

She couldn't just sit there. She had to go find him. No overthinking, no weighing every move. *Go. Take the risk.*

Her stomach pitched with nerves. He could reject her, and she'd deserve it.

But he might not.

Only one way to find out. Pushing off the door, she ran to her room, threw some things in a bag, grabbed her purse and keys, then raced to her car.

Exhilaration and nerves had her breaking every traffic law, taking more risks, but the urge to get to Justice before the loneliness and guilt over his father drove him to the streets pushed her. Turning on the street, she heaved a huge sigh of relief. His car was there.

And so was he, standing by the Jeep, in the pool of the security light mounted above the garage. The harsh illumination showcased his granite jaw, shoulders and arms tensed beneath the shirt he must have thrown on in the house. His original shirt that he'd given her at the restaurant still sat in the washing machine at her apartment.

She should have called. Texted. Something.

Parking her car on the street, she didn't let herself pause or she'd start thinking and give her fears a chance to gain traction. She grabbed her purse and got out. When did the night get so cool? Chills dotted her arms as she walked up the driveway to the man glowering at her.

His eyes never left her face. "Why are you here?"

Part of her wanted to turn and run at the flat, blunt question. *Don't be a coward, don't live in fear.* She didn't let herself flinch or retreat. "I had to tell you in person. Not a phone call or text. I'm sorry. From the moment those girls came up to you in the restaurant, it was like my emotions took over my brain." She tried to articulate the sensation of her feelings careening out of control. "I didn't want to share you. And I realized in a way I'd always have to because you're a public person. You've barely scratched the surface of stardom, and that freaking terrifies me. So I tried to get some distance and think, but then I wanted you there. And once you were in the shower you know what happened."

"I forgot the condom."

"We both did. I saw this rerun reel in my head—my life playing out like my mother's. And I got scared, so scared. She was all in too. Always. Some guy took her fancy, she was all in. Drinking? All in. Drugs? All in. Me, her daughter? All in. Maybe she was a bad mom in a lot of ways, but she loves me—the only one who ever did, and she's in a cage for loving me—"

"Liza, don't cry when I can't touch you." His voice graveled, frustration lining every syllable. "It's fucking killing me."

Oh God, his words made her cry harder. That was who he was. He wouldn't touch her because she'd pulled back, and he wouldn't physically invade her space if he didn't have her consent. He didn't cross that line. Instead he'd told her in words exactly what he felt.

No lies. No games. No macho crap.

She needed to make him understand. "You don't get it. I could love you the same way. Not yet, I mean...too soon...I know that." God, did he think her a crazy woman? He'd never said a word about love. But he did this to her, brought out her passionate, honest side. Hot, salty tears rolled down her face in the unforgiving security light. This was her with blotchy skin, red eyes and nose, and a growing certainty that what she and Justice could have together was worth the risk. "Before now I thought that kind of passion was crazy and dangerous, and maybe it is. Or maybe it's the best thing that could ever happen to me. All I know is I want this chance with you, Justice. I want us. All in." She shut up, giving him the chance to reject her.

Justice opened his arms.

Relief and hope damn near burst her heart as she stumbled forward, grabbing on to him. Her tears wouldn't stop, and she fisted his soft shirt. "I'm sorry."

He tugged her head back, his eyes blazing. "You already apologized, baby. I heard you. You don't have to keeping saying it. We fought and made up. Let it go."

Shudders rippled through her. "Just like that?" It was that easy to be forgiven?

Wiping her tears, he kissed her. "Exactly like that."

"Justice." She leaned into him, absorbing the sense of acceptance. He'd forgiven her for a meltdown, her fear, and for hurting him.

He just forgave her. Accepted her.

All in.

How could something that felt this good, this perfect, be bad?

Chapter 12

LIZA CAME OUT OF THE bathroom after washing her face and pulling herself together. She passed by the guestroom where Justice had put her overnight bag on the bed when they came in. She paused at the sight, thinking about the significance of it.

Justice came out of his room, wearing only gym shorts.

She lifted her gaze to his. "If I'm all in, shouldn't I try sleeping with you?"

He glanced in the room and back to her. "You ready to do that? Truth."

She didn't let herself think. "No. Even if I fall asleep...I might wake with terrors."

"That happens?"

"Not often anymore, but sometimes."

He nodded. "Sleep where you feel safe. As long as I know where you are, I'm okay with it."

As opposed to not knowing, like his dad. "You were going out to search for your dad when I drove up, weren't you?"

"How did you know?"

She ignored the stab of guilt and took his hand.

They walked to the couch where she pulled him down next to her. "You told me. And since I pushed you away tonight, I guessed you would feel the need to try again to find him." She wanted him to know that she listened to him too.

"Not just tonight. Whenever I'm home, the compulsion is bad. It's why I talk or text you before I go to sleep. You calm that sting of my guilt over my failure to find him, or to be enough for him to come home to."

Her chest ached for him. It'd been hard for her with her mom in prison. But she'd known, intellectually at least, that her mom hadn't wanted to leave her. And she knew where her mom was, even if she could only see her on occasional visits. One day, her mom would come home, but Justice was left in this awful limbo of not knowing. "How long has he been gone?"

"This time? A year. He came home when my grandma died. He stayed for two days, then once she was buried, he was gone again."

Liza picked at her shorts. "He just came home? Doesn't that seem coincidental?"

"Not really. He gets prepaid cell phones, and he used that to catch the announcement on our band website that we'd had to cancel a show due to a death in my family. He told me that much when I asked, but we didn't talk much beyond that." His lips stiffened. "He won't even look at me. Won't forgive me."

"Forgive you? For what? You were a kid when he was hurt, right?"

"Yeah. Fifteen. It was bad. He was pulling injured soldiers out of sniper fire, and an explosion went off. He spent months in the hospital and rehabs with shattered bones, shrapnel injuries and burns on his left side." He closed his eyes. "But the worst wounds are in his mind." He ran a hand over his face, as if trying to wipe out the memories. "Night terrors and insomnia. In the day, sudden loud noises can send him into a panic."

That was why he hadn't flinched when she mentioned she had terrors sometimes. But his dad had gone through so much more than her. "Was it hard living with that?"

"I didn't understand. I got the physical injuries, but I hadn't expected him to change, you know?"

She nodded.

"For years, he fought for our country and was a hero. If I was on base with him, I saw him commanding respect. At home, we'd hang out, do things. He took me to my first concert at twelve. He loved rock music, beer and working on cars."

"That's how you learned to change the oil."

"Yep." He shrugged. "I like doing it. It reminds me of him, the man who still wanted to be my dad."

Oh God, that broke her heart. Her father hadn't been around much, so her longing had always been for something of a fantasy of what it'd be like to have a dad who loved her. But Justice—he'd had this man who cared enough to teach him all the things he loved, working on cars, going to rock concerts. It hurt so much worse to have it and lose it.

"And then he was wounded," she prompted gently, needing to understand why he blamed himself.

"When he finally got home from the hospital, he withdrew and shut down. Drank. My mom worked more and more, finding reasons not to be home. One day, a couple of my friends came by, and we started playing a video game. There's a car crash in the game, but it sounds like an explosion."

Liza tensed. "Oh no."

"Yes. Dad had been in the bedroom, must have fallen asleep, and started screaming, 'Get them out.' By the time everything calmed down, I was embarrassed and so angry. The guys left and I..."

"What?"

Pain deepened his eyes to a harsh blue. "I told him I wished he'd never come home."

It hit her so hard she gasped.

"The next morning I got up, and he was gone."

Not knowing what else to do, she wrapped her arms around him. "You didn't mean it. Your dad has to know that."

He was too stiff, unmoving. She crawled onto his lap, trying to reach him. "Justice, all kids say things. Parents know that. I used to get in screaming fights with my mom and tell her I hate her. The very night it all happened, she'd told me no way in hell was I going to a party with my dad. I'd told her then that I hated her. I snuck out when she was at work. And she still came to save me that night."

He lowered his chin, meeting her gaze. "Your mom wasn't injured and suffering. You didn't tell her you would rather she'd died then come home broken."

No she hadn't. All she'd done was get herself into a situation that put her mom in prison and saddled her aunt and uncle with a damaged niece in the center of a Category 5 hurricane with the trial and fallout. But this was about Justice. He truly believed he'd done something awful, and now she understood his drive to find his dad and fix it.

Framing his face between her palms, she said, "Was your dad ever the type to hold back when you screwed up?"

Tiny furrows dug in around his eyes. "No. When I made a mistake, he made me remedy it."

"Did he hold a grudge?"

"No. But he changed. It—"

"Yes he did. Because he hasn't left the battlefield. It's right there, going off in his mind, torturing him." She leaned in. "It's not you. I don't know your dad, but I know a little bit about PTSD. It's not you." Her years of therapy had taught her that much.

Gripping her hips as she straddled him, he studied her. "You believe that?"

She could feel his longing to believe it, and Liza desperately wanted to give him reassurance. To support him like he did her with things like understanding she needed to sleep in her own space. "Yes. I don't know if he'll ever find peace, Justice, but you'll be here for him if he needs you. You're keeping this house for him. He has a home."

He swallowed. "You undo me, Beth. Your compassion is amazing."

"Yeah, well, don't be too sure of that. Your dad's easy, but your mom not so much." She couldn't get what the woman had said and done to Justice out of her mind. "She left you when you needed her. How could she do that?"

He brushed her hair back from her face. "She wasn't ever really into being a mom. Every time my dad was deployed, she pawned me off on my grandma. My parents married because she got knocked up with me, and you know that story from your own life."

Yeah, she did, and both of them were marked enough by it to fear a surprise pregnancy. Justice must have been even more panicked than he let on, and yet he'd been the reasonable one while Liza had freaked out. "True, but how could she not love you?"

"She loves attention. My grandma used to say it's a quality I inherited."

Liza laughed, lightening the somber mood. "Not wrong, Rooster."

"Grandma'd love that nickname." Growing serious again, he added, "My mom was fine when Dad was the big hero, but once he came home and couldn't hold a job, essentially couldn't function, they pretty much split up. Stayed-in-the-same-house-but-slept-in-different-beds kind of thing. She didn't want to be the woman who left a wounded man. After he took to the streets and I was arrested, it was the proverbial straw. She was done and took off to build her own life."

Unbelievable. Where had she gone? Did she talk to Justice? Did she know he was on the verge of winning a reality TV show?

"Forget her," Justice said. "I want to talk about you. More about your secret world."

"My books."

"Tell me, or better yet, let me read one."

"I haven't finished any yet. I get to the middle, panic and start a new one. It's a pattern."

Skating his fingers over her hipbones, he lifted an eyebrow. "No shit."

His touch feathered out in soft, seductive pleasure while his sarcasm pricked her pride. She was tired of being a coward and envious of his fearless attitude that got him out there on stage, singing in front of millions.

"I write romances. It's my escape." She'd never said that out loud to anyone, not even her mom. What would he think? "I know some people think romances are silly or unrealistic." Except she loved that in her worlds people found a way to overcome problems and hardships to be stronger together. That fantasy had bloomed bigger and stronger in her dark and lonely, terrified nights.

"You're talking to a man whose dream is superstardom. You can write any damn thing you want to, and you don't apologize to anyone."

Her chest swelled with so much emotion it felt like she'd burst.

"But no more quitting, Beth. Finish a story." He kept touching her, making her melt, and added, "And let me read some of your work."

A couple hours later, Justice stared at the wall separating him from Beth. She'd listened to him, cared about him, then gave herself to him.

The memory of her on his couch, writhing as he thrust into her—this time with a condom—threatened to send his dick right back to the hot zone. He couldn't get enough of her. Wanted her right there in his bed, working on her book or sleeping. What did Beth look like when she slept? One day he'd find out.

But tonight she'd given him a priceless gift by coming after him. When he'd seen her drive up...he almost hadn't believed it. It'd taken all his will to lock his muscles and wait, let her tell him why she was there. Find out if she thought he was worth fighting for. Hearing her say she was all in and wanted to give them a chance had seared him right to his soul.

On the other side of the wall, she was working on one of her books. She always wrote before she went to sleep. Said it helped her keep her mind from the dark places.

He wanted to give her something and reached for his guitar propped by the bed. He went through the opening riff, then launched into the song "Expired Hero."

The one about his dad.

Seconds after his last notes died off, his cell phone vibrated on his nightstand. Picking it up, he read a series of texts from Beth.

That's 'Expired Hero'?

It's giving me chills.

Powerful and poignant.

Oh, Justice...perfect.

Again?

Her words on the screen meant so much to him. He could feel her emotional sincerity in every single letter of the texts. How could he feel this close to a woman with the wall between them? Riding a wave of happiness, he teased her back with, *You want to hear it again?*

Yes.

Grinning, he typed out, *Nope. You have to earn it.*

Are you hitting on me, Rock Rooster?

He roared with laughter, the sound echoing in his bedroom. That was his smart-mouthed girl. From the other side of the wall, he heard her giggles. He called out to her, "Quit thinking about my dick, little bunny." Two could play this nickname game.

"Bunny?" she asked.

"'Cause, you know, you panic, run and hide like a rabbit. Finish your damn book." What would she do? Justice waited, his phone quiet, the room quiet. Finally his cell screen flashed a new text.

Check your email. P.S. It's a scientific fact that bunnies are always horny. Deal with it.

His fingers flew over the keyboard, *Horny bunny, this rooster has just the cock for you.* He hit send and switched to his email, and his breath caught when he realized what she'd sent him.

Pages of her book to read.

She was sharing a piece of her secret world.

Backstage at the Sandcastle Concert, Justice couldn't stand still as his adrenaline pulsed and pounded. Jagged Sin was on stage now, screaming a rendition of the cover songs they'd been assigned for this concert. Ace's too-rough voice had Justice looking up at the monitor.

The lead singer sported sunglasses, mottled skin and gave an anemic performance. Justice shook his head. "Partying much, loser?"

"Had a convo with Ace and Mick when they stumbled in earlier," River said. "They were late for the signing, and their little publicist was trying to get them there. Ace grabbed her arm, told her to get the fuck out of his face and shoved her back."

Oh hell. River had a short fuse when he saw a woman being harassed. No telling what he'd done in reaction to Ace shoving Nikki. Although if Justice had seen that, he'd probably have punched first and remembered the consequences later. They were only two days away from the next elimination show and just over a week from the finale. They had to stay out of trouble. The stakes were too high for this crap.

Justice said, "You obviously weren't arrested since you're standing here."

"Didn't have a chance. Liza was with me, and she jumped in. And, dude, she was pissed. She got in Ace's face and told him if he laid a finger on Nikki again, she'd take pictures and post them everywhere. Then she'd superglue the same pictures all over his ugly-ass truck so everyone would know an asshole drove it."

Hot streaks of protective anger hit his chest. "Did

he touch her?" His voice had dropped to icy menace. He spotted Liza bent over her laptop, her camera at her feet. Lynx sat by her with earphones in and tapping his sticks. Safe, she was safe.

He needed to know if that bastard had touched her. "What did Ace do?"

River tilted his head. "Usual. Started yelling that Savaged Illusions is stealing their publicist, he was gonna get us, file a complaint, wipe his ass...dunno. I walked away with the two girls and helped them get set up in the signing booths. Ace shut up in the event, probably 'cause I saw Frank and Colin storming over to Ace and Mick."

Ah, the show's producer and head of security would tell them to calm down. The execs might stir shit up behind the scenes, but they didn't want fights at a Sandcastle Contest and Concert where families and kids were running around.

"Might want to keep an eye on Liza, J. Ace won't come at any of us face-to-face but..." He glanced over at Liza. "I already told Lynx."

The band was closing ranks around her. But damn, they'd warned her not to tangle with Ace.

What did you expect? You saw her last night when that bastard grabbed her, she fought back. He might have teased her about being a bunny who ran and hid, but his girl had a fierce and protective side. "Thanks, man."

River strode over and grabbed a water bottle off the table filled with drinks.

Onstage, the show's host called out, "Ladies and gentlemen, Jagged Sin!"

Realizing Jagged Sin would be exiting the stage in a few seconds, Justice jogged across the backstage and stood in front of Liza.

When the band straggled by, Ace glared at him.

"Problem?" He knew that Liza telling Ace off would stick in the man's craw. He didn't even bother keeping the mocking grin off his face.

"Keep that bitch away from me and my publicist." He stomped off, all of the Jagged Sin band going to another corner. Nikki rushed up, passing out towels and drinks, like she was their assistant, not a publicist.

"River has a big mouth." Liza set her computer aside and stood to face him. "And don't start. He shoved Nikki. I know you told me to stay away from him, but—"

He held up his hands in surrender. "I didn't say a word."

"You were going to." Her expression was pure stubbornness. "I'd do it again."

"Yeah, I figured that out. I'm not trying to stop you, I just want you to be safe." His gaze shifted to the monitor, watching as Fury Run owned the damn stage. Those women knew how to rock, and they were killing it with their cover—a song by Heart. His edginess ramped up, his muscles twitching to get out there and perform.

"If I'd been alone, I'd have gotten help. But you said River trained with you and your fighter friend."

Eyes on the monitor, he answered, "He does. You're safe with him." Jagged Sin was a dangerous irritation, but Fury Run? They were the real competition.

"Nervous?" Liza's hand settled on his arm. "I can feel the energy radiating off you."

Tearing his concentration from the monitor, he gazed at her. She'd braided her hair today to keep it out of her way and wore a pretty green-and-white sundress. She'd started the day with a sweater over it, but she'd soon shed it beneath the warm sunshine and her growing confidence. The sight of her, the feel of her hand on his arm, and her scent eased some of the wildness in him. But it did nothing to dial back his protectiveness. However, he didn't want to harp on her tangling with Ace right now, especially since she'd made a good point, she really was safe with River.

"Not nervous, it's my adrenaline." He held out his hands. Both of them trembled slightly. "I'm always like this before I perform—amped up and wanting to be out there on stage."

"Ah, there's my rock-star rooster, demanding his turn at being the center of attention."

How did she make him grin like this? "Hell yeah. And later tonight, all my focus will be on you."

Challenge gleamed in her eyes. "Think so?"

"Know so." She'd agreed last night they were all in, and that meant she was his to take care of. That thought switched him to his overriding concern today about side effects from the morning-after pill. She seemed okay, but she could have nausea, cramps, or various other symptoms. The doctor wanted her to make a second appointment for the birth control shot, and Justice agreed. She was stressing her body enough, and he could damn well use a condom and a little care until then. Peering closer, he asked, "You feeling okay?"

"Fine, same as the last eight times you asked today."

"Keep it that way. But if you're tired, we'll eat something and kick back tonight." Much as he wanted her naked and begging, he also liked just sharing time with her, even through the wall late at night. "If you give me more of your book to read, I might be able to keep my hands off you." She'd only sent him one chapter last night. He wanted more.

"Not subtle, Cade. Also, I like your hands on me."

Damn right she did, but her words stoked up his pre-show frenzy until he bounced on the balls of his feet, needing a release. Either he got on that stage, or he picked up his girl and found them a private spot. "Don't torture me right now. I'm—"

"Okay, listen up, Savaged Illusions," Frank cut in.

Justice shut his mouth as she dropped her hand from his arm.

The other four band members closed in around them.

Frank went on, "I need you guys ready. Fury Run exits the stage on the left. You go on from the right after the intro. Remember, we're filming this to use for promo clips, so hit your marks." He turned to Liza. "You can stay at the curtain. Take pictures or whatever you do."

Justice's heart pounded as he slid in his earpiece, let the crew check his mic pack, then he picked up his guitar. The guys gathered at the curtain and fist bumped.

"Let's do this," Lynx said.

Gray took a breath, turned and ran out on stage first, followed by River, Lynx and Simon.

"And the front man of Savaged Illusions," their host shouted, "Justice Cade."

Excitement exploded in his veins. Hyped up, he kissed Liza, then jogged out and effortlessly hit his mark. Throwing out both arms, careful holding the neck of his guitar in his right hand, he shouted, "Hello, San Diego! How's it hanging?"

The crowd roared back, and the connection went live, that moment when he knew the band and the audience were gelling. This was the magic he lived for. They launched into their first song.

Twenty minutes later, Justice was pouring sweat when he ran off stage to thunderous applause and screams.

"Fucking awesome." Simon high-fived him.

"Sick show," Lynx added.

Justice cracked a seal on a water and drank it down, when Liza caught his attention. She was huddled over her computer. Everyone was hovering backstage, waiting for the last call when they all would go onstage together before the concert closed. Liza was probably just taking a minute to upload some shots she'd taken during their set.

Except that she was twisting and fiddling with her watch. She did that when she was anxious.

"Ninety seconds," Frank yelled out.

Justice nodded, then started toward Liza.

Simon put a hand on his shoulder. "Dude, you heard him."

"Need a sec." He shrugged off the man's hand and walked up to Liza. "What's wrong?"

Startled, Beth slapped her hand on her laptop, closing it.

He didn't think, just reacted, catching the top before it fully shut. "Beth?"

"You have to go back on."

"Talk fast." Something was definitely worrying her.

Sighing, she lifted the lid and turned the computer enough for him to view the screen. "It's posted around the web."

He shifted his gaze to the image blazed onto the screen. Oh hell. It was him shirtless with his tats gleaming and his eyes furious. A smaller picture was set into the bottom right-hand corner. It was Liza—her blue top wet and plastered to her boobs. Caption read, *Justice Cade gives drunk girl his shirt.*

"Oh shit." Rage roared into him. It was bad enough he'd pulled her into that online interview, but now this picture was out there too. More exposure meant more chances for someone to discover Liza's past, or her family to see her and be mad.

"Thirty seconds."

Aware of his time limit, he crouched and studied the image on the screen. "They don't say your name, Liza. The picture of you is small and blurry. No one will recognize you." Hopefully.

"I guess. The interview is probably more risky. But I'm still worried. This just looks bad."

"Justice," Simon called out.

"Try not to worry. It'll be okay as long as we don't call more attention to it." He didn't have time to reassure her more than that. "I have to go onstage, but we'll talk more later. Just don't panic."

Her lips tightened. "I won't. Go."

For one second, he stared at her. She wouldn't pull away again, would she? "Beth—"

She shut the machine and snagged her camera. "All in. Now go."

That relieved him. "All in," he answered her. Out of time, he turned and jogged back.

But damn it, he had to protect her better. Last night, he'd turned his attention to the fans and lost sight of Liza. Hadn't taken care of her.

He didn't care how committed she was right now, he knew the score. If he screwed up enough, he'd lose her.

Chapter 13

TWO DAYS LATER, LIZA WAS running on adrenaline and nerves. The big night was finally here.

The second-to-last *Court of Rock* show.

As Fury Run exited the stage, Liza flashed her credentials to the security guard and slipped through the door into the auditorium. It was jam-packed with five hundred screaming, pumped up people. The atmosphere was different than all the times she'd been in here during practice. Powerful lights made the stage look bigger, and the three iconic rockers seated behind the judges table added an electrified star power.

Those judges and all the viewers' votes she'd been courting with her promo would decide which band went home tonight. The other two bands would battle it out for the win in next week's show.

Savaged Illusions had to survive the elimination and go on to the finale.

The show host introduced the second band of the night, Savaged Illusions.

Liza's heart jumped into her throat as the crowd erupted in near hysteria. Women screamed, "Justice! Justice!"

Gray, Lynx, River and Simon jogged out, whipping up the enthusiasm. Gray waved and sat at his keyboard. River blew kisses, making the girls scream, Lynx did his usual devil-horn gesture, then rapped out a beat on his drums, while Simon grabbed the mic and asked, "Who are we missing?"

"Justice!" the crowd shouted back in a frenzy.

That was her rooster going for maximum impact. She raised her camera to be ready.

Justice burst out of the wings, his hair flying, wearing a leather bomber jacket over a dark T-shirt and black jeans. With the lights blaring down on him, he looked fierce and bigger than life. "How's everyone feeling tonight? Are you ready to rock?"

At the deafening response, Justice laughed, then stripped off his jacket and tossed it aside. The lights caught his bronzed, ripped arms and gleaming tattoos. "Let's do this!" He counted them into the first song.

She couldn't take her eyes off him as he sang. Up on stage, he seemed older, more intense and so raw. He held nothing back, and everyone in the crowd responded. His voice gravelled out low and sexy.

Liza squeezed her thighs together, surprised at the shaft of heated desire suffusing her. Even his voice made her wet and ready. Probably like every other woman in the audience. But the difference was Liza would be the one in Justice's bed tonight.

Get back to work. Right. After snapping the shots she needed, Liza slipped through the door to the backstage area and paused for a second. The intensity dimmed, but even here, crew milled around, and pieces of set changes were stacked on one end. Frank stared at the monitor while talking into his headset—she assumed to the camera guys or the control room. She didn't know. This whole world of rock mixed with reality T.V. was surreal and awesome. She loved being a part of it. Even with the risks, like that picture of her and Justice she'd found while at the Sandcastle Contest and Concert.

She'd been holding her breath, waiting for something to come of it. But Justice was right, it faded away. Too many other things happened. Some chick claimed Wendy from Fury Run was coming on to her man when the girls were out Saturday night, and threw a drink on the lead singer. It'd taken a couple of her bandmates to hold her back, and the pictures hit social media.

Mick from Jagged Sin had gotten into a fender bender, mouthed off to the cop that responded and got a ride to the police station. Charges weren't filed, but there were pics of him in handcuffs.

Someone bumped into her. "Sorry, Liza," one of the makeup guys said. "You okay?"

"Just taking a second, you know?"

"First show's a rush, yeah?"

"Amazing. But I'd better get back to work. See you." She hustled to the greenroom where she, Nikki and Karl were all working feverishly to solicit votes for their respective bands. She skirted around Nikki and took her spot on the couch in front of her laptop.

"Nikki, if you're going to pace like a caged animal, can you toss me a water?" Karl asked.

The girl scooped up a bottle and lobbed it. "I tried to get some pictures of the guys getting ready, but Ace was..."

Liza eyed Nikki, but she didn't look hurt. "What? Did he touch you?" Liza was pretty sure Ace had gotten his ass chewed by the brass for grabbing and shoving Nikki. She'd been called in to describe what she saw and was admonished to keep it quiet as it had been handled. She didn't like that, but since Nikki assured her it was fine, she went along with it.

"No. But he got clearance to bring in his own hair chick, and she was—no lie—giving him a blow job."

Liza recoiled. "Ewww." She didn't need that image of Ace in her head. Justice was a whole different matter, but not something she should be thinking about right now.

"Should have gotten a picture," Karl blurted out while typing on his laptop.

She and Nikki rolled their eyes at the same time.

Liza split her time between engaging on social media, with constant reminders of the number to call or text in the vote, and stealing glances at Justice and the band on the monitor. Once they left the stage, she only had twenty minutes to coax out more votes.

By the time the show ticked down to the conclusion, her heart pounded and her nerves were stretched. She'd done all she could, the band had rocked the house...

Now it was up to the judges and fans. Liza, Karl and Nikki forgot their devices and jobs as they watched to see which of their bands would make this cut. Tension thickened the air around them.

The announcer said, "The votes are in and tallied. Which two bands will stay for the finale next week? And which band will leave us tonight?"

Her heart leapt into her throat. This was it. She froze to the couch, staring up at the huge monitor. The three bands were grouped on stage, each one in a spotlight. She barely looked at Jagged Sin or Fury Run. All her attention was on Justice and Savaged Illusions.

"The first band that will be going on to the finale is..."

The drum beat an edgy tattoo as everyone waited.

Liza leaned forward, as if she could hear the answer faster.

"Fury Run!"

The crowd clapped as the girls hugged each other in excitement. Their spotlight snapped off, and the noise died away.

"And now, it's down to two bands, Savaged Illusions and Jagged Sin. Savaged Illusions are known for their hard-edged authentic rock vibe in their music. They've been a fan favorite since the first day and a huge hit on YouTube. And Jagged Sin is known for their pure grunge rock sound and consider themselves a true alternative rock. Both these bands have been neck and neck with the judges, but what will the fans decide?"

"Come on," Liza muttered, frustrated by the buildup. Savaged Illusions had to make the cut.

"And now, on our second-to-last show of the season, the band that will be going home tonight is..."

The drums picked up, beating a terrible tension. Liza squeezed her eyes shut, begging the gods of rock to let Justice and the guys make it. "Please, please, please," she whispered the prayer.

"Jagged Sin."

"Yes!" She leapt to her feet. With Jagged Sin eliminated that meant Savaged Illusions had made it to the finale. The crowd roared in excitement. Liza didn't stay to hear the rest. She tore out of the greenroom, through the halls, but she stopped when she saw Ace and his crew stomp down the stairs, bellowing, "This is fucked! The show is rigged!" They stormed out the door.

Frank chased after them, yelling about contracts and required interviews.

"I guess I should go help," Nikki said.

Liza turned to the girl standing at her elbow. "No, don't. Stay here, Nikki." Had the show even ended yet?

Frank came back in, his face mottled with rage. "Bastards," he muttered.

Liza held on to Nikki's arm. "Did they leave?"

"Gone." He rubbed his eyes. "Execs are going to be pissed."

Before Liza could think of anything to say, the other two bands raced down the stairs in a flurry of back slaps, hugs and laughs. Justice caught her eye and broke away from the group to hurry over to her. Damn he looked good.

"We made it." He swung her up in his arms and spun her.

Laughter spilled out of her. "I know."

"Justice, they need you in the media pen now," Frank said. "Hurry."

He lowered her to the floor and was swept up by the rest of his band and the *Court of Rock* executives.

Liza stared after the small crowd hustling down the hall.

This is what it'll always be like. Justice pulled away by his fame.

Could she really handle that? Wait, what was she doing? Savaged Illusions won! Tonight was about the band and celebrating their victory, not Liza and her insecurities.

Liza and Justice boarded the private elevator up to the penthouse of the Opulence Hotel.

"Relax," Justice said, taking her hand. "This is a small party."

"But a penthouse? That's pretty extravagant."

He shrugged. "Sloane's rich. And the band is already staying here, so it's easier to drink."

"Oh." She glanced away.

Justice caught her chin. "What?"

"Did you want to stay here tonight?" Could she do it? Sleep with him? She trusted Justice more each day, but what if she couldn't sleep? Or woke and panicked? "I could try. Or if I can't, maybe I could borrow your car to go home and come back in the morning to get you."

Anger darkened his gaze. "So you wake up at three and drive home alone? Is that what you think I'd ask of you?"

She hated this. "I should be able to sleep in bed with my boyfriend."

The elevator stopped, and the doors glided open. The view took her breath away. A huge room, done in whites and grays, that went straight through to a big terrace.

Justice settled his hand on her back, led her out of the elevator and stopped to stare down at her. "You'll sleep with me when you're ready. I don't mind waiting. But if you ever do wake up scared, you wake me. You don't leave, Beth. It's dangerous at night, and you don't like the dark."

His words washed over her, bringing out a profound happiness at the way he understood and accepted her. And he believed that if he gave her space and support, she would be able to sleep with him. That made her feel more confident. She opened her mouth to answer when she caught sight of two men heading toward them. Both were big, well over six feet. The one on the right wore dark slacks and a beautifully made dress shirt with sleeves rolled up to accentuate the sheer power radiating off him. The other was older, deep into his forties, with gray threading into his hair and sharp blue eyes.

"Sloane, Drake." Justice and the two men did the handshake-backslap-almost-a-hug thing guys do.

"Liza." Justice tugged her to his side. "This is Drake Vaughn."

The name clicked into place. The mentor who'd helped Justice after he got out of juvie. She shook his hand. "Pleasure to meet you."

"And this is Sloane Michaels."

The man turned his dark, assessing eyes on her as he shook her hand. "Liza, Justice tells me you're working hard for their band."

"They make it easy." She glanced around. "This is amazing."

"Come out on the terrace. The rest of the band is here, and the chefs have dinner ready."

Sloane led them out to three tables set up on one end of the terrace. Overhead, a canopy of velvety sky dotted with bright stars stretched out while the sound of the waves crashing and receding wafted up from the ocean. The other side of the terrace had couches and chairs grouped around a couple fire features and a built-in bar. Near the tables, two chefs manned a huge BBQ grill. This terrace had to be as big as the indoor space.

"Liza." A girl rose and rushed over.

"Nikki." How did Jagged Sin's publicist end up here? Well ex-publicist now since they'd been eliminated tonight. "What a surprise."

"Simon invited me. I was waiting for security to walk me out to my car, then I saw Simon, and we got to talking."

Liza glanced over at Simon. He had his head close to River, chatting about something. She turned back to the girl becoming her friend. "So, you're with Simon? Like a date?"

Nikki fiddled with her sleeve. "Just a night of fun. I followed him here in my car." She peered closer to Liza. "This last week and a half, it wasn't great, you know? I kind of hated the job. So I told Simon that, and he said come have fun tonight, finish it off with a good memory. And I thought, why not? But I'm not looking for anything more."

Liza had seen the stress building in Nikki, so yeah, she got it. "Then let's have some fun."

A popping noise made her jump.

"Champagne," Sloane announced as he opened a second bottle then started pouring. The white wine fizzed in the glass.

Justice claimed the first flute and took a deliberate sip as she watched. He eyed her. "Would you like to try it? Or I can get some sparkling water from the bar."

Her throat tightened, but not with fear. "You took a drink first. For me." He'd done it to reassure her it was safe.

His face softened. "It's not a big deal."

"It's huge." The glass was in his hand didn't scare her. Not like it had that night at Screech's nightclub. "I'll try it." She accepted it from him.

Sloane passed out more champagne then held his glass up. "Congratulations, Justice, River, Lynx, Simon and Gray. May the star power of Savaged Illusions burn bright and eternal."

As cheers broke out, Liza sipped the bubbly wine. The crisp and complex taste lingered on her tongue.

"Like it?"

She looked up to find Justice's eyes fixed on her. "I think so."

"Go light, baby. That shit will knock you on your

ass and leave you with a headache you won't forget."

"All right, let's eat." Sloane motioned, and several waiters swarmed the tables with warm, fragrant bread and chilled salads. They all dug in, and the guys talked while Liza and Nikki chatted about school.

Halfway through the bacon-wrapped fillets cooked on the grill to order, River called out from across the table, "Hey, Liza."

She looked up.

"Did you confirm with Cassie? She's coming to the finale?"

"Oh." Liza set her fork down, her excitement taking hold. "Yeah, I called her while you guys were in the interviews, and talked to her and her mom for a minute tonight. She was thrilled."

"Cassie," Drake said. "That was the girl Liza talked about in the IRB interview, and then River read her letter on the air?"

"That's the one," Liza answered. "I'm still arranging some details, but they'll be here."

River tilted his head. "I thought the show was handling that?"

She sipped her sparkling water—she'd taken Justice's warning to heart about the champagne and kept it to one small glass. "They're donating the two tickets. But they said it wouldn't be fair to fly out fans for Savaged Illusions and pay for room and board and not do it for the other bands."

Nikki sighed. "That's probably partly my fault. After that interview, Ace had a tantrum, insisting I make sure the show didn't do anything for your fans and not his. I had to send an email about it." She stared down at her plate. "I'm sorry. That poor girl lost her leg, and Ace acted like she was looking for a free ride."

Liza could feel the regret coming off the girl. "Nikki,

don't worry about it, okay? I've got some contributions coming in to help defray costs. My friend Emily and her boyfriend Ben are helping get the word out, plus a lot of the doctors Ben works with are donating frequent flyer miles. The airlines were a pain in the ass about that, but I finally shamed them into agreeing to convert the donated miles into two tickets for Cassie and her mom."

"How'd you do that?" Simon asked from the other side of Nikki.

Liza smiled. "I threatened to put the word out that they're refusing to help a disabled young woman. Worked like a charm." Shifting her gaze back to Nikki, she said, "You were doing your job."

"I don't have any money to donate, but I have a ticket for the finale. Do you need it for them? Maybe for another family member?"

Liza really liked this girl. "It'd be great if you went and sat with them. You could show them around."

"Sure. I'd love to do that."

Liza smiled. "Awesome. Just a couple more details and we'll be all set." She smiled at River. "Cassie's so excited."

"What other details?" Sloane asked.

She shifted her attention to the man. "I'm negotiating with a couple hotels to get reduced prices. And working to find a driver who can also stay with Cassie, kind of like a bodyguard, because it's a lot of walking and crowds. It all takes money, but we're getting there."

Silence fell around the table. Embarrassed, she tried to figure out what she'd done wrong. Then it dawned on her. "I'm not asking anyone here to donate. Honestly, we're getting it taken care of, and her family will pay the rest."

Sloane pulled out a business card and held it out. "Contact me tomorrow, and I'll cover the remaining costs. I'll get her a suite here in the hotel and give you the information."

Was he serious? "You don't have to do that. I got carried away talking about it."

Sloane leaned around Drake. "Take the card. Call me. And for future reference, I don't make offers unless I mean them."

She took the card. "Thank you, Sloane. I really appreciate it."

He waved her thanks off.

"I really didn't bring it up to—"

"I brought Cassie up," River jumped in. "And you should have told us this, Liza. I assumed *Court of Rock* was paying for it. We would have helped."

Justice covered her hand. "Why didn't you say anything?"

"You guys are doing enough. Plus, I didn't want anyone to say something to her about it. Her parents don't want her worrying about money right now."

"You've found yourself a very special young woman, Justice," Drake said.

"Yeah." Justice stared at her. "I have."

Several hours later, Liza and Justice said their goodbyes. "Thanks for having me, Sloane. Dinner was incredible," Liza said.

The elevator doors opened, and Justice led her in.

"Hang on, we're coming too." Simon ushered Nikki in just before the doors closed, and the car started the glide down to the parking garage.

The girl touched Liza's arm. "Call or text whatever you need me to do to help Cassie."

"I'll call you. Sloane's sending a limo for her, and he said he'd include you in the pickup so you won't have to drive. The driver will act as a bodyguard too, because Cassie can't be jostled around or she might fall. This guy, Sloane said, can handle that and, worst case, lift her if there's a problem. Sound okay?" She'd discussed a few details with Sloane. The man had a get-it-done briskness that she liked.

The girl grinned. "Let's see, limo and bodyguard, I think I can deal with that. You know, for Cassie's sake."

Liza laughed. "Rough, huh?"

"I'm tough." Her gaze strayed to Simon.

Liza eyed the two men involved in an animated recap of their win tonight. They were too occupied to pay much attention to her and Nikki's conversation. Everything in Liza wanted to warn Nikki that Simon was still in love with his wife. "Uh..."

Nikki met her gaze, her blue eyes somber. "I know. I'm going home. He's just walking me to my car."

The elevator eased to a stop, and the doors slid open. Liza hugged Nikki. "Let's talk tomorrow, 'kay?"

"I'd like that."

"Good night," Simon called as he and Nikki headed right, while she and Justice went left, passing several parked cars.

"That was fun. I really liked your friends. I can't believe Sloane offered to help Cassie. He knows I wasn't angling for that, right? I hadn't even thought of it."

Justice tugged her against his side. "He knows. Trust me, Sloane doesn't do anything unless he wants to do it. He's a bigger hard-ass than Simon." He kissed her forehead. "And they all like you. I knew they would."

Warmth spread through her. "What a great night."

"It's not over yet. I can't wait to get you home and—"

A loud scream pierced the quiet, echoing in the underground parking lot.

That scream snapped Justice into action. He shoved Beth between two cars and tossed her his phone. "Call Sloane and stay down."

Simon bellowed and swore, followed by the sounds of punches and pained grunts. Adrenaline powered into Justice as he raced toward the noise.

The fight spilled out from between two SUVs. Justice counted three men on Simon. They'd gotten him to the ground and were hitting and kicking.

"Traitor," one man snarled.

Justice roared in, grabbing an arm and heaving Ace against a car. "What the fuck are you doing?" He couldn't believe members of Jagged Sin had jumped Simon.

A fist drove into his kidneys from behind. Pain exploded. Justice whirled, ramming his fist into the face of Jagged Sin's drummer. Rage ripped into his brain, and his training kicked in. Everything slid away but the need to defend Simon and protect Beth.

"Justice."

Beth's voice pushed back some of his fury. Snapping his head around, he saw Liza standing a few feet away. She was shaking and clutching the phone he'd tossed at her. The three Jagged Sin guys were laid out on the ground covered in blood. Simon sat up, with Nikki holding his shirt bunched against his face.

Sloane and several security guards burst out of the elevator at a dead run.

"What the hell?" Sloane demanded.

"They attacked Simon," Nikki cried. "Smashed his

head into the car. He shoved me back, and they were on him before he could do anything. He's cut."

Justice stared at Beth, her face pale and horror in her eyes. Hating her anxiety, he reached out to soothe her.

"Don't." Beth drew back, her gaze zeroing in on his hand.

He froze as the word sank in. Don't touch her? Because his hand was bloody, or was she afraid of him? He was too edgy to handle the answer to that question right now and turned to check on Simon. "Let me see." He moved the shirt.

"Oh hell." Justice snapped when he saw the nasty split over Simon's right cheekbone, either from hitting the car or the ground.

"Bastards jumped me."

"No shit," Justice answered. "One of them got in a sucker punch on me too." That was going to hurt tomorrow.

"Had to get Nikki out of the way."

"Yeah." And those seconds of focusing on Nikki's safety cost Simon the chance to defend himself. He heard Sloane issuing orders and Beth talking to Nikki.

A gentle touch landed on his arm. "Let me see your hand," Beth said.

"It's fine. Don't get blood on you." He couldn't look at her, feared seeing the same disgust on her face he'd seen on his mom's. It had been a different situation, yeah. But the cold truth was he'd lost his temper and gone feral at the thought of the assholes getting anywhere near Beth, and he hadn't stopped pounding on them until she called his name. She'd just seen him stripped down to his most violent, primal self. That had to scare and repulse her. Beth needed control, he got that about her.

"What's your problem?" Beth demanded.

"You flinched when I reached for you." Everyone in the garage could hear, but right now he just didn't care. Beth being afraid of him hurt.

"Because I didn't want you to damage your hand any more than you already have. And I'm a little rattled. That's how I get when people I care about are attacked right in front of my face." She squeezed her eyes closed for a second, then opened them, determination gleaming in her green irises. "Knock it off, Justice. Whatever bullshit is going through your head, just stop it. I am not in a good mood here, and I'm doing the best I can. Now let me see your damned hand."

He couldn't look away from this fiery version of Beth. She wasn't hiding or holding back, she was right in his face. She was still pale, clearly upset and the most beautiful sight he'd seen.

Simon laughed. "Ouch. Fuck. That hurts. Shit. Liza, don't make me laugh."

Beth turned to him. "Then stay quiet. And FYI, you're going to the hospital, and if you give me any macho shit, I'll use my keys to gouge your favorite guitar."

Simon closed his mouth.

Justice stared at his girl who'd morphed into a tigress. Without another word, he held out his hand. "It's not broken." He'd broken fingers before and knew what it felt like.

She wiped off the blood with a towel—where she'd found that he had no idea. "Okay, we'll get it x-rayed to be sure. Where else are you hurt?"

"Just bruised. They only got in one good shot, a kidney punch." He couldn't believe he was telling her all this. Except...she cared enough to get right in his face and yell.

That was his sweet and sexy girl.

Chapter 14

"HOW THE HELL DID YOU turn this into a win for your guys?" Karl asked.

Liza cut her gaze from the huge TV monitor to her fellow student publicist next to her on the couch in the greenroom for *Late Night with Alicia*. The last two days had been a mad scramble. She'd had her classes, the fallout from the fight Monday night, local interviews, signings, shout-out events, and then tonight the trip to the Burbank studio for the live show.

Fury Run went on first, and the guys were in the wings, watching, while Liza, Karl and a few others from *Court of Rock* scattered around the greenroom.

"I'd love to take credit," Liza answered Karl. "But Nikki is the one who labeled Simon a hero. Some reporter showed up at the hospital while he was getting stitched, and she told the story of Simon protecting her from the three mental midgets in Jagged Sin." It had even more impact because of Nikki's connection to them as their former PR intern. The night had been awful when it happened, but in the last two days, it had been awesome for Simon publicity-wise.

"She took pictures," Karl groused. "I mean, who gets attacked and takes pictures? Are you sure she didn't join your team, start working for Savaged Illusions and the two of you didn't set that whole thing up?"

He was seriously annoyed, and it made her laugh. "Right. Like Jagged Sin would cooperate with something like that? Come on, Karl, think. Nikki had her phone in her hand to call 911 and snapped pictures of Simon fighting all three guys, then Justice jumping into it. Which she tweeted all over."

"You added the label Savage Hero."

Her grin probably radiated glee. "Just doing my job. But to be fair, yesterday Nikki tweeted pictures of your band doing the jam session with the high school girls. Encouraging them to go after their dreams, even in male-dominated fields. Clever."

Karl smirked. "They're naturals at it, you know, because they're girls. Guess who votes the most in reality show contests between males and females?"

She made a face at him. "Yeah, well, they all want to date my guys."

"They want to be my girls. Guess who they want to win more?"

"Savaged Illusions." Hopefully. Liza had seen the polls. Right now the two bands were running close, with her guys having a slight lead. So slight anything could shake it. She glanced up at the monitor. Fury Run had performed and done their chat session. The show went to commercial, which meant Savaged Illusions would play next.

The Fury Run girls poured into the room, high on performance adrenaline. The energy ramped up, and they raided the food table.

Liza tuned it all out as the show resumed. Alicia

introduced the band, and they launched into their song. Damn they looked good, despite both Simon and Justice still being sore. The white bandage covering the stitches in Simon's left cheek added to his sexiness.

"I'll think of something to give us the lead," Karl said. "Maybe have Fury Run rescue puppies. Everyone loves puppies."

Liza focused her attention on the monitor. "Hush now, their song is over." She leaned forward, fixating on the TV. She had one concern. Alicia was known to drop bombshells and try to get answers. One of the show's producers had asked about Gray and the sister he'd mentioned in the IRB interview, and why he'd walked away from his classical career in such a dramatic fashion. But when Liza broached the subject to Gray, he refused to elaborate, forcing Liza to tell the show the topic was off-limits. Would Alicia respect the boundary?

Once the applause ended, Alicia strode across the stage to where the band had performed and said, "Doesn't look like getting jumped by Jagged Sin slowed you guys down any."

Relief cascaded through Liza. Okay, they were on solid ground here. Ace and his two moronic sidekicks had been arrested. There was no dispute as to what happened.

Justice eyed the camera. "It takes more than a couple sore losers to stop us from doing what we love."

Liza smiled. He had this down.

"How about you, Simon?" Alicia asked. "Ace from Jagged Sin says that you betrayed their band by quitting abruptly and leaving them without a lead guitarist. He claimed that you were trying to sabotage them in the contest. How do you answer that?"

Simon's diamond-hard gaze glinted. "It's total crap.

That was long before we tried out for *Court of Rock*."
He turned to the camera. "I left Jagged Sin because
they wanted to party and pose as rockers, but they
didn't put in the work. When I met up with this
crew...and let me tell you they can be clowns..."

Laughter spilled from the audience.

"But they're clowns who want nothing more than to
get onstage and play music. Jagged Sin sabotaged
themselves."

She moved on, talking to River, Lynx and Gray.
Then she circled back to Justice. "Do you think you can
beat Fury Run?"

In the greenroom, the girls spun to face the
monitor. Wendy called out, "Not a chance, Savages."

"Hell no," agreed their drummer.

"Shh." Liza missed Justice's answer, and the
camera panned back to Alicia. "From your IRB
interview, it looks like you guys have an enthusiastic
publicist."

A flash of surprise briefly registered on Justice's
face, then vanished. "Liza, yes. It's part of *Court of
Rock* and Tangent's program to involve college
students in the business end of music."

Alicia leaned closer. "I'm hearing rumors that you
two are dating. Any truth to that?"

Justice flashed a big grin. "Is that right?" He turned
to Lynx. "You hear that rumor?"

Lynx didn't miss a beat. "I started it. Wanted to
class up your image a little." He looked into the camera
with a hangdog expression. "Sorry, Liza."

The audience laughed.

Justice turned back to Alicia. "There you go. Liza is
out of my league." He got serious. "Right now, all five
of us are focused on winning *Court of Rock*. We don't
have time for distractions."

Good. Okay, yeah, she had a tiny pinch at being called a distraction, but it was better to keep the focus on the band, not her and Justice.

Alicia said, "That might be a problem. We have a video that may very well turn your publicist into a major distraction."

What? Liza leapt off the couch. Her heart rate launched into the stratosphere. A video of her? From where? They'd already mentioned the Indie Rock Broadcast video.

"A video of what?" Justice asked.

"Another rock star who also knew Liza. One who couldn't be here in person. The reason for that will become obvious." She turned to the massive screens sliding down for everyone in the audience and stage to see. "Watch."

While a camera honed in on one of the big screens, a distant roar filled Liza's ears. There was only one that would remember her.

She cringed internally, not wanting to believe it.

"Liza?" Karl's worried voice floated vaguely in her head, but she ignored it, her focus one hundred percent on that screen.

Gene Hayes's image burst to life. Liza lurched back a step, all her muscles tensing in an elemental reaction. Her heart thudded, sweat pricked beneath her arms and on her back, while her brain screamed, *Danger. Run.* Tremors rocked her as she struggled to get control of herself. *Breathe, he's not here in the room with you. He's in another country. It's just a video feed, he's not here.*

She calmed enough to take in a few details. Hayes wore his dark hair pulled back, his thin face grim. His eyes made her shudder. She remembered thinking in the first moments she'd met him that his eyes were dark and sexy, like bedroom eyes. What had she known of bedroom eyes?

Hayes sat on a barstool in a room filled with what looked like a sound board behind him. Was he in a recording studio?

"My name is Gene Hayes, and for nearly seven long years, I've kept silent. Until I saw the IRB interview online with the group Savaged Illusions. A woman named Liza joined in that interview. The second I saw her, shock hit me like a train and knocked me back to that terrible summer almost seven years ago.

"That woman is Elizabeth Ranger, the very same girl who set out to, and succeeded in, destroying my life."

She destroyed *his* life?

Hayes shifted on his stool, sincerity flowing out of those dark eyes. "I decided then to tell the truth. But you know what? Some people don't want the truth, and that includes Indie Rock Broadcast. I contacted IRB and offered them an exclusive to the story of what really happened. They refused. That's the kind of slanted reporting that allows innocent people to be demonized and victimized, forced to flee their own country to live in a foreign land. But I'm determined to get the truth out there, so I'm doing this myself. Here's the real story: Eddie Ranger was a washed-up hang-around, a guitarist who played in a couple garage bands but never had the chops to make it big. He was working on my road crew. My first album had topped the charts, and my second album had just dropped and hit number one.

"I was on top of the world and ready to party. It's no secret I like women. Hot, young, and wild. Eddie told me that his adult daughter, whom he claimed was eighteen, was dying to meet me and asked to bring her to a party.

"I said sure. When they showed up, I met Liza, and she looked at least eighteen. She was more slender then, but totally built. She came over wearing shorts cut up to expose her butt cheeks, falling out of a scrap of a shirt, and she was all over me. We went to my room.

"But her father, the conniving bastard, set me up. He burst into my bedroom screaming rape, taking pictures and telling Liza to drink something in a glass. I don't know what. All hell broke loose.

"Eddie Ranger then demanded I make him part of my band or he'd ruin me.

"I was stunned and outraged. I mean what the hell, man? Who does that? With their own daughter?"

Liza shook her head in frantic denial. That was not what happened. It wasn't. But in her head, a tiny voice said, *How would you know? You were drugged. Maybe you did come on to him. Maybe you told him you were eighteen.* "No."

Wendy grabbed her hand. No words, just a warm hand holding hers as her past exploded in her face.

Hayes went on, "After that, things took an even more bizarre twist. I mean, I can't make this stuff up. Screaming started in the hallway. Eddie rushes out there, yelling. A woman screams back, 'It was my plan. Mine!' A second later, a gun goes off." Hayes looked away in dramatic silence before adding, "I hustled out there and found Eddie dead on the floor in a pool of blood. And Amber Ranger holding the gun." He swung his gaze back to the camera.

Liza almost flinched at the impact of his hard, bitter eyes. He hated her, truly blamed her.

"I got out of there. I had no idea what was happening. I was trapped in some nightmare in my own house. So I booked it, and later that night I was arrested for rape."

Hayes leaned forward. "I did not rape that girl. She was fully conscious and begging me to have sex with her. But my life was shattered, ruined. I'd been seduced by a fourteen-year-old who swore she was eighteen for a blackmail scheme that went wrong. The irony of it all? Liza's mother, Amber Ranger, killed Eddie that night. Not to protect her daughter as Amber claimed. Oh no, but because the greedy woman was mad that her ex-husband stole her plan to shake me down." He shook his head. "Every guy knew that chick. She had a reputation as a hardcore groupie into wild sex, drinking and drugs."

Greasy sickness slithered in Liza's belly and burned her throat. This was on late-night TV. It would spread like a virus by the morning shows.

"So all these years, I kept quiet. Because come on, I'm not a monster. No, I didn't rape that girl, and yeah, she seduced me to ruin me. But she was fourteen. So I'm like...okay. Let's not blame the kid, right?"

Was he for real? Liza had the sense of being in a carnival fun room filled with distorted mirrors and tilting floors.

"Then I saw her on the IRB interview, involved with another band rising to fame. And all my alarms went off." He tilted closer to the camera. "She's not a kid anymore, and she's doing it again, looking for a meal ticket or planning some shakedown. I don't know, but what I do know is I don't want what happened to me to happen to some other schmuck. So let me ask you this, if this girl was so hurt and traumatized by what supposedly happened with a rock star, then what's she doing back in the rock world? Looking like this?"

A picture flashed on the screen. Liza gasped in outrage. It was from the night of her date with Justice at Wylie's. Her wet tank clung to her breasts obscenely. Her expression was dazed...as if she were drunk.

She hadn't been drunk, she'd been shocked and mad.

Hayes reappeared. "I'm done hiding. I'm done paying for a crime I didn't commit. I had my career destroyed and my life ruptured because of her. No more. I'm fighting back. It's time for Elizabeth Ranger—I guess she calls herself Liza Glasner now—to tell the truth by recanting her allegations of rape and getting that bogus verdict against me overturned.

"I want my name cleared, so I can return to the U.S. and live my life."

The video stopped.

The camera homed in on Alicia, her eyes bright with barely suppressed glee. "Do you think this is going to impact your chances to win? Did you guys know who Liza is?"

All five of Savaged Illusions guys stood together, their faces furious. Justice turned his glare on Alicia.

The woman stepped back.

"What I think..." Justice's voice rang out, harsh and guttural, "...is that you just exposed a sexual assault victim's identity to the entire fucking world. Congratulations, lady, you win the asshole journalist award." He stormed off stage, and the show cut to a commercial break.

"Control room's gonna bleep that out," someone in the greenroom muttered.

Liza should be concerned about Justice swearing on TV, but she couldn't get her breath enough to think or react. A brutal hand squeezed her lungs, and sweat burned her skin. Her worst nightmare had exploded right in front of her eyes. Voices cranked up in her head.

Her aunt crying out, *What have you done? Elizabeth, you can't do this!*

People yelling, *Whore! Lolita! Slut! Cunt!*

The signs of the protesters when Hayes left the country after her court testimony. *Run, Hayes, Run! She asked for it! Recant! Hayes is the Real Victim!*

Her aunt's constant reminder, *Don't talk about it, Liza. You're making it worse. People are judging you. Actions count, not words. Make the right choices. People judge. Just keep your head down and stay quiet.*

She jerked against the violent searing in her left wrist, like hundreds of fire ants were chewing through her scars. Liza fought the black fear enveloping her. She had to get out of there. But she couldn't move, couldn't look at anyone.

For the last three years, she'd been just Liza. She had friends, a life, and now it was all shattered, ruined.

"Liza, that's you?" Karl turned, his eyes huge in his face. "That dick with a mouth assaulted you?"

What could she say? She eyed the door. *Escape. Run. Get away.* Everyone was going to know who she was. She could get in her car...hell, she didn't have her car here. She'd come with Justice.

And it didn't matter.

There was nowhere she could go to hide from her past now. She couldn't do this, didn't want to live through it over and over. But there wasn't any way she could deny the truth.

She forced herself to look at the other publicist. "Yes."

Silence settled around her except for the TV and the murmur of voices from the *Court of Rock* execs eyeing her across the room while whispering into their phones.

Karl shook his head. "That's...huh...what's the word?"

"Fucked up." Wendy squeezed her hand.

Karl rolled his eyes. "That's two words." He shifted his gaze back to her. "I was thinking bombshell."

Liza tugged her hand from Wendy, tears prickling her eyes. *Don't cry. Keep quiet.*

Wendy refused to let go. "A fucked-up bombshell."

Karl tilted his head, as if considering. "That should destroy Alicia's career. She did this knowing full well she was exposing Liza's identity."

"That bitch is lucky she pulled that stunt with Justice. If she'd done it with me, I'd have punched her." Wendy's eyes burned with sincerity, anger and caring. "No one treats our friends like this, Karl. We need to do something."

Liza had expected them to hate her, to put as much distance between her and them as they could. So why did Wendy have a tight grip on her hand?

"Let's move fast and get ahead of this." Karl pulled his phone out and started typing. "Wendy and the entire Fury Run band..." He looked up expectantly.

Wendy finished with, "The only thing more powerful than our love of music is our support of women. We stand shoulder to shoulder with our sister Liza Glasner."

He put his phone away. "Done."

Liza's head spun. This wasn't what she'd expected. They weren't screaming at her or staring at her like she was a freak. The buzzing in her head dialed down, and her breathing eased.

"What?" She swallowed, trying to get her thoughts in line, but she couldn't think of a way to ask them if this was real and they believed in her.

Karl touched her arm. "We're your friends. I'll fight

you to the final minute of *Court of Rock* for my girls to win over your guys. I totally think Fury Run is the better band. But this bullshit?" He gestured to the TV. "We aren't letting that happen. Gene Hayes is a scumbag pervert sporting a sick dick. And Alisha is a ratings whore who doesn't care who she hurts."

Wendy nodded. "But you aren't his victim anymore. You're a woman who can fight back."

The impact filled her chest. She wasn't alone or helpless. Two of her friends stood at her side, and her phone was going off nonstop too—that would be Emily.

After the rape, she'd been isolated and scared. But Wendy was right, Liza wasn't that same girl anymore.

In the hallway just outside the greenroom, a hand came down on Justice's shoulder.

He spun, rage banging in his head.

Anger glinted in Simon's eyes and bearing. "How long have you known who she is and not told us?"

He needed to get to Beth, but one look at the four men staring at him, and reality struck full force. He'd screwed up. At least in their eyes. "She told me that first weekend."

"Fuck," Simon said. "You didn't tell us? Let us all get blindsided out there in front of the goddamned TV cameras?"

Urgency jerked and popped in his muscles with worry for his girlfriend. "I don't have time for this. I need to get to Liza."

The vein in Simon's temple throbbed. "What the hell, man? Now you're putting a chick before the band? Five days until the finale. Five. We just got hit with a ticking bomb, and you can't focus."

Shit. He was torn. Could almost feel half of him being pulled one way and half the other. But Beth...he couldn't leave her alone right now. "We'll figure it out after I get her home."

"She can get a ride with someone else."

"No. Get off my ass, Simon. I just lost my shit on national TV after my girlfriend had her worst nightmare exposed to the world. I don't need my band in my face." He couldn't fuck this up with Beth.

Simon leaned in, rage burning in his gaze. "You put her before us. While I went on TV to spill my guts about Julie—the one thing I never wanted to talk about, but I did it for the band—you kept Liza's secret. The very one that could ruin us now." Anger vibrated between them before Simon added, "You're turning her into a Yoko." He spun and stormed out of the building.

In his wake, unease settled. Lynx, River and Gray looked as torn as he felt. "I have to get to Liza," Justice said.

"That I get," Lynx answered. "But not warning us? Not telling us that our publicist was part of a news story that could explode? Why, man?"

Yeah, why? "I didn't think of it. She told me, and it seemed like her business. In the three years she's been at school here, no one bothered her about it. No one knew." That wasn't true though, Justice admitted silently. Her ex-boyfriend's father had found out. But Liza had confided in Justice, and telling the others would have breached that.

"Look, I like Liza. Hell we all do. She's cool, and she doesn't deserve this." Lynx rocked back on his heels. "But, dude, this is our shot. Do you get that? This is it. We lose this, we lose the chance to sign with the label and hire Christine Castle. We'll be back to begging for gigs."

His guts twisted. "I hear you. I'm in. I'm always in. I just need to..." What? He should be going with the band and getting a game plan in place.

Lynx shook his head. "Sort out your shit, Justice. This isn't the time to lose your head over a girl."

River hesitated as Lynx and Gray left. "Thing is, we had your back. Out there on that stage you lost it, and every one of us walked off with you. Not even a hesitation."

True. He'd known they would.

"So let me ask you this, did you have our backs?" River left without waiting for an answer.

Fuck. They weren't mad at Liza. Nope, this was on him. He'd had information he hadn't told them.

The door to the greenroom opened. "Justice?"

Forgetting everything else, he pulled Beth into his arms. "God, Beth, I'm so sorry." Why the hell hadn't he kept her out of that interview? Or protected her better in the restaurant instead of posing with fans?

Everything was spinning out of control.

She burrowed into him. "I'm sorry too. You walked out of an interview. After swearing at Alicia."

"She got off lucky. If she'd been a man, I'd have punched her." The one he really wanted to go after was Hayes.

Pulling back, she looked up at him. "Don't do that. You have to..." She squeezed her eyes shut then opened them. "You can't punch anyone."

He felt like he'd been kicked in the chest. Her eyes were too wide, and the green in her irises appeared sickly under the overhead hallway lights. He imagined her at fourteen. She said she fought with her mom, so she'd been feisty. He could see it in her most of the time, streaks of boldness in her personality that matched the rebellious threads of red in her brown hair.

Too many people hurt her as a kid. She was his now, and he was going to do better. "Wrong. If that asshole ever worms his way back into the states, I'll do more than punch him." Gene Hayes had raped an unconscious girl, and now he was trying to lay the blame on Beth.

"I didn't tell him I was eighteen. At least not that I can remember—"

He cupped her face. "Stop. Now. You don't ever need to explain to me. Not like that. You want to talk about it, I'll listen." He'd try anyway. It ripped a hole in his guts to think about it. "But don't you defend yourself. You were a kid."

"You believe me. So does Wendy and the other girls. And Karl."

"So does Emily and the guys in the band." Rumors had swirled about Gene Hayes before that night. It didn't matter how pissed they were at Justice, the other guys wouldn't blame a fourteen-year-old girl.

"The band, are they mad?"

"Not at you," he reassured her. "Let's go home, Beth. You're staying with me. On the way I want you to call Em. Make sure she stays at Ben's, or she can come to my house if Ben's not around."

"I already texted her that I'm okay and will call, but why should she leave our place?" She pressed her lips tight, sighed and answered her own question. "Because the media has my name now. They can find where I live."

Justice wrapped his arm around her, wanting to shield her from the fallout.

Why had Hayes surfaced now? What was he after? How much danger was Beth in?

Chapter 15

LIZA STARED UP AT THE ceiling of the guestroom, thoughts racing and bouncing around. Sharp claws raked the inside of her head. The bright bedside lamp made it worse.

But closing her eyes...

Terror knotted in her throat. She'd see it again—that hand holding out the pink frothy drink. Not wanting to take it, but her dad...

Bolting up, Liza scrabbled until her back hit the wall. Drawing her knees to her chest, she grabbed her glasses off the table and searched the room.

Nothing there. She was fine.

Breathe. Calm down.

She glanced at her laptop sitting next to her. She'd tried to lose herself in her story, but all she saw was Gene Hayes and that hand.

That drink.

Waking up in the hospital, vomiting, begging for her mom.

A burn of pure, raw anger surged up, so powerful it screamed in her mind, hacking at her brain, until she could only think in red. The lies out of Hayes's mouth in that video had ignited a physical urge to fight back by shouting the truth over and over.

It wasn't her fault. She didn't trick anyone. She'd been a stupid girl who trusted her father.

Don't talk about it, Liza. People judge.

She dug her nails into her wrists, drowning in the violent rage. "Get control. You have to be in control." She whispered it over and over. "You can't lose your temper. Control." Dug her nails in deeper.

Not enough pain.

But she had a razor. In the hall bathroom right across from her door. *Remember how it felt?* Digging that chunk of glass into her skin, the pain flashing through her like a clean wave washing everything else out. She craved the relief.

A tiny spot of blood bloomed on her wrist around her index fingernail.

The sight of it shocked her senses. She ripped her fingers away, disgusted with herself. Dropping her head back to the wall, she stared up at the ceiling.

"No. Just no." She wasn't that girl anymore and she wouldn't let Hayes drive her to self-destruction. Liza had friends. She could call Emily, or Nikki or—

Justice. She had Justice.

She needed him.

Justice strode into the kitchen, opened the fridge and stared inside.

For the seventh time.

He fucking hated that closed door. Liza hadn't said much, just that her head hurt and she was going to bed. He'd tried to get her to lay with him for a little while, but she went in the guestroom and shut the door.

Slamming the fridge, he dropped his hands on the counter. The muscles in his neck and jaw were rigid. Would she leave? Every time he tried to go to bed, he feared he'd get up in the morning and she'd be gone.

Vanished from his life.

He couldn't stay in his bedroom. Instead he had to keep watch to make sure she didn't leave. But what if she was in that room cutting herself? The helplessness infuriated him. He couldn't do anything but pace around his house like a caged animal. He raised his hands, ready to slap them down again, when he heard a noise.

The sound of a door opening. Even his blood stilled. Was she leaving? At one thirty in the morning? Oh hell no. Justice strode out of the kitchen to find the living room and dining room empty. He could see Liza's door open, and he sprinted into the hall.

She stood at the doorway to his room, her shoulders bowed in her tank top.

"Beth?" He closed the distance.

Her head came up, and she turned around.

Her face... Jesus, too pale and strained. "What's wrong, baby? Are you sick?"

"I... Can I sleep with you?"

It punched him straight through the chest. She hadn't left, hadn't cut, she'd come to him and wanted to sleep with him. All his muscles unlocked, powerful relief pushing him to her.

"Always." He settled her in the bed and put her glasses on the side table by her phone. Turning on the bathroom light, he tugged the door partway closed. Once he snapped off the bedroom lamp, a slice of illumination cut through the dark. If she did fall asleep, he didn't want her waking up in pitch blackness. Getting in, he pulled Beth against him and covered her.

"Do you want to talk?" He brushed a hand over her hair.

"Can't."

Thick and raw wounds vibrated in that single word. Too many years of being silenced. "You came to me, that's all that matters."

She trusted him, and that was everything. He couldn't hunt down the man who threatened Beth's world right now, so he did the only thing he could think of.

He sang to her until she fell asleep.

Loud pounding woke Liza. Groggy, she tried to sort out where it was coming from and where she was.

Awareness slid back in. She was in Justice's bed, his arms around her. She'd slept with him. The last thing she remembered was him singing softly to her, and then...she'd slept.

Another round of pounding cut into her thoughts. "Is that the front door?"

"If that's a reporter, I'm turning the hose on them." Justice rolled out of bed, dragged on shorts and vanished.

Alone, memories flooded back. Gene Hayes. What had made that weasel slither out from under his rock? Seeing him again had shaken her. She'd spent years trying to be anonymous, and now she was exposed. What should she do?

"I brought donuts."

Liza shoved up to a sitting position and grabbed her glasses. "Em?"

"Yep."

"What are you doing? You have class..." She looked at the clock. Almost nine a.m. "...in ten minutes."

"Screw class. Get up. Your boyfriend is making coffee, and my boyfriend is apologizing for us barging in." She rolled her eyes. "Justice didn't seem upset though. He told me which bedroom you were in. Said to take as long as we wanted." Em sat on the bed. "You okay?"

Her throat tightened. "I don't know what I am." She glanced toward her phone. Had her aunt or grandmother called? Had they seen the show or video yet?

Em snatched it up.

"Hey." Liza tried to grab it, but Em leapt back, unlocked her screen and eyed it. "Missed calls from *Court of Rock*, Nikki and Keith." She looked up, confused. "Who's Keith?"

"He owns Indie Rock Broadcast." Liza got up and dragged on some clothes.

"Oh right." Em dropped her gaze back to the screen. "A text from Cassie." She tilted her head. "That's the girl we're raising money for to bring to the show, right?"

"Yes. And Sloane is covering what we can't raise, plus a few extras." Sloane had been all business when she'd called him, then she'd emailed him her itemized projected expenses, how much they had raised and what they needed. Liza got back, *Approved, make it happen.* The man got to the point. She liked that about him.

"We need to be friends with her. Know what she says?"

Locating a brush in Justice's bathroom, she worked on taming her hair. "I would if I had my phone."

Em ignored her sarcasm. "Cassie texted, 'I want to kick Gene Hayes in his lying mouth. I can't kick that high, heck sometimes I fall down trying to walk. But I can take my leg off and smack that smirk off his face.

Wink, wink, smiley face.'" Em laughed, her entire face lighting up. "This girl is funny." The laughter died. "And sweet."

She really was. "Her mom is too."

Em's face darkened. "Nothing from your family."

Liza sat on the edge of the bed. "I—" She cut herself off when her phone started vibrating.

Em dropped her gaze to the screen. "It's your aunt. Talk about freaky timing."

Liza's stomach clenched.

"You can let it go to voicemail."

Tempting, but instead she held out her hand.

"Do you want me to stay in here?" Em asked as she gave Liza the phone.

"No. Go have a donut." She needed to handle this and get it out of the way so she could figure out her next step. Accepting the call, she answered, "Aunt Mari."

"Liza, where are you? I'm worried. The video is all over. People are talking..."

Shame, guilt, and that sick feeling of regret weighed on her chest. She'd carried those feelings for so long, but over the last few years, they had eased. Now they were back. "I'm at Justice's house."

"So it's true? You're dating that singer?"

Obviously Mari saw *Late Night with Alicia,* or at least clips of it. What could Liza say? "Yes."

"What are you doing, Liza? I saw the other video too. You're working for a rock band? How long have you been lying to us?"

Wincing at the accusation in her tone, she said, "Not lying. I told you I was trying to get the paid position this summer." Quickly, she explained that she was competing with other student-publicists to win the prize of the Tangent internship.

"Hiding it is the same as lying," her aunt snapped. "You're dating a guy in a rock band. It's like your mother all over again. A nightmare that won't end."

"Justice isn't like my father. He's different."

"Different? There's that picture of you at a bar, your shirt plastered to you. You looked drunk."

"I wasn't drunk." She paced the room, trying to control her growing resentment that she had to defend herself. Just one time, couldn't Mari give her the benefit of the doubt? "I didn't do anything wrong. It was an accident, beer was spilled on me. I wasn't even drinking that night." She rubbed her forehead. "I'm not doing anything different than any other college girl."

"You're not any other girl. And now they know who you are. Is that what you want? Everyone to stare at you? To know that you went to that man's house that night at fourteen years old? Dressed that way? Drinking? They'll judge you, Liza, say you deserved it."

She deserved it. Something ugly ballooned in her chest and throbbed in her head. That was the implication over and over.

You snuck out.

You dressed like a slut.

You took that drink.

She closed her eyes, struggling for control. "What do *you* say, Mari? Did I deserve it?" The question shot out before she could think. Hadn't she always wondered?

"You have to ask that? I took you in, finished raising you. I was there through that trial, through it all. Of course I don't think you deserved it. But we've tried to help you understand that choices you made that night put you in the situation. Just like choices you're making now. Look what's happened." She took an audible breath. "You have to accept responsibility. You more than other girls." She paused. "We love you, but this isn't something we can support. I won't live through all this again."

For years and years, she'd stayed quiet, done what she was told, never had friends and didn't go out. Her only escapes were gardening, eating candy and writing her books. And it wasn't enough. She fought a wave of choking anger. "What does that mean?"

"Quit the show, and end this thing with that musician. Your quarter is almost over, and you can come home for the summer."

"And if I don't? If I keep seeing him?"

"I'm not going to watch you destroy yourself. You can come home when you end it."

She squeezed the phone, desperate. "I care about him. He's different. I've never felt this way for anyone."

"You've only known him a few weeks. You've known us for years."

That was true. But they made her feel like she had to hide, had to pay a penance for the rest of her life. While Justice made her feel like it was okay to talk about the rape and be herself. He made her feel sexy, safe and strong enough to live with the truth instead of hiding a secret.

"You're making me choose? My family or my boyfriend? All these years, I did everything you asked, tried to be good..." She'd found something amazing. Who else would hold her in the middle of the night and sing to her?

"I'm not going to debate this. He's not good for you. Look what's happened already. There are crazies out there. Don't forget the threats we got when you testified."

"What am I supposed to do, Mari? Live in fear forever? Hide?" She swallowed, struggling to find a way to make her aunt understand.

"Be responsible, quit that job and the guy, or don't come home."

Liza yanked the phone from her ear and saw the call had ended. Her aunt had hung up on her.

Silencing her again.

Liza threw the phone on the bed.

Justice stood on the side of the living room, flipping channels on the TV. Ben and Emily sat on the couch, equally tense. All the morning news and gossip shows were covering the story.

"I remember when all this happened," Em said. "I didn't know her then. It was all about Hayes. Did he or didn't he? Was this girl trying to ruin him? What kind of family let a girl go to a rock star's house at that age?" She tossed her uneaten donut on the napkin on the table. "Then I met Liza, and she told me who she was." She looked at Ben next to her. "I was one of them. Talking about her like she wasn't a real person."

"I didn't know that our Liza was that girl. Not until last night." Ben rubbed his hand over his chin. "It's still hard to believe. Liza's just Liza."

Justice paused his channel-surfing to study Emily. "You never told him?"

She shook her head. "Not that, no. It was too hard for her. She told me who she was, but not much more. She can't talk about it. That's how I knew you were different. She told you."

The weight of Liza's trust settled on him. She'd given him a real part of herself almost from the start. But hadn't he done the same by telling her about his screwed-up family, and why he was keeping this house?

"I want to hear this." Emily leaned forward, her eyes on the TV.

Justice shifted his attention to a national morning news show. The show's anchor asked, "What reason could Gene Hayes have for releasing that video? Is he trying to get a new trial?"

The camera swung to a well-dressed woman. "It's possible. Hayes was tried in absentia. That's a fairly rare occurrence with strict legal standards."

"You're a criminal attorney who's tried many high-profile cases. Can you explain what trial in absentia means?"

"Of course. It means that the trial was held without the defendant in the courtroom. In the case of Hayes, he was there the first couple weeks. At that point, there was a general feeling that he'd get off, or a slap on the wrist. Then the victim—"

The anchor cut in. "Gene Hayes revealed her identity, but our practice is to protect the names of sexual abuse victims. The media outlets usually called her Girl X."

The expert nodded. "Girl X testified, and she was powerful. I was in the courtroom those two days they had her on the stand."

"The media was blocked from the courtroom, correct?"

"Yes. No cameras or audio at all. Sketch artists were strictly instructed to not show her. The judge protected her identity, and she was very serious about it." The legal expert added, "Her testimony ended Friday. Monday morning the defendant, Gene Hayes, didn't show up. After that, it was quickly discovered he'd fled the country. The judge continued the trial without Mr.

Hayes, thereby trying him in absentia. The jury handed down several convictions, and he was sentenced to twenty-five years."

"Do you really think it's possible to get it overturned?"

"If lawyers file it, it's possible he could get that conviction vacated and a new trial ordered. Gene Hayes was extremely famous, his trial as big and divisive as O.J. Simpson's murder trial. Many people believe Hayes was innocent, that the real culprits, the victim's father and mother, were punished. Her father's dead, her mother in prison for his murder. Hayes's defenders believe it was a blackmail plot gone bad and Girl X was in on it."

"What would be different this time if he had a new trial?"

The lawyer looked into the camera. "They have the same physical evidence from the first trial, but it was Girl X herself, I think she was fifteen at the time of the trial, who made it all real to the jury. If Mr. Hayes were to be retried now, I'm not sure the adult version of that girl would have the same impact. Especially if they ruin her image in the media beforehand, thereby swaying potential jurors' opinions. She may not even want to testify again."

"So essentially, Hayes's strategy is blaming the victim?"

The professional-lawyer demeanor cracked, and the woman leaned forward. "That would be my guess, and it's disgusting. But unfortunately, it works. Once juries dehumanize or objectify the victim, see her as less than a good girl, some—not all—but some are willing to believe they brought it on themselves." She compressed her mouth then added, "Blaming the victim and smearing her reputation is an effective strategy, especially now that she's an adult."

"That's what that picture was about."

Justice jerked his gaze to Liza. She stood in the hallway, her hair waving madly around her, wearing a T-shirt and yoga pants.

She stared at him. "They're trying to prove I'm a groupie whore and was part of some blackmail scheme."

Emily jumped up, but Liza ignored her, storming into the kitchen.

Justice spun around and followed her.

"Em, stay here," Ben said.

Justice paused in the doorway.

Beth grabbed a cup, clunked it down on the counter and poured in coffee. Anger vibrated off her.

"What happened?" He had an idea, but he wanted to hear it from her.

She thunked the coffeepot back on the warmer. "When is it going to end, Justice? How long do I have to pay for one mistake? One." She opened a drawer and grabbed a spoon. Dumping sugar in her coffee, she stirred hard enough to slosh out some liquid. "The DA, lawyers and the counselors all promised it would be over once I testified. But it wasn't. He ran, and I'm left here facing the judgment."

He'd seen her pissed but this... Her tight, jerky movements indicated she was fighting hard not to completely explode. Last night she'd needed comfort from him, but today? His girl was ready to fight. What had she told him in the shower the night the beer had been spilled on her? *I don't lose my temper. I readjust my expectations.* That was about to change. She'd been holding this in too long.

"Beth, did you argue with your aunt?" Justice asked. Emily said she was talking to her aunt on the phone.

She spun, the spoon flying out of her hand and hitting the floor to dance across the linoleum. "It's never enough. I tried. I did everything they wanted. I got caught up in school, then I excelled and got straight A's. I won a scholarship, a full ride." She slapped her hand on the counter. "I didn't date, didn't drink, I didn't go out. I didn't even have friends. I was good so they wouldn't send me away. I cut, but I stopped to protect them from social services."

Her rage collided with the pain in her eyes, and it fucking killed him.

"Beth." He started toward her.

"No. It's not enough. Mari told me not to come home."

Justice froze, his chest going hollow. "Your aunt told you that?"

"If I don't quit *Court of Rock* and drop you, they won't let me come home." She turned away, staring down at the counter. "I don't have a home."

Jesus Christ. He heard Ben and Emily talking, Em's voice rising and Ben trying to calm her, but he didn't give a shit about them right now. What the hell should he say to Beth?

"I have to be out of my apartment soon," Beth added, worry heavy in her tone. "If I don't get that internship..."

He didn't know what to do. "Do you want to go home?"

She twisted her head, her long hair flying around her. "No. I don't. I'm so damned tired of the judgment. The silence." Her back expanded beneath the shirt, and she added, "I just want them to love me. Is that so hard? I told them I really like you, but that's not enough."

He started toward her.

"They want me to hate my mother and to blame her. But I don't." Her green eyes darkened. "I hate my dad and Gene Hayes. They cooked up that sick scheme. I saw my dad maybe a couple times a year, and for whatever reason, he showed up on my fourteenth birthday. Starts this story about how he's going to be in Gene Hayes's band. My mother laughed in his face."

Justice wanted her to be able to talk and let her anger out with him, but— "Uh, Beth, do you know Emily and Ben are still here?"

Her eyes narrowed. "So? Am I supposed to keep it all quiet, Justice? Not talk about it? Will it embarrass you that your girlfriend was so stupid? Slutty?"

Oh he was so done. The gloves were off. He closed the distance between them and glared down at her. "You want to scream at me, go right ahead. But don't call yourself names, Liza."

Fire lit in her eyes, and color stamped a blaze across her cheeks. "Or what? You'll throw me out of the house? Out of your life? Talk about me in the media? What will you do, Justice? Huh?"

Somewhere in his brain, it registered that she wasn't afraid of him physically. Amazing. For having been hurt by a man, that was incredible and showed him just how strong this girl was. A survivor. "I'll get right back in your face and tell you that my girlfriend can be as pissed off as she wants, but she can't call herself names. It makes me mad, baby. Seriously fucking mad."

"I'm mad too."

"I'm not blind or deaf. I'm right here, witnessing you getting real, telling the truth. You have every right to be mad. You don't deserve this, Beth. Not that rapist asshole spreading lies, not the media shitstorm, and you sure as hell don't deserve your family giving you an ultimatum. If you don't care that Ben and Emily hear, then I don't. Tell me."

Beth had lived in fear of losing the only family she had left, so she'd bottled up everything to become the perfect good girl. Now that bottle was cracking, the real Beth coming out, spreading her wings to show the world her true colors.

She didn't even glance toward the living room. Nope, Beth's eyes were on him, her chest rising and falling. "My dad always had this story, this scheme to be in some great band or something. But when my dad asked me if I wanted to meet Hayes, maybe be in a music video, my mom lost it. Screaming no way, not a chance. Later, my dad told me she was jealous, that she'd always tried to keep me from him, and that I was growing up into a beautiful girl while she was growing old. I wanted to believe him and to be in that music video. Then I'd be somebody. Anyway, he told me he'd come pick me up when my mom was at work and introduce me to Hayes. Told me to wear something sexy and impress the man."

It took everything Justice had to stay still and quiet. Beth needed to tell this her own way, and his job was to listen.

She waited a beat, but when he didn't say anything, she went on. "I told you my mom and I fought. She told me no way in hell was I going. Hayes was a known pervert—her words. She wasn't letting her daughter near him. I yelled back all kinds of things I regret."

He winced, unable to contain it. He knew what that felt like. The things that flew out of your mouth at that age.

She leaned back, gripping the counter behind her, and looked up at the ceiling. "She went to work, and I dressed exactly like Hayes described. Short shorts, a crop top. My dad picked me up. We arrived, music played, a few people mingled, drugs were everywhere, and guests were already getting stoned. The place was huge, like that penthouse we went to the other night. We walked around, and finally we were told to meet Hayes in his bedroom."

She met his gaze. "I got nervous. I told my dad, but he said to grow up. Hayes wanted to talk to me about his music video, and he couldn't do that in front of other people. So we both went in there, and Hayes was in a pair of sweatpants and nothing else. The room was massive, bigger than the whole trailer my mom and I lived in. We sat on these couches, and Hayes asked me if I wanted to be in his video. I said sure, while being secretly pleased that my mom was wrong. He went to the bar in his room, turned on the blender, then poured pink, slushy stuff in a glass. He held it out and told me it was a strawberry margarita." Liza shivered. "I hesitated, growing more uneasy.

"My dad leaned over and said, 'Elizabeth, don't be rude. Do you want to ruin this for both of us?' So I took the drink and sipped it. They kept encouraging me to drink more. Soon I felt strange and really scared. That's when I told my dad that I wanted to go home. He said he'd take me home as soon as I finished the drink. So I did.

"But I realized my dad was gone. When had he walked out of the room? I was confused and really frightened. Hayes smiled, said we were all alone...and all I thought then was my mom had been right after all. I remember thinking I needed to call her, but...that's when I went blank. I don't remember anything after that.

"The tape of me calling my mom—my voice is

slurred and I'm crying. She asked where Hayes was, and I said bathroom. I must have managed to use my phone to call her, but I don't remember it. I don't remember anything until later in the hospital."

Rage beat a harsh thump inside his head. Justice tried to breathe past it, but his muscles twitched and burned. Unable to contain himself, he swung around and slapped his hands on the cool refrigerator.

It didn't help. He had to hit something. Doubling up his fist, he pulled it back, aiming for the fridge—

"Justice, no!" Beth grabbed his arm. "You'll break your hand. It's already bruised from the fight with Jagged Sin. What are you doing?"

Her frantic voice pierced some of his fury. He dragged in air, trying to calm the violence thundering in his blood with the drive to find Hayes and kill him. "He got away with it. He raped you and got away with it. Did your aunt and uncle try to find where that bastard is hiding? Did they do anything? Maybe try to getting a civil judgment against his remaining assets for you?"

Her fingers dug into his forearm. "They couldn't bear another trial."

"*They* couldn't. Jesus Christ, Beth, you're the victim. Not them." He was so furious, it actually hurt as if a probe were shocking his nerve endings. "They didn't protect you, they protected themselves." Twisting around, he pulled her against him, desperate to feel her safe and warm in his arms.

She tilted her head back. "You're shaking."

Her sweet concern softened his temper. "Part of it is that I want to kill Hayes. Then I want to go meet your mom and high-five her for shooting your dad."

"And the other part?"

He hated himself for it, but she deserved to know

the truth. "In a way, I'm as bad as your aunt and uncle. It's my fault Hayes found you. You warned me that something like this could happen, but in the IRB interview, I didn't think about what it might cost you to join in. It was an unforgivably stupid and selfish action. And now you're paying the price. Not only dealing with that pervert coward showing up on video and stirring up the worst nightmare of your life, but now you're forced to choose between dating me or your family."

Which choice would she make?

Chapter 16

THE BOILING FURY INSIDE LIZA deflated. Once the adrenaline rush settled, her chest ached with sadness and fear.

Her aunt was really forcing her to choose. Did her family even want her around at all? Or would they be relieved to be rid of her? What about her cousins, Kristen and Rafe? They were more like her siblings than cousins. How could she bear not seeing them?

Her eyes stung, and Liza dropped her forehead against Justice's chest. "What do I do?" She squeezed her eyes shut. "You were right when we fought in my apartment. I'm a coward and desperately tried to hold on to something safe." But it wasn't safe, it was tearing her up that she meant so little to her aunt. And that her cousins would be hurt in this too.

He settled his hand over the back of her head. "I should never have said that. You stood up to that bastard in the courtroom and told the truth at fifteen years old. I can't think of anything more courageous than that. But you didn't stop there. You kept surviving, and now you're this amazing woman in my kitchen forced into an unbearable decision. One that I could have prevented if I'd taken more care with your privacy during the interview. I regret that so much. And not just because it might cost me you, but because you don't deserve any of this."

His chest vibrated against her face, his hand on her head warm and sweet. It tore her up to feel his caring and comfort. He always offered it freely and never made her feel like a burden.

And now she was supposed to give him up? That was what her aunt wanted, for Liza to give up the one thing she hadn't had since that awful night of her rape.

Gathering her hair his hand, he tilted her head back. "I've never felt this before—a raging passion mixed with that massive tenderness that makes my heart feel too damned big in my chest. You're my song, that one that every singer craves and can't stop singing because it fucking owns them and they want the whole damn world to know it. You, Beth, you're my song."

Her heart fluttered wildly, like a swarm of beautiful fireflies bursting to life in the darkness.

"I don't want to come between you and your family, and I can't tell you what to do. But I can tell you this— you'll always have a place here in this house if you need it. Anytime. Whether we're together or not. You won't ever be homeless. So if you need your family, then..." He sucked in a breath, sadness devastating his eyes. "I'll let you go. But you aren't going back to them because you think you don't have a home."

"No." The word erupted from her chest, from the place where fiery love broke free. "When I said what do I do? I just meant it hurt, Justice. Not that I'd choose my family." She placed his hand over her heart. "Feel that thump-thump? Do you know what I hear every time my heart does that?"

"What?"

"All in." She clutched his hand tighter. "I'm all in with you because I love you. I love your fearlessness, the way you back your friends and care for your father. I love that you have the blue jay tatted over your heart for your grandmother. You believe in me, but more importantly, you make me believe in myself." He hadn't said he loved her, but he deserved to know the truth and that she wasn't bailing on him.

He swung her up, planting her butt on the counter. "You love me. A rock star."

The fact that he added rock star poked at her. He'd told her once...*the world only wants the hero, not the man.* Justice was trying to turn himself into a hero—a rock god that people would love and not leave. She had to make him understand.

"No. Lots of women love the rock star." Liza took his face in her hands. "But I love *you*, Justice. The man who is striving to live up to his name. You almost slammed your fist into the fridge because my rapist escaped his punishment that you consider justice. That's the man I love."

He dropped his forehead to hers. "You had your chance, baby."

"For what?"

His gaze burned into hers. "I'd have let you go if that's what you needed. But now you're mine." Pulling back, he added, "I love you, Beth, and I'm not letting you go."

They really were all in.

Four days later, Liza was completely exhausted. She'd picked up Cassie and her mom, Patricia, from the hotel and ferried them to the auditorium to meet the guys. Now she was driving them back.

Cassie looked over at her. "Is it always like this? All these reporters and stuff?"

Outside the auditorium, reporters and their vehicles clogged up the parking lot and surrounding roads. She ignored it. After a talk with the DA in Beverly Hills, she'd agreed to not make any statement. If Hayes filed to get the case overturned, the DA would likely retry him. If she made a public statement and said the wrong thing, it could cause problems in her future testimony. Liza chafed at not being able to defend herself, but she understood the ramifications, and so she'd cooperated, refusing to talk to the media.

What bothered her more were the small groups of protesters with their ugly signs.

Recant!

Bring Gene Hayes Home!

False Accusations of Rape!

They could say anything they wanted about her. Nothing ever seemed to happen to them.

As they passed by a group of three stringy-haired men holding signs, Cassie shuddered next to her. Shoving her long brown hair away from her heart-shaped face, she frowned. "How do you endure this?"

Pulling out of her own thoughts, she looked at the girl. Cassie was pretty in that girl-next-door way, with deep-set hazel eyes and a tiny scar across the bridge of her nose. She'd been shy meeting the band, but after ten minutes she'd loosened up, played bass guitar and even sang with them. The guys had had her laughing in no time.

The girl's laughter had made her mom cry. Liza wasn't doing much better. That was Savaged Illusions at their best. Liza had secured permission to use the auditorium for an hour before the crew set up for dress rehearsal. She'd gotten a ton of pictures, then she and

Cassie had chosen the two she wanted posted on social media. It had been all up to her. Liza wouldn't have posted any pics unless she was okay with it.

Cassie had amazed them all with her obvious resilience and fun sarcasm. And this girl asked her how she coped? "Same as you, I guess. No one gave us a choice, did they?"

"Yeah, but I've been kind of feeling sorry for myself."

The shame in her voice pissed Liza off. "Cassie, do you think I didn't?" She took the girl's hand. "Many times I wished I'd died that night. That I just never woke up and had to face it all." Too late, she wondered if she'd said the wrong thing. She glanced in the backseat to Patricia.

Cassie's mom looked tired but nodded reassuringly. Obviously Patricia encouraged her daughter to express her feelings, no matter how grim or scary. Unlike Liza's aunt and grandmother. But that wasn't entirely fair either. They'd been through years of frustration and pain with her mom, and in their minds, all the tragedies of that night were a result of her mom's actions from as far back as college. They'd been desperate to keep Liza from going down the same path.

Now wasn't the time to think about them.

Returning to the girl, Liza added, "I'm here, and I'm making the best of it. You can do it too." She squeezed her hand. "But it's okay to acknowledge that something really crappy happened to you and that sometimes it plain sucks."

"Do you think that after this is over, I could still text you sometimes? I won't do it a lot, but you know, sometimes?"

Liza smiled. "I'd like that. By the way, my friend Emily wants to meet you too. She thinks you're funny."

She told Cassie how Em had snooped in her phone and found the text.

"Some people kind of hate when I joke about my leg. It makes them uncomfortable."

"Yeah, well, maybe they should try walking a mile on your leg."

Cassie laughed. "That was awful, Liza. Seriously."

Grinning, she made a turn and said, "I'll practice and get better."

"Hey, so the guys, are they nervous about tonight? Do you think they'll win? I want them to win. I mean Fury Run is good and all, but Savaged Illusions, I just love their music."

It made her head spin how fast Cassie went from mature beyond her years to a teenage girl. Liza's stomach writhed with nerves, anxiety and everything else. They had to win. "I love their music too. And yeah, they're nervous. Seeing you today was really good for them. It gave them a break from the pressure and mounting tension." After pulling into the hotel entrance, she stopped right at the door. "Okay, tonight there will be a limo coming for you guys. Cassie, the driver is going to stay with you. If you need assistance or people are too close or shoving, he's there to help. He works for my friend Sloane, and you can trust him. With them will be my other friend, Nikki. She's going to be your guide. She knows the auditorium and routine, so she can help you guys through the security checks and anything else you need."

Cassie leaned over and hugged Liza. "I can't wait."

Patricia squeezed her shoulder. "Thank you, Liza. This whole trip means the world to her."

Once they were on their way into the hotel, Liza drove to Justice's house, where she'd been staying since the Hayes video released. The one time they'd gone to her apartment to get some of her stuff, reporters had been lurking around. Now she just wanted a little time to herself. Justice and the guys were at a lunch with Christine Castle, who was in town for the show and to sign them if they won. They all had so much riding on this, for Savaged Illusions' big break and her to get that internship.

A while after the harsh conversation with her aunt, Liza had called her grandmother, hoping to mend fences and offering to have them meet Justice. Maybe if they got to know him... But Grandma refused.

Had they been looking for an excuse to cut her out of their lives? What would she do if she didn't get that internship? She wouldn't be able to finish her degree in the fall quarter without those credits.

She sucked in a breath. One step at a time. She'd work, borrow money if she had to and figure it out.

Turning down Justice's street, she breathed out a sigh of relief. No reporters that she could spot. They were all at the auditorium, or maybe another, more interesting news story broke. Once she parked, she grabbed her purse, got out her shiny key Justice had made for her and rushed to the door.

She noted that the rosebushes had perked up, stroking her pride. Any free time she'd had, she'd spent working in the yard.

Quickly Liza shoved the key into the deadbolt when she heard sounds behind her. Footsteps. Uneasiness tightened her neck muscles.

"Liza?"

Adrenaline spiked at the unknown voice, and she spun. "If you're a reporter—" Her words froze in her throat. This was no reporter. The man was easily six feet, but scars covered one side of his cheek and temple above his ragged beard. He wore a shabby jacket, stained jeans, black athletic shoes and a battered backpack was slung over one shoulder. His hair was mostly gray, but his eyes...a mix of blue and gray so familiar to her.

"Didn't mean to scare you. I'll leave. I just..." He shook his head. The left side of his face didn't really move. "I'm sorry." Turning, he retreated.

She snapped out of her surprise. "Mr. Cade?" Justice's father. "Don't go, please." How did he know her name? Caution warred with her excitement. She didn't know this man.

He slowed and faced her.

She ordered her thoughts and asked him, "You know my name?"

"I saw you on the interview with IRB and on the news. I wanted to meet you."

Her stomach clenched. What did he think of her? "The Gene Hayes video?" The question popped out before she could think. Inside her, rage and ugly insecurity clashed and fought.

Anger blazed into his eyes. "I don't listen to a rapist who fled the country I fought for. My friends and comrades laid down their lives so he could have a right to a trial and he runs? Coward."

"Oh." What else could she say? Clearly she'd jumped to the wrong conclusion. "Justice is in a lunch meeting, but I can call him. He'll come home." She shoved her hand in her purse, happy to have a plan and a way to help after all Justice had done for her.

"No. Don't." He threw his hands up, retreating. "I can't see him. Can't talk to him."

Her excitement withered beneath the raw agony in his voice and the pain in his eyes. All thoughts of herself fled. "Why? He loves you. He misses you." She desperately tried to make him understand. "Mr. Cade, he's keeping this house because it's your home. He wants you here, you just need to trust—"

He shook his head. "Not me. It's not me. You don't understand."

His angry frustration pierced her good intentions. Liza lowered her arms. He'd sought her out for a reason, and she really doubted it was to be told what he must know about his son.

"You're right. I'm sorry." She pulled in a breath, grasping that she was making assumptions about Justice's dad, not unlike strangers had done to her. "I don't understand, and I'm not giving you a chance to talk to me."

The tightness around his eyes eased.

"I won't call Justice." Not right now anyway. "Please, Mr. Cade—"

"Noah."

"Noah." Justice's middle name. "Why did you want to see me?"

"He cares about you. I saw the way he looked at you in the interview." Tapping his hand against his thigh, he added, "How is he?"

The hunger in that question reached past any concerns about her own safety with a man she didn't know. She was close to Justice, and his father was trying to connect to his son through her.

She didn't know why he couldn't just talk to Justice, but it was clear he was locked in a prison as surely as her mother was. What did he want to know? "He's going after his dream to be in a rock band." Duh, he knew that already. "He's in a good place, I think. He and the band are really tight. They fight, man do they fight. But the thing is, Justice knows they have his back."

"Like on *Late Night with Alicia* when they walked off."

Pride had deepened his voice, and Liza guessed he followed Justice closely.

"Yeah. The band was pretty pissed at him." It bothered her that she was causing trouble. "He hadn't told them who I am. They felt betrayed."

His bushy eyebrows lowered. "He'd do the same for them. Don't they understand that? Justice won't leave a man behind."

Interesting way to phrase it. But Noah was a former Marine, so she guessed it made sense. "They must know it. One of the first things Justice told me was that he didn't want to get signed to the record label and then leave his band behind. He's loyal to them."

"That's the boy I remember."

"He wouldn't leave you behind either."

The glaze of memory in Noah's eyes vanished, replaced by sharp intensity. "I know."

Two simple words vibrating with a wealth of meaning. It took her a couple beats, then she gasped with understanding. "That's why you left. Why you keep leaving." He thought he'd be a burden of some kind. A weight. She opened her mouth, then shut it. Noah, Justice had told her, had been severely injured and had PTSD. He'd been through a hell she couldn't even pretend to imagine. "It's not that simple, is it?"

"No."

What could she do? "Noah, do you have a place to stay? Is there something I can do to help you? If you need anything—"

"Just for Justice to be happy. Take care of him, Liza. I failed him, and so did his mother. He needs you."

This man loved his son. She needed to keep him

engaged with her until she could figure out what to do next. "How do you follow his career? You obviously know a lot."

"I have a phone and service."

Of course, Justice had told her that.

"I have one more thing to ask you," Noah said.

"Sure."

"Tell him to stop looking. Forget about me. I'm his past. You and the band are his future."

Sad conviction ached in his voice. He believed that was what was best for his son, even though he hungered for any scrap of information about Justice. It hurt to witness his private hell. She wanted to ease him, but she wouldn't lie. This was too important.

"I'm sorry, Noah, I won't do that. Not now, not ever. Justice won't do it anyway." She took a risk, moving closer to Noah. "You're his father. A man he looks up to."

"Not anymore." He looked around the front yard, at the house, the sidewalk. Anywhere but her. "If you won't tell him to forget me, then tell him I said good luck tonight." He pivoted and walked partway down the driveway.

"Noah, wait." She kept her voice calm and followed him. She didn't think Noah Cade was dangerous, and he didn't appear insane. He'd held a perfectly reasonable conversation. But he was troubled, haunted and clearly wary.

"What?"

"Justice is singing a song he wrote tonight."

A real smile tilted up the good side of his face. "Thank you."

The gratefulness in his words touched her. His craving for information on Justice was almost a visceral thing. "It's a song for you. One he's hoping you'll hear." She took a breath. Was she doing the right thing? "Would you consider coming tonight?"

The agony in his face tore at her. "I can't talk to him. I just can't."

She thought fast. "Okay, I have an idea." Staying a few feet back, she outlined it, hope filling her chest.

The man's eyes, so like Justice's, stared at a spot somewhere behind her. "I don't know if I can."

Moving closer, she touched his arm. "That's okay if you can't. Let me give you my cell phone number. If you come, let me know, and I'll get you in and out. You won't have to talk to anyone but me."

He pulled out his phone, swiftly recording her number. Yeah, nothing wrong with this man's mental faculties. Once he was done, Liza added, "Noah, I'm going to wait to tell him I saw you until after the show. I hope you'll come. But if you can't, I'll tell him you tried."

He watched her, his gaze so like Justice's. "You really do care about him."

The words escaped before she thought them out. "So much it scares me."

"The song. Have you heard it?"

"It's called 'Expired Hero.' It made me cry." Silent tears she never told Justice about. "He's desperate for you to hear it. He needs you to."

He angled his head down. "I don't know."

Liza hung back as the Savaged Illusions band did preshow interviews in the backstage media pen. The reporters with access credentials clustered around while their photographers took pictures. Out in the auditorium every seat was filled, and a crowd of fans lined the parking lot. Protesters against her were out there too, carrying their signs full of hatred.

The Gene Hayes video had changed everything. But no, she wasn't thinking about that tonight. This was Savaged Illusions' big moment.

One reporter asked the guys, "Did you see that Jagged Sin has thrown their support behind Fury Run?"

Simon turned, the lights catching the black stitches standing out against his cheek since he'd refused to wear a bandage any longer. "Don't hold that against Fury Run."

Liza smothered a laugh. That was the perfect answer.

"Do you think you can still beat them? Jagged Sin has a strong following. That's a lot of votes for Fury Run."

"Not strong enough. They were cut," Lynx pointed out. "The fans will make their own decisions."

"Jagged Sin is calling you Savage Traitors. They claim they have talked to Gene Hayes, and he has assured them that just like Liza set him up, Savaged Illusions set up Jagged Sin in the garage incident."

Justice spun, his eyes blazing. "Hayes is a convicted rapist. Now Ace and his crew are joining forces with him? That shows who they really are. As for the *garage incident*, Ace and his two sidekicks were drunk and stoned and jumped Simon. Do you not see the stitches in his face? How are we the bad guys here?"

"They claim Liza got Nikki, their former publicist, to turn against them. Their story is she screamed first, and they thought Simon was hurting her."

Liza's stomach churned, and she slapped her hand over her mouth. My God. Did Ace hate Simon so much they'd make up huge lies?

Stupid question. Three of Jagged Sin's band

members jumped him in the garage. Of course he did.

But had Ace really talked to Gene Hayes? Anything was possible with the Internet.

A new voice interrupted her thoughts. "Liza, didn't you know about Jagged Sin aligning themselves with Hayes and supporting Fury Run? Justice didn't tell you? We discussed the problem at lunch."

Turning, Liza faced Christine Castle. The business manager wore a designer dress and Louboutin heels, her blonde hair cut longer on one side. Christine's whole look was polished, trendy and very expensive. She radiated power.

"I, uh... We haven't talked since then. I mean not alone. There was dress rehearsal, then he got ready here, and all the preshow meetings and interviews..." She studied Justice as he answered another question. He'd dressed for the show in slim dark jeans and a blue T-shirt that left his tatted arms bare. His jaw was rock hard, and she saw him tap his thigh—his only sign of nerves.

Exactly like his father had done earlier today.

"If they win tonight, they're going to the big time. Everything changes then. You get that, right?"

Liza dragged her gaze from Justice to the manager. "What do you mean?"

Christine sighed, and the hard edge in her voice softened. "You know Justice is fame driven. The whole band wants it bad."

Fame driven. Same as her father. "I know." But Justice had proved he wasn't anything like Eddie Ranger.

"I'm not trying to be cruel, Liza. I've seen Justice with you and heard the way he talks about you. He does like you. But it just won't last. It can't. This kind of life is all-consuming and requires a hell of a lot of sacrifice. The travel alone kills relationships. But I'm also speaking as their manager." Her eyes took on a determined glint. "The guys need to focus on their passion—music—not get caught up in the drama of relationships outside the band."

"Drama. Like my past." There it was, the bald truth.

"Yes." Christine touched her arm. "Hayes is a dangerous adversary. The man's a greedy, narcissistic personality who truly believes his talent makes him entitled. And you, a mere girl, destroyed him. For a while he hid, then he started stepping out, playing small concerts...but that's not enough for someone like him."

Chills dripped down her spine. She'd done her best not to think of Hayes over the years. "You know him?"

"You weren't his first victim. I knew girls, or more specifically their families, that he paid off for the exact kind of thing you went through. Guys like him need to have their man parts whacked off."

She shook her head, unable to believe this. "But why didn't you speak up? Why are you protecting him?" Anger sparked. "He could be hurting other girls. You're a woman." That offended a deep part of her. Shouldn't women try to help each other?

"I'm protecting myself. I had to fight longer and harder than any man to make it in this business. It's more difficult for women, that's a fact. I pick my battles, and those battles are about my clients' success and ultimately mine. That's reality."

That wasn't Liza's reality. She lost all respect for the other woman. She had chosen her career over helping stop a rapist. "So what is this conversation about?" What did Christine want? And would Hayes find a way to come back to the U.S.?

"Believe it or not, I'm trying to open your eyes to

the facts, as well as protect my client. If you get in the way, if push comes to shove, who do you think Justice will choose? You or his career?"

Liza flinched, the worry too close to her deepest fear.

"All right," Frank the producer announced. "Ten minutes."

The band headed out to the backstage area by the stairs. Liza followed, her thoughts swirling. Makeup people and crew members swarmed the guys, doing last-minute fixes and checking mic packs.

She watched the highly choreographed chaos with a pounding heart. Forgetting her own worries, all she could think was, *This is it*. The two-hour show that would decide their fates, either launching Justice to stardom and keeping Liza on the path to her degree or leaving them both in the dirt.

"Places," Frank yelled.

Everyone moved toward the stage, but Justice broke away, stopping by her.

"Jesus, look at my hands." He held them out.

Liza eyed the way they trembled slightly, and laced their fingers together. "You're always amped before a show." Once the assistant handed him his guitar and he ran on stage, all the wild energy would focus. Smiling, she added, "This is what makes you so good. You give them everything when you're onstage."

"Tonight is different."

Yeah it was. This was the finale, the pressure insane. But that wasn't what he meant. "'Expired Hero.'" As much as he wanted to win and gain fame, he also hoped to reach his father.

"It's mine, Beth."

Oh she knew. He'd written it and convinced his band this was the song that would take them to the next level. Justice was laying the most vulnerable part of himself out there for the world.

"Suck it up, Cade," she teased, trying to make him laugh. This was his big night, and Liza wanted him to enjoy it. "I let you read pages from my book. That was way scarier than singing the most important song of your career in front of millions of people. I swear, if I'd known the rock egos I'd be forced to deal with, I'd never have taken this gig."

His eyes crinkled, shifting his face from hard to almost boyish. "Been a tough road, huh?"

"The worst." If she didn't count that she'd met a man who made her feel like she didn't have to bury her past and be perfect every second. He gave her more security and encouragement than she'd ever experienced. "But I've never believed in any other person like I believe in you."

"Beth."

The way he did that, saying her name with reverence, always got to her. But this wasn't their moment, it was his. "Now get out there, and get me that internship."

"I'll give it my best shot." He kissed her. "Win or lose, I need this, Beth."

"What?"

He released her hands to take her face in his palms. "Us."

God she hoped so. Because this man owned her heart.

Chapter 17

MORE THAN AN HOUR AND a half into the show, Justice took his mark in the center of the darkened stage. To his left, Simon found his place. River settled just behind them as Gray took a seat at the piano and Lynx perched on drums at the back.

The whole show was a massive production tonight, a real battle, with each band going on stage three different times to perform a classic, modern and an original rock song. Video packages led into each song, with a lot of emotion roiling through the auditorium.

This was Savaged Illusions' last set. Once they came back from commercial, they would play their final song.

"Expired Hero."

Don't fuck this up. Don't lose this.

"One minute," a voice warned them.

Anxiety rippled up his spine. Had the band made the right choice? All week long, they'd worked together on some changes and perfected the song. But it was still his song, the one he'd written. The one that told a story...

The world only wanted you when you were on top.

Justice and the guys had to win. He couldn't let his band down. And failing in front of millions of people?

His dad would never come home.

His mom would be right about him.

And Beth...she'd chosen him over her family. If he lost now, would she regret that choice?

Pressure closed in on him, trying to shake his nerves. A slow smile curved his mouth. Fuck that. Justice didn't do stage fright. He'd made it this far, to the moment where he stood ready to prove to the world he was a rock star. Worthy.

Not just him, but his entire band. Savaged Illusions would conquer tonight.

Glancing over at Simon, Justice held out his fist. "Ready to own this, man?"

Simon bumped fists, heat boiling in his gaze. "Born ready."

"Time to unleash the savages," Lynx said behind them.

The next warning came. "Ten seconds."

Justice fingered his guitar strings, preparing for the blast of hot lights once they were cued in. His heart pounded, and he loved every damned second. All the work, the travel and long days, frustrations and fights.

It came down to now.

A movement caught his attention in the wings of the stage by the stairs. While he and the band were in the darkened center, there was enough light on the side to get a clear view of Liza. Seeing her watching fed his confidence, flooding him with the desire to preen for her. Like a damned rooster. He almost laughed. Her just being there made this moment perfect. She did this to him, stoked his passion higher and stronger.

His girl believed in his dream, believed in him. They were all in, together.

He was more in love with this girl each day. But right now he had a show to win. He gave her a quick thumbs-up, but she missed it when she turned and whispered to someone.

Weird. Was someone else with her, or maybe on the stairs telling her she shouldn't be there? Liza had watched them from that spot before and no one had bothered her. His scalp prickled. Justice leaned toward her, trying to see.

Another person came into view.

The prickle ran straight down his spine and slammed into his gut. How? Was it really him?

"We're back in three, two, one, and go."

Lights blazed on, and the jumbo screen behind them sprang to life. Piano music haunted the air.

But Justice stayed rooted, unable to look away from the large man. One second later, the stage spotlights focused on Justice, blinding him until all he could see was a shadowing figure in the wings.

That quick glimpse was long enough for Justice to recognize his father.

His dad was here with his girlfriend. How was that even—?

Something jabbed his back and snapped him back into reality. He guessed that River had nudged him. Turning his head, he got an eyeful of the close-up camera tight on his face catching his shock.

He'd fumbled his cue on stage in front of millions.

Oh hell no.

Adrenaline exploded, the rush hitting his system. Justice turned his gaze straight into the camera and launched into "Expired Hero."

Behind them, the massive screen flickered with images of war juxtaposed with pictures of Justice as a kid with his dad. He didn't look at the screen; he knew what was there. Didn't care about that. What did matter was that one glimpse of his dad was seared on his brain. He'd looked old, ragged and tired. A shadow of the hero in Justice's memory. Pain and regret opened up, spilling more of his blood into the song.

He wouldn't fail now. Not like he had that day long ago. *I wish you'd never come home.* His own words ricocheted in his brain, paired with the absolute devastation on his dad's scarred face. Those memories gushed from his soul into the song. River's dark bassline throbbed with emotion, Lynx pounded home the rage on his kit, Gray brought out the pain, and Simon...he played like a monster, ripping up his guitar, his vocals so powerful it forced Justice to push his voice to the next level.

Sweat poured from Justice, his throat raw by the time he sang the final note.

Silence dropped for a single heartbeat. Then applause exploded like rockets, going higher and longer than he could ever remember. Like a wave, the audience surged to their feet in a standing ovation.

The huge swell of energy crashed over the stage, filling a part of Justice—but another part of him, the youngest part of his soul that was still a lost teenage boy, craved the reaction of one person. The one man he'd looked up to and still wanted approval from. His father.

Justice turned to the wings, needing to see his dad, desperate to glean some acknowledgment or understanding in his eyes.

But his dad was gone.

Liza wanted to beg Noah to stay, but she'd made a deal. Plus she could see the man was trembling, with sweat dotting his forehead. Every loud noise caused him to twitch.

What had it cost him to stand there in the wings for those four minutes?

"Thank you, Noah." She walked him outside into the dark, staying close to the door to avoid encountering a Hayes groupie. They were all herded behind a barricade by the street, so she was safe here and focused on Noah. "This will mean so much to Justice."

"Not as much as it means to me," he said in a low, thick voice.

"Are you sure you can't talk to him?"

"Can't."

She didn't let any further protest escape into words. Noah coming to the show was a step in the right direction. "He loves you."

Noah faced her. "I hear the screams every time I close my eyes. I failed them, and they died. Not easy deaths, but horrible and agonizing. Because I made a mistake. I can't face my son. I can't." He walked away, a tall, lanky man with shoulders bowed from an internal weight no one could see. She wanted to run after him and...

What? Hug him because a hug would make it all better? What could she do? Oh, they might get the police to pick him up, get him locked down for seventy-two hours for a psychological evaluation. And then what?

They'd release him, and he might be more traumatized. Not a good plan.

Her heart broke for Justice. She got it now, the frustration he lived with every day.

"Liza," Colin called from the door. "The show's coming back on in one minute."

Her stomach clenched, her nerves twanging hard. At this rate, her intestines were going to resemble overcooked spaghetti.

Justice stood beneath the spotlights, struggling to keep his face relaxed and confident. River waited at his left, Lynx and Gray on the right, and Simon crowded behind him.

A few feet over, the lights caught the bright purple zigzags Wendy had added to her blue hair. She and the girls all held hands.

"Waiting's a bitch," Simon muttered.

Justice silently agreed.

"And now," the show's host announced, "after ten weeks of competition, we're in the final minutes of the eleventh and last week...and down to two bands, Fury Run and Savaged Illusions."

The audience leapt to their feet, their excitement palpable.

Once they settled, the announcer went on, "Voting has officially closed, and the computer is tallying those, along with the judges' scores." He turned to the judges. "Now's a good time to thank..."

Justice wanted to wrap his hands around the guy's throat and shake him until he stopped delaying by naming each judge, talking about how wonderful they were and kissing their asses. Sweat trickled down his back, and he worked to keep his hands loose at his sides. Was his dad still in the building, or had he left? Would it matter if Justice won? Would his dad come home? How had Liza found him?

"It's been an incredibly exciting season, our best so far. This is the hardest part, as only one band can take home the title of *Court of Rock* Champion."

They could have another entire season while this jerk-off delayed.

"Ah." He tapped his earpiece. "Yep, the final votes have been double-checked and locked in. The winner of Season 4 of *Court of Rock* is..."

The host trailed off as the drums tapped out a tension-filled beat. The cameras zoomed in on both bands.

Swear to God, his heart slammed harder than Sloane punched. He stared straight ahead while thinking about all the practices and shows, the fights and negotiating, every single note he'd sung and hours he'd played, all the sleepless nights...and it came down to this moment.

They had to win.

"Fury Run!"

Justice got off the stage and went in search of Liza. He waved off the assistants telling him to get into the media pen. The guys were on his heels, but right now his head rang with failure.

You're a loser. You'll always be a loser. No wonder your father takes off. He can't stand to be around you.

His mom had recognized it when he was sixteen, and now eight years later, he'd just proved her right.

And his dad? Well, he wasn't here now, was he? Justice scanned every face, unable to find his dad or Liza. Finally he made his way to the greenroom.

Liza sat there alone. Everyone else had spilled out to the halls and backstage.

"Where's my dad?"

"Justice." She shot to her feet and rushed toward him. "He couldn't stay. I tried, but he just couldn't do it."

His last shred of hope died. "He saw me lose."

"What?" She took his hand, her face softening. "No. He saw you sing, and he was so proud of you. But he was sweating and anxious. Every noise made him jump. I don't know what caused it exactly, being inside, all the people, or the sounds, maybe the war scenes on the video, whatever it was, he fought through it long enough to watch you. He didn't stay to see the outcome."

"But he won't talk to me."

Her eyes filled with tears. "He can't. I don't understand it either."

Her pain pierced enough of his misery that he pulled her into his arms. "Don't cry."

"I can't help it. None of this is fair. You should have won, and your dad should have stayed."

The enormity of what Liza had done sank in—she'd found his dad and persuaded the man to come see Justice. No one else had managed to do that. "How? I don't understand. How did you find—?"

The door opened, banging into the wall. Simon stormed in, followed by Lynx, Gray and River. Simon's scowl took them in. "You're supposed to be in the media pen, not in here with your troublemaking girlfriend." Simon crossed the room to get right up in his face. "You, this..." he gestured to Justice and Liza, "...is the reason we lost."

Oh, he was done. Frustrated rage poured into his veins. Making sure Liza was behind him, he glared at Simon. "Don't blame her."

He leaned around Justice. "What the hell was that, Liza? Coming onstage with some guy? Were you trying to knock us off our game?"

"That was Justice's father," Lynx said. "But I gotta agree with Simon here. What the hell? Shocked the shit out of me."

Simon narrowed his eyes. "Your father? Did you know? Was this some little game you and Liza are playing?"

"He didn't know," Liza jumped in. "I'm sorry, I was trying to help. Justice wrote that song for his dad, and—"

"It was *our* moment. The band's. Not Justice's goddamned family reunion." Simon slapped his hand down on the refreshment table. "You had no right, Liza. None."

She drew back. "I'm sorry."

"Stop yelling at her." Justice wasn't letting anyone blame Liza. The real problem stood right in front of him. "What sank us is your feud with Jagged Sin. If they didn't hate you, they'd have kept their fucking mouths shut."

"Now you're blaming me?" Simon bellowed. "Don't you get it? They weren't voting for Fury Run over us, they were voting against her. Look at all the Hayes groupies outside. They hate her."

Justice's brain drenched in red. From the very pit of his soul, all his muscles coiled, ready to drive his fist into Simon's face.

"No," Liza screamed.

A door slammed.

Dropping his arm, Justice spun around.

Christine stood there, arms crossed and her face a blank. "Everyone can hear you."

Justice took a breath. This night was so fucked up he had no idea how to save it. None.

Gray dropped onto the couch. "Does it really matter now?"

The manager perched on the arm of the couch. "That depends on you. Is this where you guys fold? Give up? Then go right ahead, fight with each other and let the whole world hear you."

Justice leaned against the wall, head throbbing. "I don't quit. None of us here are quitters." Getting control, he swung his gaze to Christine, and asked, "What about you? Are you giving up on us?" The deal was she'd only manage them if they signed with Tangent and she got her cut.

She looked them over. "Depends."

Tension vibrated in the room, so palpable his muscles twitched with it. "On?"

"Prove yourselves to me. Pull it together and record an album. Despite your loss, I can get you gigs and keep you going. But without Tangent, you have to pay for the album yourselves. That means studio time, sound engineer, marketing and promo materials. I'll get you a tour, but you have to do the work and finance it all. It'll be long and grueling. Anything you've done up to now will be a cakewalk in comparison. You have to decide soon, while you still have some exposure." Her assessing stare slid over each of them. "If you want it bad enough, get your asses into the media pen and do the interviews."

Silence settled around them.

Simon made the first move. "You'd better decide, Justice. Because if we do this, it's one hundred fucking percent. All our time and money will go into trying to make it indie without a label. We'll be paying for everything."

He glared back at the man, the weight of the eyes of his band—and Liza—on him. "I've been in a thousand percent. I've made sacrifices and worked my ass off."

Simon glanced at Liza then back to him. "You kept a secret about our band publicist that exploded in our faces, and that shitstorm is still growing. Are you getting this, Justice? She was supposed to help us, but you knew something that had the power to hurt us and didn't tell us. I get that Liza's a victim too, but you put us all in the line of fire. How are we supposed to trust that next time you won't do the same thing?"

Christ, he couldn't defend himself. He'd done exactly that, no matter how he tried to justify it. "That's on me. I'm the one who promised her I wouldn't say anything."

Simon shook his head. "She's becoming our Yoko, the thing that divides us. The whole world is tuning in now, half for Liza and half against. You're going to have to choose which you're committed to." He walked out, and the others followed.

Choose between the band he'd poured his soul into, or the woman he loved who had chosen him over her family?

Her hand settled on his arm. Justice turned, catching her scent of warm peaches and distress. Her eyes hurt to look at, too damned vulnerable and shadowed. "Beth—"

She shook her head. "Go to the interviews. It's important. Show your fans that you guys are united and that Savaged Illusions will keep playing the music you love. Then come home, and we'll talk."

Did she think he'd leave her? He wouldn't, damn it. The weight of it nearly crushed him. Much as he loved the band, he needed her too. The girl who trusted him enough to sleep in his arms.

"Don't leave. Wait here. I don't want you out there alone." He'd seen the crowds and protesters, and people were still leaving the auditorium, creating more chaos.

She drew her phone out. "Ben and Emily are waiting for me."

Right, he'd gotten her two friends tickets to the show tonight. Okay, she'd be safe with them. Tugging her to him, he spread his hand on her back bared by the dress—the same dress she'd worn to the USS Midway. "You'll be there? At the house?" He needed that much tonight. To just know she'd be there.

Her brave mask cracked, streaks of fear and dread glittering in her eyes. "I don't want to be your Yoko." She sucked in a breath, visibly pulling herself together and stepping back. "We'll talk at the house." Grabbing her bag, she headed to the door, her back stiff and tense, almost as if she was shielding herself.

Her pain ripped straight down the center of his chest. Foreboding spread from the crack. *Don't let her go. Don't let her walk away now.*

"Justice? You coming?" Christine's sharp voice sliced into him. She was the future of his success.

But the girl walking down the hall held his heart.

Chapter 18

YOKO.

The word flashed in her head like a neon sign in a dark room.

She was ruining everything for Justice. His band. His life. A hot lump knotted her throat and burned her nose. The screen of her phone blurred as she sent a text to Emily. *Coming out now. Side door by staff lot.*

Her thoughts wouldn't stop. Simon blamed and hated her. All of the guys in the band were angry, and now they wanted Justice to choose: them or her.

Yoko. Yoko.

Don't cry. Just hold it together.

Beelining for the exit, she kept her head down and didn't look at anyone.

Finally, she hit the door, escaped out into the night and flinched at the frenzy of shouts, hysteria and honking horns. An endless row of cars snaked along the alley bisecting the theater from the staff parking lot. To the right, protesters and groupies were held back by a barricade and a line of cops. Two police cars had their blue-and-white lights flashing as part of the crowd control, adding to the chaos. Huge signs bobbed. One had an obscene picture of Liza soaked in beer with *Slut Not Victim* stamped across it. Additional signs blared phrases like, *Tell the Truth! Bring Hayes Home!*

Next to her, Colin and one of his guards were dealing with a determined man insisting he was a reporter. No, he didn't have credentials, but they should recognize him.

She could tell him that being recognized was overrated. Memories tugged at her, and she squeezed her eyes shut. Her head buzzed, and pain slashed at her heart. Everything was crumbling around her. She'd wanted to believe she could be normal, just be a college girl who took a few risks and fell in love.

So much in love. Justice...oh God. What was she doing to him? He'd kept her secret, and look what happened. And taking his father into the wings? What had she been thinking? The knot in her throat swelled. She'd wanted to show Justice his dad did love him, but instead she'd shocked him—shocked them all right as they were going to perform, throwing them off their start.

Shame flashed hot and miserable over her skin. Even the cool night couldn't touch it. Justice and his band had lost.

It killed her to see his dream shattered.

"Hey, Liza."

The voice pierced her agony. Forcing her eyes open, she focused on her friend and roommate. "He lost."

"I know." Emily hugged her. "It's going to be okay."

Pulling back, Liza said, "Everyone in the band except Justice hates me. They blame me. Called me Yoko."

Sympathy hardened into fury on Emily's face. Her gaze slid to the door.

She'd seen Em's ready-to-kick-ass expression before. "No. You can't get in there." Security had it locked down tight. "I just want to leave. Where's Ben?"

"Here." He strode up to them. "Had to answer a quick call. We're in the staff lot. Let's hustle." Taking her arm, he tugged her between him and Emily.

"Liza," Colin called out. "You good? Need an escort?"

She glanced over at the security guard. He really didn't miss anything. "They're friends. I'm fine."

He lifted a hand in acknowledgment. "Night."

"You want to come to our place?" Emily asked as they wove between the line of cars trying to exit.

Our place. Emily didn't mean the apartment she and Liza shared, she was talking about Ben's condo. She hadn't even officially moved out of their apartment, but she'd already left in her heart.

Another worry. Where was Liza going to live? She had to be out of the apartment soon. She couldn't go home—her aunt didn't want her there. More tears threatened. No, damn it. She'd survive and find a way to take care of herself. But tonight she'd be there for Justice...if he still wanted her. "Thanks, but I'll go to Justice's house."

On her right, screams pitched up from the protesters. Liza ignored them. The police kept them back far enough, plus it was dark, so she doubted they could recognize her anyway. Especially since they were headed away from the street. She didn't have enough energy to care how much strangers hated her when her heart was breaking over Justice and Savaged Illusions losing tonight, and that scene in the greenroom.

Em said, "We'll stay with you at Justice's house until he gets home."

She hadn't thought that far ahead, but it made sense. "Thanks, I'd feel better with you guys there."

Gratitude for her friends eased some of her turmoil.

"You won't be saying that once I clean out your kitchen," Ben said. "I'm starved. The car is the next row over."

"He's always hungry," Em complained while she pulled out her phone. "I'll call in a pizza. What do you guys want on it?"

"Get what you guys want, I'm not—"

A force slammed into Liza so hard, she sailed through the air and hit the ground on her left shoulder. Her head smacked onto the asphalt. Pain slashed into her brain. Blackness sprang up at the edges of her vision. Inky darkness spread, trying to pull her into unconsciousness.

No. Terrified of the obscurity, of what could happen if she lost consciousness, she bucked and fought a crushing weight on her hips pinning her down.

"Message from Hayes, you cunt," an ugly voice snarled.

A man was on top of her. He'd attacked her. Confusion muddled her thoughts.

"Liza! Oh God, get off her!"

Em was screaming. Desperately trying to figure out what was happening, Liza forced her eyes open and struggled to find her friend. But all she saw was the knife slashing toward her face.

Instinct took over, and she turned her head away an instant before fiery pain sliced into her neck and shoulder.

Justice grabbed Simon, spinning him to the wall in the hallway outside the room set up for media interviews.

"Enough," River snapped. "No more fighting."

Justice shrugged off River's hand and faced the man he considered a friend and a brother. "You have every right to be pissed at me. But you don't ever do that to Liza again. Ever."

Simon's eyes heated. "Me? I didn't keep a damn secret. Or—"

"You're a hypocrite. You went on TV and gave the whole story about how your wife killed herself after vicious words hurt her unbearably. Then you turned around, blamed Liza and called her names like Yoko." Justice struggled to stay in control this time. He needed to make a point to clear this between him and Simon. He'd make things right with his girl at home later. "I'm not saying we, Liza and me, didn't screw up. But as you said in that interview, *words matter*. And Liza has the scars on her wrist from trying to escape cruel words in the past."

Comprehension dawned like a tornado touching down, instant and devastating. A storm of grief and regret ravaged Simon's face in just seconds. "Oh damn."

Justice dropped his hands, stepping back. "Let's do this interview and—" He cut himself off when his phone vibrated insistently in his pocket. Yanking it out, he expected Liza's name, sure she'd tell him she wasn't going to his house. That she was going to Ben and Emily's to think, or some fear-laced bullshit. No way was he letting her run.

But it wasn't Liza. Instead it was a text from Emily. *Liza's been attacked in parking lot. Get out here.*

His guts clenched as he read it a second time. Oh hell, she was in danger. "Liza's been attacked." He had to get to her, turned and raced down the hallway. Hitting the door, he burst out and skidded to a stop. Where in the parking lot were they? A sea of cars snaked along in front of him, and more cars were trying to get into the line. Groups of people milled around, and by the street, protesters bellowed and chanted. Where was Beth?

Simon caught up to him. "Over there." He pointed to a group of cops running to the staff lot.

Justice raced to the area, shoving people out of his way, his desperation rising.

Some cop grabbed him, but Justice tore free, too jacked to explain. "Liza!"

"Over here!" A blonde waved at him. Justice traveled closer, recognizing Emily. Then he looked down. Liza. "Oh Christ." She was curled on her side, her face streaked with tears, dirt and blood. She panted, her eyes glazed. He crouched down, afraid to touch her.

Behind her knelt Ben, who was bare-chested and holding what must be his shirt against the curve of her neck and shoulder. Blood soaked the material.

"What?" Justice croaked out his dry throat. "The blood. What happened?"

Ben's gaze lifted to his. "She was right between Em and me, and some guy tackled her from behind. She hit the ground hard, and he cut her. It's bad. I need an ambulance. Now!" No sign of the funny, gentle man Justice had met at the restaurant. Ben vibrated competence, determination and anger.

A cop ran up to them. "Ambulance around the corner. Police are clearing a path through the protestors. I have a blanket and kit from the rig. Told them you're a doctor." He tossed the white blanket to Justice and set a big, plastic toolkit on the ground. "I'll hold a flashlight for you."

"Em, IV now," Ben ordered.

Emily ripped open the lid, and the two of them

worked. Her hands shook, making it clear she wasn't anywhere near as sure as Ben. When Justice had seen her at the medical clinic the day Liza took the morning-after pill, Em had been in a clerical position. But she followed Ben's directions, and right now that was all they had.

"You." Ben lifted his chin to Simon. "Hold this while I start the IV." He held out a bag attached to a tube. Once Simon took that, he shifted his gaze. "Justice, talk to her. She's going into shock. I want her to see you."

He tucked the blanket around her. "Beth, baby?" The nickname came out automatically.

Her eyes slid to his, slowly focusing. Tears pooled, communicating her pain and fear.

She was ripping his damn heart out. "I'm here. Right here." He didn't know where to touch her and settled for her hand. Broken nails. More blood. What the fuck happened? How? Helpless agony wrenched his chest. Someone had attacked and cut her.

"Dark." Her lips trembled. Her bloody fingers gripped his.

"What?" He pressed his cheek to the ground so she could see him easier. Feel him.

"Dark spreading." Her eyes fluttered, as if she fought unconsciousness. "Don't leave me. Please."

Oh God. She was afraid of the dark. So afraid. "I won't leave you." He held on to her hand. "I've got you. I'm here."

Her eyes slid shut, her hand going lax. Into the darkness. "Beth. Liza."

Hands pulled him away. Two men in uniform shirts took over. Ben swore, issuing more orders, his voice tinged with a frantic edge. "Have to find the bleeder. Keep that flashlight on the wound."

Justice fought the arms holding him. He had to get to her.

"Hold it together." Lynx got in his face while someone else bear-hugged him from behind. "They're trying to save her. That doctor guy has his fingers inside her skin, clamping something. You can't touch her."

Save her? No. Beth couldn't die. A shudder wracked him. How the hell was this even happening? Around Liza lay bloody cloths and discarded paper. The two paramedics lifted her onto a gurney, while Ben kept his fingers on—or in—the back of her neck or shoulder. There was so much blood, her hair was soaked with it.

Jesus. His whole world narrowed to the woman. He didn't dare take his eyes off her, as if he could will her to live. The paramedics braced her on her side, with Ben snapping out directions. Once they had her secured to his satisfaction, Ben said, "Go," and they ran toward the ambulance.

Breaking free, he hurried after them. Had to get to her. *Don't leave me.* She'd begged him to stay with her. He'd promised. A million thoughts stabbed him. Liza laughing. The night she stood up to him, refusing to take the drink in the club. Kissing her. The feel of her body against his.

The night she'd told him who she was and that she'd woken alone in the hospital. That wasn't happening this time. He'd be there with her. He wouldn't let her be scared and alone.

Lynx caught his arm as they loaded her in the back of the ambulance. "You can't go in there. The doctor is working on her."

Wrong. Liza knew Ben, but Justice had told her he wouldn't leave her. "I'm going with her." She was afraid of unconsciousness; he couldn't leave her alone in it.

This whole night was a nightmare. Who attacked her? He knew it had something to do with her past. It had to be one of the crazy Hayes groupies she'd warned him about.

He shrugged off Lynx's hold and climbed in the back of the rig just before the door closed. As the vehicle sped away with sirens blaring, Ben and the paramedic worked on her at a frantic pace. Justice gently folded her cold, limp hand in his. The blood pressure cuff on her arm hissed as it automatically went on.

A minute later, things in the ambulance calmed, and Justice looked at Ben. "Now what?

The man studied the small cardiac monitor he'd hooked her up to. "We wait. As long as she doesn't code, there's not much more I can do until I get her into the hospital." He ground his teeth. "When the guy attacked, Em was thrown to the ground. I helped her up and didn't get to Liza fast enough to stop the crazy bastard from cutting her."

Vividly aware of her unresponsive hand in his, a part of him wanted to lash out. But Ben was fighting to save Beth and deserved his gratitude not anger. "You said the man attacked from behind you. Obviously he snuck through the security and waited. You couldn't have stopped him." Justice swallowed the knot of hot fear for Beth. *Please let her live*, he prayed silently. If Justice had the power, he'd switch places with her and bear any amount of agony to spare Beth this. But right now, it was Ben he needed to reassure. He dropped his gaze to Beth. "She knows you're trying to save her."

"Wasn't just me."

"You mean Em? I know, she—"

"No. The man who attacked Liza wasn't going to stop. He'd raised his arm for another knife strike when another man came out of nowhere and tackled him."

Confused, Justice tore his gaze from Beth. "What man?" Who else had been with them?

"I don't know. The two of them were fighting on the ground, then the knife guy ran, and the hero chased after him. I focused on Liza."

A strange sensation like déjà vu rippled over him. "This hero, what did he look like?"

"Ragged. Your height, long hair and scars on one side of his face."

Shock gonged in his brain, stunning him. "That's my—"

Something beeped. The blood pressure cuff? The heart monitor? Worry chased out everything else in Justice's head. He pressed his fingers around Beth's. "I'm here, Beth, I'm here."

Her fingers tightened around his. Her eyelids fluttered, and she muttered something he couldn't hear.

"Good girl, Liza," Ben said. "That's it, fight."

Justice jerked his head up. He could see waves shooting across the screen of the heart monitor Ben stared at, but he couldn't interpret what they meant. "What's going on?"

Ben's shoulders relaxed a fraction. "Her blood pressure's rising and heart rate's getting stronger. Still shocky and not out of danger yet, but better. She's rallying hard."

Justice leaned closer to her too-pale face, furious hope rising in him. "You're going to make it, and I'll be with you every second." He had to swallow the knot of emotion. "I love you, Beth. You're not alone, I swear. Just keep fighting."

Her fingers flexed around his once more, then she settled into a calmer state and her lips lost the bluish tinge.

As his panic eased, the harsh reality of what had happened hit him. Someone had come too damned close to murdering her. But a mysterious hero had saved her from that last, fatal knife strike.

Justice had recognized Ben's description of the hero. Gratefulness filled his chest.

His father had saved the life of the woman Justice loved.

~The End~

Coming July 24, 2017

Savaged Vows

SAVAGED ILLUSIONS TRILOGY • BOOK TWO

JENNIFER LYON

Turn the page to read Chapter One!

Chapter 1

LIZA GLASNER GAVE IN ON the wheelchair and allowed herself to be rolled out into the bright sunshine. God, she detested hospitals. But she loathed the reason she'd landed there for three nights even more.

Someone had tried to kill her. A man she didn't know had hated her that much. Nothing like an attempted murder by a stranger to make a girl feel special. Okay, not special so much as seriously pissed off. She hadn't been bothering anyone, she'd just been walking to her car when she was tackled and stabbed.

Chill bumps splattered her arms despite the warm day in San Diego. She rubbed her palms over her biceps as her stomach knotted, and pinged her gaze around, careful not to move her head. The orderly had stopped a few feet back from the curb of the horseshoe-shaped pickup zone. Beyond that lay a road and huge parking areas. People milled around, coming and going at a brisk pace.

Did any of them want to kill her too?

Jeez, paranoid much? Liza squeezed her eyes shut, determined to get control. No one was trying to murder her here. She was fine.

"Beth." A warm, comforting hand settled over her fingers digging into her arms.

When she opened her eyes, her world filled with the man crouched in front of her. Justice Cade's blond-streaked brown hair refused to be tamed, and his irises sizzled an angry blue flecked with moody gray and warm concern.

"That was fast," Liza said. He'd gone ahead of her to get the car out of the parking facility, and now the Jeep idled at the curb a couple yards away.

"I figured you'd be in a hurry to get home to your stash of candy." He flipped up the footrests of her wheelchair.

That coaxed a smile from her. "You better not have eaten any, rock star. I don't care if we're living together, some things are off-limits." She stood carefully, trying not to jostle the healing slash that ran from the center point of the back of her neck down to her right shoulder blade. Or the bruises and split lip from getting slammed to the asphalt. The pain pills helped, so she managed.

Justice wrapped an arm around her, avoiding any tender spots. At the car, he opened the passenger door, helped her in then tugged her seat belt across her.

"I can—"

He lifted his head, his eyes hard and his jaw unyielding. "I'll do it. You'll sit there and be a good girl, or all your candy will vanish."

She could almost feel the rage, frustration and worry snapping out from his pores, yet he was gentle and caring with her. "Are you threatening me? I'll have you know I survived a stabbing, and that makes me a bona fide badass."

His face softened. "Definite badass and a tough-as-hell survivor." After locking in her seat belt, he cupped her jaw. "But anyone tries to hurt you again, I'm going badass on them, and when I'm done, they'll be bleeding on the ground. Breathing is optional."

He hovered over her like a shield, and yet he'd called her tough. He didn't see her as weak and reckless, but as a survivor who wouldn't let some maniac with a knife kill her. "Lot of badass in this car." She sank back against the seat, surprised at how tired she was just from dressing, arguing over the wheelchair and getting into the car.

Justice leaned in, kissing her on the side of her mouth to avoid her sore lip. "You're my tough girl." After closing her door, he slid in the driver's side and got them on the road. "We'll get your stuff moved Saturday from your apartment to my house. I'm borrowing a truck and rounding up Sloane and a few friends. We'll get Emily's stuff moved to her boyfriend's for her too."

"But I haven't finished packing." Before the attack, she'd been so busy with her internship and finals, there hadn't been time. Now reality dropped on her like a ton of bricks. She had to be out of her apartment by the end of the weekend, and since she was injured, it fell to her best friend and boyfriend to do everything.

"Emily said she'll handle that." He shot her a look. "You're not going to the apartment. Reporters might be there. And you—"

"I'm not hiding." Not anymore. She'd had enough of that before she met Justice, when she lived with her aunt. "I didn't do anything wrong."

"Damn right you didn't."

"Tell that to my aunt."

Justice clenched his jaw, his head snapping around. "What the hell did your aunt say to you?"

She fisted her hands at the memory of the phone

call. Despite having been on morphine, she could recite it verbatim. "She said I told you something awful would happen if you kept dating that rock star. You put yourself in danger with bad choices. You have to leave Justice and stop behaving like a drunk groupie."

He slapped his hand on the wheel. "That cold bitch. How the fuck is this your fault? Blaming the victim is bullshit." He narrowed his eyes. "I didn't see your oh-so-fucking-perfect aunt getting her ass in the car and coming to the hospital. You almost died, goddammit."

His arm bulged, making the beautifully inked guitar on his upper arm swell. His shirt sleeve cut off the old-school microphone above it. The whole design was wrapped in a crown of thorns with drips of blood—the only spots of color in the intricately shaded gray-and-black tat. She loved the ink, loved the man who wore it, and she loved the way he defended and cared about her. He'd slept at the hospital to be there with her if she had night terrors.

Stroking his arm, she could feel his fury in his rigid muscles. And it wasn't just her he was worried about. When he wasn't at the hospital, he'd been out searching for his dad. "You haven't found any sign of Noah?"

His jaw tightened. "No. Both he and the man who attacked you vanished."

The worry for his dad poured off him. Had Noah been injured fighting the assailant? "He'll turn up when he's ready. If something happened to your dad and he was hurt, or worse, the cops would have found him." She had to believe that.

He stroked his thumb over the back of her hand. "You're right. And he saved you. I'm grateful to him for that."

The sweet warmth of his words washed over her, more comforting than any of the drugs they'd given her in the hospital. This man loved her, stood by her, no matter how bad things were. "So am I."

Justice squeezed her hand then released it to steer the Jeep around a slower car. "Let's not worry about my dad right now. The important thing is that you're out of hospital. We'll be home soon, and you can rest. I had a security system put in too. You'll be safe."

"Home," she repeated. "I can't believe I'm actually doing this, not only dating a rock star, but living with him." If she thought too much about it, her head would spin. She'd met Justice Cade and the world as she knew it shifted into a new, exciting place.

And more dangerous.

"I'm the man who's going to keep you safe, Beth. Trust me."

Beth. The name she'd been called for the first fourteen years of her life, until her aunt changed it, trying to erase a huge part of who Liza was. But Justice latched on to that name, making her feel whole and accepted.

"I do. And I appreciate everything you're doing for me." That was what her aunt and grandmother didn't get. Justice made her feel like she mattered and supported her dreams, while they cut her out of their lives when they didn't agree with her choices.

"I won't lose you," he added. "From now on, your security is my first priority. Especially with that fucker who stabbed you still on the loose." Anger vibrated in every syllable.

Concern for Justice welled in her chest. He'd suffered this week too. "Are you and your band okay?" The four other guys in Savaged Illusions were like brothers to him.

His jaw flexed. "Yeah, the guys are in L.A., meeting with Christine and handling things. We're not giving up."

The cold-hearted business manager wasn't Liza's favorite person, but she was more troubled by the tension riding Justice. "That's good, right?"

He glanced over at her. "*Court of Rock* offered us a spot on their summer tour in July. Christine's negotiating that contract now. We need the money and exposure, but will you be okay when I'm gone?"

Was that what had him anxious? They were only a week into June now. But more importantly, this was the life she'd signed on for by loving Justice. He was a rock star—well, right now his star had taken a beating and gotten shoved into the shadows. But he and his band would fight their way to the top. He'd never once lied to her about his goal.

Fame.

Darkness weighed down on her lungs, trying to suffocate her in fear-soaked memories. But Justice wasn't her father, or the bastard her dad traded her to for a shot at stardom. She wasn't letting her past dictate her choices, not anymore.

Lifting her chin, she said, "You have to go on this tour. I'll be fine. I'm going to be working anyway. I wonder if Wylie will let me go back to my waitressing job?" Or would her notoriety be a problem?

"Not until the doctor clears you."

"I can't just sit around."

"You can write your books. Then you can send me chapters when I'm gone. Maybe I won't miss you so much if I can be a part of your secret world."

She hadn't told anyone about her writing until she'd shared it with Justice. It had been her way of escaping her fears and feeling in control. He'd embraced it and encouraged her to write, believing she could one day publish.

Now it was *their* secret world.

"I had this idea about my heroine," she blurted out. "What if she's a groupie who falls in love with the lead singer and—"

Her cell phone rang. It took her a second to remember she'd tucked the device into the plastic bag of all her stuff that Justice had put in the car. She tried to twist to find— "Ouch." Pain streaked out from the cut and her sore muscles.

"Don't move." Justice steered with one hand and reached back to grab the bag and set it on her lap.

Liza fished out her phone and eyed the screen. Her heart jumped. "The police station." Quickly she hit the speaker button so Justice could hear, and answered, "Hello, this is Liza."

"Miss Glasner, this is Detective Jenkins."

Her stomach tightened. "What can I do for you?"

"I'm calling to inform you we may have a break in your case."

Finally. The knot of anxiety in her stomach eased. "Do you have my attacker in custody?" She desperately wanted to feel safe and to know who hated her enough to try to kill her.

"Not for your attack specifically. We've arrested our suspect on another charge, and that led us to evidence that suggests he's involved in your stabbing."

She couldn't stand it. "Who?"

"Noah Cade."

Her fingers went numb. Oh my God, they'd arrested Justice's father.

Justice swerved into a gas station parking lot and shoved the car into park. He couldn't believe this. His dad arrested?

Glaring at the cell phone in Beth's hand, he

shouted, "What the blazing hell, Jenkins? My dad didn't stab Liza, he saved her."

Beth winced, which pissed him off more. She was in enough pain without him losing his shit.

"Detective, as you can hear," Beth said, her gaze wide in stark contrast to her pale, bruised face, "Justice is with me. You said Noah is under arrest, but not for my attack?"

"Correct. He was picked up early this morning for an outstanding warrant. He's failed to pay several citations for encroachment."

Justice gripped the steering wheel to keep from punching it.

"What's encroachment?" Beth asked.

"A way to hassle homeless people for setting their stuff on public property," Justice snarled. "I'll pay his damned tickets."

"It's more complicated than that. Mr. Cade was in possession of a jacket covered in dried blood that matches Miss Glasner's blood type. And there's more evidence we're following up on."

"Of course he has her blood on him, he tackled the assailant right off her." He forced calm into his voice and settled his hand on Beth's thigh. "I had her blood on me, and so did half a dozen other people."

"It wasn't Noah," Beth jumped in. "I would have recognized his voice. It's a rusty version of Justice's." She lifted the phone closer to her face. "Why are you doing this?"

"Because I don't have a choice here," Detective Jenkins said. "This story has exploded. People are scared that someone is going around stabbing college girls in our town."

Fuck. Justice didn't require a flashing sign to tell him that Detective Jenkins and the police department were under pressure and needed an arrest. And a homeless man with a coat soaked in Beth's blood?

Too easy to pin the blame on him.

His head throbbed. After yanking out his phone, he checked for missed calls. "My dad hasn't called. He gets a phone call. Are you allowing him his rights?"

"Yes, he refused to call anyone or talk at all. He stares at a wall and says nothing."

"Don't do this, Detective," Beth pleaded. "Noah's not well. He has PTSD, and you can see he's suffered from his scars." Her eyes filled with tears. "Don't do this."

"I need Mr. Cade to talk to me." Jenkins's frustration vibrated through the speaker. "All we have is a vague description from eyewitnesses—medium height, average build, wearing dark clothes and a beanie. I need more than that to rule out Mr. Cade, and he's not communicating."

Beth squeezed her eyes shut. "I didn't see my attacker, I just heard his voice and saw the knife." She shifted her gaze to him. "I'm sorry."

She was sorry? For what? She'd been fucking stabbed, while Justice had been inside trying to save his career instead of making sure his girlfriend was safe. He'd failed, not her. He took the phone from her ice-cold fingers.

"I'm getting him a lawyer, and I'll be there as soon as I can. You try to pin this on him, we'll go to the media and let them know the guy with a knife is still on the loose while you hassle a former Marine who was seriously injured in the line of duty." He cut the call, ready to kill someone.

Pull yourself together. Beth doesn't need you losing it right now. Get to the police station and sort this out.

"Do you know a lawyer?" she asked.

After handing the phone back to Beth, he put the

car in gear and drove while mentally ticking off what he needed to do. "No. I'll call Sloane once we get to the house. He manages MMA fighters now, and a few of them have gotten into trouble, so he knows a reputable law firm." But he couldn't leave Beth alone to work on getting his father out of jail. "Can you call Emily? See if she'll come stay with you?"

While Beth made the call, he eased around a corner. He lasted five seconds before he asked, "Is Emily answering?"

"Not calling Em, I'm— Sloane, hi, it's Liza."

Justice jerked. "What are you doing?"

She held up a hand. "The detective on my case called..." She summed up the conversation, then asked, "Do you know any good criminal lawyers who can get over to the jail right away and try to get him released today?"

Justice gripped the wheel as he heard Sloane's deep voice answering, but he couldn't make out the words.

She sank back against the seat and closed her eyes. "Thank you." She held the phone out to him.

He stared at her for one heartbeat. This was why he loved her so damned much. She was in pain and miserable, yet here she was helping his dad. He took the phone but said to her, "You're amazing."

"We have to get Noah out of there. I saw him after being in the auditorium for less than five minutes, and he looked bad. I don't know how he's handling being dragged to a police station, interrogated and arrested."

Her very real concern for his dad eased his own anguish, outrage and frustration. He didn't have to handle this alone, he had Beth. Putting the phone to his ear, he said, "Sloane."

"I'll contact the firm I use and have a lawyer call you in the next hour."

Justice headed into the decades-old track of homes. "I don't know if my dad will talk to the lawyer. Sounds like he's not talking to the cops." Had his dad shut down entirely? Or was he having panic attacks? He rubbed his chest to ease the crushing anxiety and regret.

"He'll talk to me," Liza said softly. "I'll go with you to the police station."

Oh hell no. She was too weak and sore, and the doctors had been clear—total rest for a few days, and no lifting. The police station surrounded by chaos, desperation and germs wasn't the place for Beth right now. "You're going straight to bed." This was one thing he'd do right—take care of Beth.

Justice turned on his street and hit the brakes when he spotted at least a dozen media vehicles in front of his house. "Goddamn it." Tossing the phone, he threw the Jeep in reverse, shot back up the road and spun around. Flooring it, he glared at the mirror.

Had any of the reporters spotted them? No one seemed to notice.

"Oh crap," Beth blurted out. "Why are they at your house? No one knew I was being released."

Frustrated fury pounded in his head. He couldn't leave Beth there with the media vultures circling. "I don't know." He sucked in air to calm down and took in her pale face, bruised eyes and scabbed lip. "Hang on, I'll figure something out." Seeing her phone where it'd landed in the cup holder after he'd pitched it, he remembered Sloane. Picking up the device, he switched it to speaker. "Sorry, Sloane, reporters are swarming my house."

"The news that they arrested your father is breaking all over social media and TV. They're calling him a suspect in Liza's attack. They're saying a cop found a bloodstained jacket."

"But we just found out," Beth said. "How did they...?" She dropped her head back. "It doesn't matter, they know."

Exactly. He needed to get her somewhere safe where she could rest. "I'm going to take Liza to her friend's house. I'll call you back."

"Can't," Liza cut in. "Emily's at work."

His neck muscles bunched as he tried to think of an alternative.

"Go to my penthouse suite at the Opulence Hotel," Sloane said. "It's secure, quiet and big enough that Liza can rest in one of the rooms and you can meet with the lawyer in the living space after he finds out the situation with your dad."

It was a good solution, and if he had to leave, she'd be safe and comfortable. He glanced over at her. "You okay with that?"

"Yeah."

The utter fatigue in her voice stabbed him with guilt. She'd hit her limit. "Thanks, Sloane."

Liza said goodbye and cut the call. "What a mess."

He'd done this to her—coaxed his way into her life, and despite her warnings, exposed her past. Her aunt wasn't wrong. If Liza wasn't with him, no one would have paid any attention to her. Beth would have blended in as just another college girl in a college town. He really was a fuckup.

Beth's warm touch settled on his arm. "It's going to be okay. We'll get your dad out."

He took Beth's hand in his, keeping his hold gentle around her scabbed fingers. She looked like hell.

And never more beautiful to him.

It was the love and trust in her green eyes that

pierced his heart. She'd chosen him over her family, and even after he'd lost *Court of Rock* and she'd been stabbed, she hadn't left him.

As bad as this week had been, she was the one person who made it bearable, made it feel like together they could handle anything.

Dear Readers,

Thank you so much for reading SAVAGED DREAMS. But it's not over yet! In SAVAGED VOWS (book 2) Justice and Liza's love is tested by the blazing glory, and the dark underbelly, of fame. And in SAVAGED DEVOTION (book 3), they come back fighting hard for their love and happily ever after against all odds. I really hope you continue the journey with Justice and Liza!

SAVAGED VOWS will be released in July 2017, and I'm striving to release the third book, SAVAGED DEVOTION, in September 2017.

To get all the latest news on releases and contests, sign up for my newsletter on my website at www.jenniferlyonbooks.com

Happy Reading!
   ~ Jen

Other Books by Jennifer Lyon

Jennifer Lyon writing as Jennifer Apodaca

The Sex on the Beach Book Club
Good, Bad & Sexy, a novella

Writing as Jennifer Apodaca

ONCE A MARINE SERIES

The Baby Bargain (Book #1)
Her Temporary Hero (Book #2)
Exposing The Heiress (Book #3)

About the Author

Jennifer Lyon is the pseudonym for *USA Today* Bestselling Author Jennifer Apodaca. Jen lives in Southern California where she continually plots ways to convince her husband that they should get a dog. After all, they met at the dog pound, fell in love, married and had three wonderful sons. So far, however, she has failed in her doggy endeavor. She consoles herself by pouring her passion into writing books. To date, Jen has published more than twenty books and novellas, won numerous awards and had her books translated into multiple languages, but she still hasn't come up with a way to persuade her husband that they need a dog.

Jen loves connecting with fans. Visit her website at www.jenniferlyonbooks.com or follow her at https://www.facebook.com/jenniferlyonbooks.

www.ingramcontent.com/pod-product-compliance
Lightning Source LLC
Chambersburg PA
CBHW030420180626
46812CB00005B/2094